All rights reserved

The characters and events portrayed in this book are fictitious. Any similarity to real persons, living or dead, is coincidental and not intended by the author.

No part of this book may be reproduced, or stored in a retrieval system, or transmitted in any form or by any means, electronic, mechanical, photocopying, recording, or otherwise, without express written permission of the publisher.

ISBN-9798714848636

Cover design by: Cmallorydesign

Printed in the United Kingdom

WE ALL HAVE DEMONS BATTLING A WAR INSIDE OF US. BUT YOU NEVER HAVE TO FIGHT THAT WAR ALONE. STAY STRONG, LOTS OF LOVE LJ XOXO

I want to say a massive thank you to my family, fiancé and friends for their never ending support. Through the mental break downs and the endless self doubts. Your support made me complete my dream.

I love you all.

CHAPTER ONE

Hadley fell onto the empty bed, the covers her mother had picked twenty years ago had long been disposed of after the church removed her lifeless body. Hadley had not been in the room let alone the house she spent the first ten years of her life in since the church took her in after her mother died. The mattress was stained and old, Hadley knew the dark splotches were where her mother had purposely slashed at her arms.

'Going to get the demon out on my own if no one will help'. She remembered her mother telling her while walking around the house.

Deep in her thoughts Hadley heard a creek on the floorboards.

"Oh sorry, didn't mean to scare you darling, big house tho eh!"

Hadley looked over to the door where her husband was examining the room she was sitting in. His dark brown hair was slicked into a low ponytail, his acid washed tight jeans looked too lived in and his plain t-shirt fit snugly across his nearly there muscles.

She smiled and shook her head telling him she wasn't startled, just remembering. He walked over to where she was sitting and held out his hand to help her to her feet. Holding on to his hand always made her feel safe, looking up at him, she smiled.

"Thank you, but don't you think it's a bit to big for us? Jace, don't give me that look."

Hadley knew her husband had already fallen in love with the house. Growing up Jace lived in a small two-bed flat in Edinburgh with his parents and older brother. She supposed living below the poverty line was worse than living in a home someone had been possessed in.

"If you don't want to live here, we don't need to. We can live anywhere, as long as we are together."

Jace was always the man she had wanted to be with, strong, loving, green eyes and he loved her despite her past. Hadley shook her head and wrapped her arms around her husbands waist. She knew this was the best place to be, this is where she lived with her mother, where they would celebrate Samhain and where their sacred tree stump stood in their garden. This house was her home, she had inherited everything her mother owned.

However, moving back to Gloucestershire was like stepping back into the past, stepping away from the world Jace and her had made in Edinburgh since leaving university.

Walking down the stairs Hadley became aware the handling men were standing staring wide-eyed at one of the boxes which had been opened.

"Can I help you gentlemen?"

Hadley knew the small town where she was from were aware of her career. She also knew many would be deceived into thinking her and Jace were devil worshippers. Jace had already beat her to them, and took the book they were looking at.

"That one is a classic." Jace told them "See how old the leather is? This one is a first edition. Sir Walters Scott's Demonology and Witchcraft."

Hadley noticed the man who had been holding the book, quickly wiped his hands on his trousers, as if to brush away the evil which was encased in the book.

"You collect these?" He asked.

Jace looked at Hadley before he replied.

"Of course these are collectable, but we have these for research, for reference. You can be at the highest in your craft, but that doesn't mean you can never relearn or reinterpret something differently. Walter Scott published these in 1829 to 1847 to teach us in the future, that there are forces in this world we are very unaware of. And although we age and grow weaker; those forces grow older and stronger."

Hadley knew she had to interrupt her husband before he scared the handling men away with the rest of their belongings. She took the book out of her husbands hand and placed the book back into the box.

"I believe there are more boxes to be brought in, Jace why don't you go help them?"

Hadley picked up the box she had just placed the book in and carried it into the room they would use as their study. The study held an extra room she and her mother used as their altar, but she couldn't open that door just yet.

Later that night the couple ordered pizza and began sorting through their many boxes of belongings. Jace began rearranging the bookshelf, while Hadley sat and watched him eating pizza crossed legged on the floor. Hadley watched him examine every book before placing them onto the shelf.

Each book held stories of possession, of demons and monsters. A lot of them were ancient, wrote in English, Hindu or Latin. They each explained different religions hold different beliefs on how to rid a demonic presence. Hadley and Jace had chosen to learn every religion while studying Parapsychology at Edinburgh University. While there, they had spent their years perfecting their knowledge on Buddhism, Christianity, Hinduism and Judaism. Years on the study of demons within these religions and the beliefs held about them.

However, neither were any of these religions and although Hadley was taken into the church after her mothers failed exorcism; her mother was not christian either. Her mother had brought Hadley up pagan, however, when a dark phantom, a demon took over her body, the church intervened and told her they could perform an exorcism. But only if she and Hadley renounced their faith. Unable to control herself with whatever was inside her, her mother agreed.

"Lets finish this tomorrow." Jace whispered in Hadley's ear as she lay resting on the dusty sofa. Wrapped tightly in a blanket, she nodded and stood up waiting for Jace to turn off the lamps within the room. Walking up the stairs they walked into the second master bedroom, Hadley knew she was not ready to sleep in her moms bedroom. There were to many memories, too many nightmares attached to the room.

"Mom!" Hadley cried out "Mom, you have to come back, you are strong please don't leave me."

Hadley watched her mothers head turn unnaturally to stare at her, thick black bile leaked from her mouth and her arms and legs were tied painfully tight to the bed posts. Hadley no longer saw the beautiful fair skinned woman who used to tuck her in at night and kiss her on the cheek. This thing inside her stained her skin black, her face had become hallow and her body was frail. Hadley watched as her mother slammed her head onto the headboard, causing the once glossy blonde hair to become a nest made from blood and splintered wood.

"Mommy can't come right now." Hadley's mother screeched in Latin out to the room.

Father Anderson continued throwing holy water and chanting his prayer. Hadley felt confused. What did she say? She did not understand what her mother screamed at her. Hadley looked to the Fathers right hand, his eyes were wide and his knuckles white as he held on to his cross.

"What did she say? What did my mother say?" She pulled his arm down so he would look straight into her eyes. She sensed he did not want to tell her, she knew the words spoken were not English.

"Tell me what she said!"

He quickly grabbed her as if to protect her from the words.

"It said mommy cannot come right now." He whispered into Hadley's ear.

A deep laugh filled the room.

"Pauper pauper Hadley."

"Speak English demon!" The father demanded. "Leave this woman's body, go back to the fire pits of hell where you belong."

"Poor, poor Hadley. Is that better for you father?"

The room became ice-cold and Hadley could see everyone's breath, except her mothers.

"I spit on the book in which your species revels in believing it shall save you. I do not come from the fire pits of hell, but from your depraved nightmares. You cannot summon me away; for when I leave this vessel, I shall find new flesh and blood to curdle and drain."

A guttural demonic scream engulfed the room as Hadley watched her mothers body convulse.

Hadley fell up against the wall her hands covering her ears. She felt tears fall from her eyes as she slowly sank to the floor. The chaos in the room became blurred to her, she could no longer hear the fathers lord prayer or his second in command blessing the shell which was once her mother. Hadley looked at the figure on the bed one last time, her childhood was gone, her mother was already gone. The demon locked eyes with her, the black eyes showed no love, but the sinister smile shook Hadley to the core.

"Hadley it's okay it was just a dream."

Hadley awoke drenched in sweat. Her hair stuck to her neck and shoulders, the sheets on her side of the bed were no longer covering the mattress. Hadley struggled to breathe as Jace soothed her with hushing nosies.

"You know that shush thing doesn't work right?" Hadley finally managed to say.

"But you"re breathing better now my sweetheart." Jace smiled "Want to talk about it?"

Hadley stood from the bed and took off her damp pyjamas to change into dry ones.

"I think its just being back in this house, back in this town." Hadley stood staring at the damp patch on the sheets.

"Don't worry we can change them." Jace got out of bed and took clean sheets out of the cupboard.

"Was it about that night?" Jace asked, as he took his pillows off the bed, matching Hadley's actions.

"Yeah, I guess I should have known something like this would happen as soon as I came back."

Jace pulled his side of the sheet off the mattress and tossed the sheet onto the floor.

"Whatever that demon was it's gone now. You know that right?" He told her as they put on the new fresh sheet. The smell of flowers lifted her senses when she pulled the sheet over the corner of the mattress.

"Yeah, I know its just being back here. But I thought if we slept in my old room and not her room I wouldn't." Hadley sighed again as she sat on the newly made bed.

"I know." Jace said as he got off the bed and left the bedroom. Hadley waited on the bed until Jace returned with a white candle, a silver ribbon and a silver coin, she smiled.

"I haven't done that since we went to Kempton Park Hospital on our international paranormal investigation." Hadley took the candle, the ribbon and the coin from him and sat on the floor staring out the window, so she could face the moon. Placing the candle in front of her, Hadley tied the silver ribbon around the candle.

"Can you turn the light off please?" She asked Jace.

Jace turned off the bedroom light and laid back on the bed. Hadley sat with her eyes closed until she felt complete peace.

'The moon is my friend
Who's listening to me
Bringing the beauty into my dreams.
The stars are here forever to shine
Bringing serenity and peace of mind.
When I close my eyes, they won't be gone
Keeping me safe till the dawn.'

Hadley picked up the snuffer to snuff the flame, she then gently unwrapped the silver ribbon from the candle and tied it around her wrist. As she stood up Hadley felt relaxed and at peace and put her arms above her head to stretch.

"Feeling better already." Jace noted. Hadley turned and saw him already below the covers smiling at her.

"Put the candle and coin on the windowsill and come back to bed."

CHAPTER TWO

After two weeks Hadley was beginning to put her mark on the house, she had also begun using protecting remedies and cleansing the home. She tied cinnamon sticks over the door and her decorative jars of salt were placed on the side table.

Jace would always joke about the jars, but he still helped put salt in all corners of the home. Most importantly Hadley blessed the house. Jace had agreed to help her do this as the house was so big. Hadley lit a candle in every room downstairs and Jace did the same upstairs, arriving back at the entrance of the house, she took the sage and used the candle in the hallway to light the sage smudge stick. The smell began to fill the hall, as she waved the sage wand round all the doors and windows before moving to the next room.

She needed to bless every room, she needed to feel safe inside the home she once feared. Jace followed her around the house, also chanting to the goddess Hestia to protect their home. When she reached her mothers old room, Hadley was unable to hide her doubt.

Jace placed his hand over hers on the door knob and together they opened the door. The room looked exactly as it did the day they moved in, bare, untouched and unloved. Hadley looked at Jace who nodded and in unison they both recited the blessing.

"Lady Hestia, Goddess of hearth and home, please join us as we continue to bless our home, bless this bedroom with peace and love. Show this room kindness and forgiving for its past."

They continued with the blessing and made their way back to the entrance, thanking the goddess for the blessing before continuing with their day.

From her kitchen window Hadley could clearly see over the fields and into the small town. She knew she had to eventually leave the house, Jace had already told her the gossip going around about them which he had overheard when he had gone to get supplies at the grocery store.

Jace was sitting at the kitchen table reading the local newspaper. Hadley stopped what she was doing and read the same headline she had read the previous day.

"Oh, you seen it's out of date then?" Jace said noticing Hadley staring at him. "I was waiting until you did, so we can finally go into town together."

Hadley laughed, she knew she needed to leave the house, more evil had happened inside these walls than outside of them.

"Fine, we will go. But I need to shower and get ready." She said back to Jace as she headed upstairs. Coming down the stairs Hadley felt anxious, her tight blue jeans needed to be worn in after coming out the dryer, she knew her black bomber jacket wouldn't keep her warm and her dark blonde hair curled down past her shoulders was left as it dried.

"Wow you look amazing, are you ready?"

Hadley nodded her head as her husband held open the front door.

Walking together down the country paths into the historic market town Hadley grew up in, they both took in the beauty Wotton-under-Edge was. Hadley had forgotten how beautiful and how quiet country living was. Living in Edinburgh had made her used to the hustle and bustle, the over crowding a university city brought; was Jace really going to be at home here she thought.

"Wow I love it here, look at this place." Jace waved his hand in the air to emphasis his remark.

"It's lovely isn't it? I'll show you the walk mother and I used to take Bones on."

She quickly looked at Jace who had begun laughing, she knew he always laughed at the name of her old childhood dog.

The walk took them to North Nibley where the Tyndale Monument stood tall on top of a hill.

"What do you think?" She said to Jace when they finally made it to their destination. Jace turned to her and smiled, she knew he thought the view was beautiful. Autumn had turned the trees her favourite orange and the grass had lost its summer glow and became a dull straw like hue; however, still beautiful for the season she thought. Jace turned back to the monument.

"So this is where the great William Tyndale translated the New Testament."

Hadley knew he hadn't been paying attention to her talk on the way up here.

"No" She sighed. "He was from here, so they built this to honour him. For someone who has a masters and can understand many languages." Hadley spoke her final sentence in a language she knew he knew.

"Hey I understood that Mrs Fernsby"

Arriving back in Wotton-under-Edge, the town had become more lively as afternoon shoppers began filling the streets. The air was filled with the smell of coffee and children were out picking their halloween costumes for two weeks time. Hadley squeezed Jace's hand tight, they had always wanted to have a baby, but the time was never right.

They wandered around, exploring the surrounding roads. A striking yet aesthetically appealing building owned a small lane came into view. The half-timbered black and white building was where Jace had chosen they would stop for a drink. Walking through the courtyard Hadley began to feel her muscles contract and the hair on her ams and neck stood up.

She let go off her husbands hand and stood still, in one of the top floor windows she saw a figure, a shadow. She squinted her eyes and stared, she couldn't understand why she could not see a single feature on the face. Not only that, but she knew it was staring at something. She looked behind her and saw rows of picnic benches. There, sitting round one of the tables sat a group of children. In the middle a young boy with a wooly hat on and seven other children sat round him. When she turned back to the window the shadow was gone.

"Are ya alright? What's wrong?" Jace realised his wife was no longer following him into the pub. "Hadley!"

Just as if she had come out of a trance, Hadley looked at Jace. She shook her head; she had a feeling something was wrong with the building and the grounds in which it sat.

"Sorry my love, something doesn't feel right here, can you not feel it?" She had hoped Jace would pick up on whatever she was feeling.

"Probably because the place is old, lets go in and see the inside."

Hadley looked back at the picnic table and to her surprise, only the boy in the wooly hat was sitting there.

Walking in Hadley could smell beer which hadn't been cleaned up. The room was framed with timber beams, lamps made the room seem cosy and fitting for this time of year. The chairs and stools were topped with green fabric and the bar curved to make an L shape. Jace was already walking towards to the bar; eager to be served his first pint of the afternoon.

Hadley wanted to take in more of the pub while she picked a table, so she observed every nook and cranny. The pub wasn't full, she could see what looked like four locals scattered about. She noticed every few beams had a dark brown bold wooden cross bolted to it, she had no doubt; they were placed there for a specific reason.

"Afternoon, welcome to the Ancient Ramm Inn, what can I get you?" The barmaid looked frail and anaemic.

Her mixed race skin was washed out, her dark curly hair was tied in a bun which sat on the top of her head. Her smile forced, her eyes showed lack of sleep and her clothes re-worn yet clean from the day before. Hadley could see her looking at Jace urging him to order something or go away from the bar. Hadley found a seat just a metre away from the bar area and sat down. She noticed a thick wooden door, the window hidden by a bright red sign saying Do Not Enter. She could hear Jace trying to make small talk with the barmaid, and wished for him to hurry up as the Ramm's Inn locals were beginning to stare.

"You're Laurie's kid aren't you? Wow, that one went mad. She killed herself didn't she?"

Hadley closed her eyes and took a deep breath before looking directly at who spoke to her. She knew the towns folk didn't believe the real story, she knew they didn't want to believe. Because if they did, they would be faced with powers that challenge humans in ways which they cannot always be protected from.

"You seem to have gone a little mad as well if you ask me. Kids from the cities ruining their bodies with that stuff. It doesn't fit into this town"

Jace was still at the bar and Hadley knew the local drunk was talking about her tattoos. She always understood they were a stance of rebellion, but not to her. She needed to have these on her skin to protect herself. If she protected herself, she could protect others, if she protected others, she would stop others ending up like her mother.

"Like her ink do you pal?" The strong Scottish accent from her husband made her body release the tension she had been building up. He put the drinks on the table and sat opposite Hadley on the small round table, took a sip of his beer and continued talking to the drunk.

"See that one there?" He pointed to Hadley's chest. "That one there, the hamsa or hand, it is believed to ward off the evil eye. On her arms, is the pentacle, it has a few meanings, however we use it as a protective glyph. That one is the Solar Cross which is used for entering calming air when under threat, it also banishes negativity and cast out shadows. The crossing spears are used to block adversary, we have both got more, gotta have them in our line of work." Jace drank more of his drink as he gave Hadley a wink.

"Satanists."

"Enough Mike! Here, drink this." The barmaid had made her way over to the local; now known to Hadley as Mike, and placed a full pint of bitter on his table. She collected his empty glass and walked over to the table where Hadley and Jace were sitting.

"Can I ask you something?" She whispered.

Jace pulled out the extra chair giving her the go ahead to take a seat. She placed the empty glass she had just collected onto the table and didn't say a word.

Upon being closer to her, Hadley could see her eyes were red, she was thin and looked petrified. Hadley started the conversation again:

"Well, I'm Hadley this is my husband Jace, you said you wanted to ask us something, please ask away."

Hadley stared at Jace as she sipped on her beer and shrugged her shoulders.

"I think you are the ones that can help me."

Neither Jace nor Hadley spoke, they knew she needed to speak.

"I'm sorry I just haven't slept properly in days. I'm Cindy, the owner of the Inn. You have probably seen my son Marty playing outside."

Hadley half smiled and nodded her head but remained quiet.

"I need your help, I heard what you said to Mike, I have also heard what people are saying about you in the town. There is something evil in this place."

Hadley began to ask what she meant before she was quickly cut ofF by Cindy. Cindy started to shake as she told the couple about her Inn.

When Marty and herself first moved in, she had big dreams, she was mixed race in a very white market town. But she was not afraid to stand up for herself and live a peaceful life in the town she had come to love. Hadley and Jace didn't move, they were worried if they moved she would stop talking. As Hadley was listening, her eyes darted towards the entrance of the pub, she could see Cindy's son standing there. Marty, just like his mom, looked frightened and sleep-deprived. He didn't resemble a happy five-year-old, he resembled a soul who had been through torture.

"Baby boy, are you okay?"

Cindy had also noticed her son entering the pub. Marty didn't answer, he just walked further into the pub, with his head down showing the pom pom on the top of his hat.

"Why don't you go help yourself to some pop. You know where it is."

Marty walked over to the bar area, his small height made him disappear when he went behind the bar.

"It is really affecting him. He doesn't talk any more, he won't sleep on his own."

Hadley could see Cindy's eyes were becoming glossy, she reached out and took hold of one of Cindy's hands.

"Tell us what is going on." Hadley asked.

"This place, my home, my business. It's already owned. I have seen things move, doors open and slam shut, glasses thrown across the bar. Had my covers thrown off me while I try and sleep. We don't go upstairs any more, we sleep in the pub area, it seems to be the safest place. I wanted to renovate, bring this place more up to date. When I started, I found bones under the floorboards along with occult artefacts. You know daggers and some sort of chalice with what I presume were devil markings. But the worst thing, the bones looked like they belonged to children."

Cindy stopped talking and looked at Jace, whose eyes darted to Hadley. The silence was beginning to become tense, Hadley knew no supernatural beings would rise from the wooden floorboards. But she could not help but deepen her breathing.

"Cindy" Hadley began "We want to help you, but we need to get more of an idea of what could be happening. I saw someone in the window when we walked in watching Marty and the other children."

Cindy shook her head "Marty is the only child here today."

All three turned to Marty who had sat at an empty table with a colouring book and old crayons.

"Hadley, why don't you and speak to Marty while I have a quick chat with Cindy, if that's alright with you of course?" Jace spoke softly to Marty's mother.

Cindy nodded her head and Hadley left them to talk. She could hear Jace whispering, asking Cindy about the past of the Inn and if there was any place he and Hadley could find out a more in-depth history.

When Hadley got to the table she asked Marty if she could sit with him. Taking his one nod of his head as a yes, she sat down and began picking up the colour crayon he had just put down. Marty didn't look up from his colouring and so she watched him while trying to come up with a way to open up the conversation.

She noticed a silver chain around his neck with a bold but delicate cross. Marty grabbed his cross as he noticed Hadley staring.

"That is a beautiful necklace, did your mother give it you?" He shook his head

"Oh so your father then? I never knew my real father, when my mother left I was taken in by the church."

Marty made eye contact for the first time, he began to say something but stopped.

Hadley spoke again "I really want to ask you some questions, is that okay?"

She waited for him to respond vocally but he once again just nodded his head.

"Your mom told me you sleep in this room now, do you know why?"

Marty anxiously bit his lip, Hadley remained silent and gave him a reassuring smile. A moment later he replied.

"Mommy is scared to go upstairs. There is a lady up there who doesn't like us."

Hadley was surprised about the calmness in his voice. She asked him if he knew who the lady was, Marty nodded his head.

"She was killed here, she doesn't like people and the others have said she wants us out of here."

"Others?" Hadley speculated. "You mean the other children I saw you sitting outside with."

Marty nodded his head. Hadley continued.

"Do they live here with the woman?"

Marty shook his head and whispered.

"They don't live here with her, they are made to live here, they don't want to be here, they are scared. The woman won't let them leave." Hadley felt the hairs on her arms stand up again. She could see he was frightened, she was beginning to feel frightened for him. Without any prompting Marty asked,

"Are you here to help my mommy, my friends and me?"

Hadley knew he was being serious, she knew a young child would be able to see the darker things in life more prominent than an adult.

"Yes Marty, Jace and I are going to help you."

CHAPTER THREE

Hadley loathed leaving Marty and Cindy at the Inn. Before they left Cindy had told them the library had historic papers and newspaper articles but there was so much history to look at; she was unsure what she was looking for. Hadley looked back over the courtyard, the children she saw before had returned and watched as she and Jace walked away. She tugged on his arm and got him to look back, the children had gone but in the window the dark shadow was there, and this time she knew it was looking at her.

Arriving back onto the high street, the nights had begun to draw in early and many cafés were now beginning to close. The library 'open till late' sign was encased in a lit frame on the thick wooden door.

Walking in, the musty smell of the century old books was meet with vanilla and almonds. Decades of literature sat on the shelves ready to be discovered by a defined community, who love exploring a world that is not their own.

Jace had walked over to the desk where an old man was sitting reading a book he seemed engrossed in. He had a welcoming face with puffed out red cheeks. Thin white strands of hair had been combed over his bald scalp. The jumper he wore over his crumbled stripe shirt had a stain which looked a few days old.

Hadley felt peace within the building, she had spent most of her childhood within the churches' library, learning the dead language her mother had spat out during her last moments on the earth. Jace found her in the non-fiction aisle. He told her the librarian had said the history of the town and the articles were at the back of the library, and they were welcome to take whatever they needed.

The back of the library smelt more musky, heavier dust covered the spines of the books; showing they hadn't been opened for years. Dark green paint covered the walls, but they needed a fresh new coat. The lights seemed dimmer and the windows were smaller and separated further apart. Jace found the filing cabinets which held the towns' historic news reports. They were filled with crumbling, yellow papers, dating back to the 1800. They understood why Cindy was unsure and overwhelmed by what she was searching for. Hadley began pulling out papers, she knew she needed to find any writing that mentioned the Inn. Jace had found a book titled:

'The History of Wooten-Under-Edge'.

They had been reading for hours. After checking out the old leather-bound book Jace found, the librarian told them the news articles could be taken as long as they were taken with care. Hadley presumed someone in the past must have taken the librarians' kindness for granted. Wanting to stay on the good side of her former community, she smiled and assured him they would all be taken care off.

Stopping at a local chip shop to get some food to take home, the couple were once again looked upon by other residents as devil worshippers. Hadley had to keep reminding herself Wooton-Under-Edge was English town, of course they would stand out acknowledge the stares or the whispers, he or food, paid and lead Hadley out the shop.

On the way home, Hadley was right, her jacket not keep her warm. Unable to hold hands due to the amount both were carrying, the couple walked side by side up the hill to their home. Jace was amazed at the stars, he told Hadley he had always wanted to live somewhere, where the stars could be seen. Bright, beautiful diamond dust thrown across the night sky, shining hope for those who are lost in the world.

Although Hadley knew there was beauty in the world, natural beauty, which would remain even after the last human took their last breath. She also knew that there could never be one without the other. No beauty without repulsiveness, no good without evil and no gain without loss.

Hadley was unable to stop her mind going over what little Marty had told her, *'They are scared, she doesn't want us here'*. What did he mean by this? Who was this woman and what sinister secrets was she hiding? She knew they had to find something that would help Marty and his mother.

After dinner the couple decided to read more on the towns' history. Jace started with the book, it was old, centuries of the towns' history wrote down on paper. Hadley worked on going through all the news articles they had brought back.

ow this wee town is mentioned as far back as 940, in Saxon royal charter. But in the Doomsday Book as Vutune."

Looking at her husband, Hadley knew this was going to be a long night. They read through the 1400 and 1600 century with little to no prevail. Reaching the 1700 and 1800 centuries they discovered Wotton-Under-Edge produced red cloth for the British Army, leading them to build the local church.

"This is hopeless." Hadley sighed from exhaustion. Jace went back to the beginning of the book. Page after page containing the same sentences they had already read. They were not even halfway through the book which meant the Inn had to be mentioned somewhere further along. Hadley brought in a fresh pot of tea, and sat down on the couch she had fallen asleep on when they first moved in.

Jace began flicking through the pages, looking for any page which had the words Ramm Inn on. Hadley hoped he was about to say lets go to bed, but with joy he announced "Finally, I found something!"

Hadley blinked multiple times and rubbed her eyes. She walked over to where Jace was sitting and sat beside him. The pages were headed with The Ancient Ramm Inn. Jace was right, he had found what they were looking for.

Built in 1145, the site was home to a multi-millennia Pagan burial ground that lies on the Ley-lines. Here they performed a blood sacrifice or blot ritual for those who lived near the site. The ritual was performed out in the open, among the nature and closer to the gods and goddesses. It was law that no violence among those who attended was allowed. The ritual would be performed over an altar made of stones and once the animals were sacrificed the blood would be collected in a bowl. Songs would be sung to honour the gods in which the sacrifice was for, and the blood collected would be sprinkled on the priest and those attended, and whatever blood was left, would be poured onto the altar.

Hadley imagined how the landscape would have looked, the buildings they walked past earlier, not built until the distant future. The trees multiplied, like a glowing carpet of gold coloured leaves. The roads dug out by the hands of those who rode on horses and travelled in carriages. Families lived in small wooden houses with thatched roofs and fabric covering the doors and windows. Inside the homes, fire pits were placed in the middle of the living area and the smoke danced out the chimney.

To show their faith, symbols of their gods and goddesses were drawn onto the walls. The pagans would use the Inn as their temple. During October barrels would be full of apples and they would bob for them, asking the dead for guidance and foretell of the future. On the days leading up to Samhain they would prepare to welcome the new year, those selected would be preparing to invoke the Cailleach, or Crone.

But knowing how her faith was in the past, she imagined how the pagans were wiped out.

'Devilry peasants, this land holds no place for your necromancy.' Christian soldiers declared as they descended upon the quiet peaceful village. They would destroy the homes, the temple and callously murder those who wouldn't convert to the lands new faith. All accoutrements of the old gods and goddesses were then wiped out and replaced with the new and only god.

Hadley was thrown out of her thoughts as Jace asked if she wanted more tea. She had always loved learning about her true religious beliefs, and how other religions shaped their actions and views on the world. How the country she came from was changing over and over again

"Sorry my love. Please, but no sugar."

Jace poured the tea and carried on reading the book.

The Ramm was home for slaves, masons and other workers building the St. Marys Church near the Inn. Due to streams which ran on the grounds surrounding the Inn and the building site for the church. They had to be diverted away from the church. This is believed to have opened portals for the dark energy which was once used by pagans in their rituals. Once the masons left, a priest made the Inn his residence.

"The dark energy is being seen as a woman. Marty said he has seen her. But what about the children? From all the books I have read, and from what I remember my mother telling me, yes some pagans did human sacrifice, but never children." Hadley told Jace, who merely just shrugged his shoulders showing Hadley he was also confused.

"What about the papers? They may be our best bet." Jace replied after feeling the shrug of his shoulders was not the best answer to give. They pushed the book to one side and began scanning through the endless amounts of paper articles they had brought back with them.

> London has Jack the Ripper does Gloucestershire have a copycat? – 1889, Gloucester Citizen.

> Murder Strikes Again – 1880, Gloucestershire Chronicle.

> Ancient Ram Inn back up for sale – 1904, Gloucester Citizen.

> 3 Children Missing Suspected Occult Causes – 1920, Gloucester Citizen.

> Tales of the Woman Burnt at the Inn for Witchcraft – 1790, Gloucester Journal.

"Wait, Jace what was that last one? 'Woman burnt at the Inn for Witchcraft' Hadley suddenly asked, hopeful they had found something.

Jace handed over the paper with the proposed title and waited for Hadley to go through the article. Hadley skimmed over the article and frowned.

"Why have parts been scribbled out?" Hadley cursed as she threw the paper article back onto the table. Hadley went back to the stack of books.

"Jace did you bring this?" She asked as she held up a battered small book.

Jace shook his head and took the book off Hadley to look through. Hadley moved to Jace's side and tried to peer at the pages.

"What is it?"

Jace stopped reading and looked at her.

"It seems to be someone's diary from when the witch hunts were going on in this area."

Hadley's eyes widened as she took the book back from Jace and sat down at the table flicking through the pages.

Date 16th October 1550

Another lady was captured tonight. Alice Yorke, my friend and fellow sister. Alice had a hard life along with her sister and many called her one of the ladies of the night. I think yesterday she must have been working. Although I always worried about her, last night that feeling intensified, and I had known something would happen. I found out from gossip that Alice was working the alleys by the tavern waiting for her usual patrons to wander past drunk. But I heard whispers today that someone named Thomas Tuswell was the one who caught her. He is an ugly man who wears a black suit and a top hat to show his statue. His thin moustache turns up whenever he seems happy or smug.

They talked about how wonderful he was and when poor Alice began her job Thomas pushed her hair back and saw her birthmark on her neck. I can't imagine how she must have felt. I heard he dragged Alice out of the alley and kept her looked up until this morning. I tried to see her but was pushed away by Tuswells merry men. All I could hear was Alice pleading for mercy and no one listened. I moved away from where she was being kept. My heart was breaking for my friend, my sister. I stood back beyond the crowds as I couldn't watch Alice be dragged and branded a devilish witch.

Likewise, I felt as if Tuswell could read my mind as he shouted to the cheering crowd:

'Here is your devil worshipping witch'.

Just the other day Alice and I were picking apples near the woods and then today I watched her be placed in the stocks, so she could await her trial.

Date 19th October 1550

I haven't been able to write for a while, Alice had her trial yesterday and before the trial her sister and me were the only ones to show her mercy. We tended to her wounds and her dehydration, I asked mother why the townspeople were doing this. Everyone loved Alice, she was kind and loved those around her but no one seems to care anymore. My mother explained that a woman is never safe when a man of power takes control.

To humiliate her more on the eve of her trial someone had rebranded a W on her forehead for all to see. When the trial began the whole town was there, all happy I might add. Such cruel inhumane mortals. I heard someone spit on the ground when Alice walked by, and I watched with tears in my eyes as she was tied to the pole.

Margret begged for them to reconsider, we both pleaded with them and told them she is not a minion of the devil which they claim her to be. But we were ignored and Tuswell looked down on us from his platform and smiled with that repulsive moustache. It was then I knew in my heart he was the real demon.

Loving sister Margaret moved closer to look up at him, I remember her words so clearly:

'It is too windy, please, do not do this. She is a good honest woman who doesn't deserve a slow torturous death'.

That is when the merry men pushed Margaret and I away into the crows who were shouting burn the witch. The towns priest was there, I remember him blessing the townsfolk, and yet, he did not once look at Alice. I smelt it before I could see what was happening, I told Margaret not to look, I pulled her close, so she could not see what was about to happen. The final words we heard Alice cry out were

"Murdering me will not stop the plague that haunts this town, for I am no black magic witch. I shall not go into hell but sit with my god and goddess in Summer-land, and watch as you all burn here in this mortal realm".

I hugged Margaret tighter as we heard the flames begin to burn and the piercing scream from our beautiful Alice. I told her to recite with me, but she could all but wail in pain, so I did it myself

'Mother Goddess, father God, I release myself from those who have left this plane. And let them walk the blessed gardens of Summer-land' Alice took two hours to die and all that was left of her was ash.

Date 23 October 1550

Thomas Tuswell murdered another woman yesterday, no trial, no evidence just an assumption was what he told everyone was his reasoning. Mother knew her, she was a widower and her name was Catherine Seymour. Tuswell mocked her appearance, he said she had a crone look to her and hair above her lip. Mother told me Tuswell had said she was possessed by the Evil Eye.

I think the day before there was a towns meeting, mother said I did not need to go due to Alice not long being killed. But she kept me informed on what happened. Mother said Tuswell said

'This woman who lives alone possess something we call the Evil Eye, I am certain she is the one that is causing this plague.

Living alone in her home, she is just waiting to strike again. We need to terminate those who are involved with the Devil'.

My mother also said Tuswell confined in the town and accused Catherine of hating children. But dear Catherine loved children, her husband died young, and she never remarried, so she saw us as her children. We would pick apples from her tree. A beautiful memory only to be slandered by the demon himself saying she poisoned them. I did not go to her execution yesterday, I couldn't bare to see another person die under this man's command. Mother told me with tears in her eyes, Catherine walked in shackles to the gallows and was branded the same as Alice. Mother recited the prayer Catherine cried as the noose was placed around her neck

"'Thou lord shall protect me, he knows the truth. The apples will still be there, still with no poison, for the children to eat after I am thrown into the ground. Forgive me father and forgive those whose path have taken a dark turn, they are under a spell not from a witch but from a mere mortal man".

I had never seen someone be hung, so I asked mother what happened she was reluctant to tell me but eventually, she gave in to my pleads. She said her eyes bulged, her hands instantly went to her neck as she struggled to breathe. But what shocked mother most was that the town was silent and there were people who cried as she hung. Mother got angry as she told me Tuswell smiled as Catherines dead body emptied her bladder.

Date 26th 1550

A town meeting was called today by Thomas Tuswell, mother said I had to go despite my hatred for the man who killed my Alice. She was not a bad witch, she would never cause people harm. Tuswell spoke of how although the deaths and disappearances were still occurring, he believed the numbers had gone down. Of course that means he killed two innocent women, but he made the town believe that the only acceptable answer to all this was there must be a coven of black witches.

I was Sitting next to mother and we by our neighbour John Asper and his thirteen-year-old daughter Mary. While Tuswell was giving his speech Mary went into one of her fits, my mother who has been helping John since his wife died helped Mary back onto her seat and made her calm.

The town is used to Mary having fits, but Tuswell could not stop staring at her as he continued his speech. I noticed John had put his arm around Mary even tighter. When we came home, mother and I spoke over dinner about how Tuswell kept looking at Mary. Mother said she was worried.

Date 28th October

I had to write as soon as I came home, excuse if the pen leaks from my tears, but my heart is aching. John asked my mother and me if we would accompany he and Mary on their walk. Mary seemed delighted when she saw us leave our house to join them and greeted us with hugs. We made our way through the town, I walked with Mary talking about how beautiful the leaves looked this time of year. As we walked past the town hall we heard a commotion and Mary flung her arms around me.

I saw them before anyone else, Thomas Tuswell and his merry men were walking towards us. I tried to protect Mary until her father got to us, but my efforts just wasn't enough as I was pushed to the floor and saw two men hold Mary down.

I called out to Mary to stay calm as they have made a mistake, but Tuswell stood above me and stared into my eyes shaking his head. He said I was wrong that Mary had the witches' mole on her chin and the fits she kept having were her demons trying to escape. John and my mother were held back, I could see him shouting but all I could hear was Mary. Pulled away from looking at my younger friend I heard Tuswell command his men to take her straight to the gallows. I screamed, my mother screamed and John pleaded to let his daughter go. No one listened to us, as we chased after them, we pleaded with the townspeople, but they all looked away.

My home where everyone was once happy and said good morning to each other, now they were willing to let a young woman die from a lie a stranger fed them. Mary looked terrified, by the time we got to the front of the crowd she had already been branded a witch, the red W on her forehead could be smelt from where we were standing. Lovely sweet Mary had to stand on a stack of wood in order for the noose to be placed around her neck. John had been put in cuffs and held down on the muddy floor. My mother took my hand as Mary started to speak. Her words will stay with me forever, and I hope if anyone else ever reads this, her words will stay with you

'Father my lord and my mortal father, you know I am no witch. Please forgive me for what I must say as this noose is tightened around my neck. I curse all your future sleeps. When you cry I hope your tears will burn for killing Alice, Catherine and myself. For you have not been saved by killing us but only anger those above us'.

I was so proud of her for saying that, but I could see in her eyes she was terrified, she looked at me when they moved the wood away. Her eyes bulged and she turned an unnatural colour. My mother and me stayed with John long after everyone had left. His cries must have been heard from everyone who had made it back to their homes. It took us most of the day to make him stop watching his daughters body sway in the light autumn breeze.

Date 29th October 1550
Mother went to take John his morning meal today, his door was open, so she let herself in and found him in bed covered in his blood. A small knife was on his bed.

Date 30th 1550

The village is different, the only people who seem chipper is Thomas Tuswell and his merry men. No one leaves their homes any more, mother and I have tried to see Margaret, but she is nowhere to be seen.

Date 1st November 1550

Oh, Margaret, what did you do. After Johns death the village lost two more children, but this time someone saw something. A well-known homeless man saw a lady walk to an abandoned building holding a Childs hand and reported it to Tuswell straight away.

I heard people ran to the building with pitchforks, an angry mob ready to find out who took the children. Mother and I stayed near our home, we didn't want to be part of it, mother said she had a bad feeling she knew who it was. Out from the shadows Margaret ran out covered in blood, symbols carved up her arms and legs. Mother tried to call her, but she hissed and ran towards the Inn.

We followed not long after as mother gave me a pouch of dill to wear around my neck, but I had to make sure it was hidden under my garments. We got to the Inn we saw Margaret bow down to where her sister had burnt only a few days prior. We heard Margaret swore to get revenge on those who lived here. She cut into her wrist so the ashes of her sister could be soaked in her blood. Her last devilish hocus-pocus before running and hiding in a blackened out room.

The town caught up to us, we heard what people had found in the abandoned building. Marks resembling demonic and magic were left of the Childs dead body. His body was left on a slab for all to see. I'll never forget the look my mother had on her face as she went over everything Margaret had just done. We watched her be pulled out and tied to the same spot her sister was executed. We could hear her shout, and it made everyone stop

'You shall never rid of me and my magic, the blackest of evil cannot be purged, I shall remain on in this realm but not alone, no I will be one you will not be able to burn!'

Tuswell put a piece of cloth in her mouth, so she could no longer speak and quickly set the fire. The smell of someone burning gets stuck in your nose, I can still smell death now and she was burnt the 30th. Just like my mother, I am worried about Margarets last words.

Hadley stopped reading, her mind filled with questions. Jace stared wide-eyed, unable to come up with a sentence to cut the sudden silence.

"So we are dealing with a black witch. An actual ancient witch" Hadley finally said.

"Why would Cindy move in there, if that was the Inns past. Jace can you please say something".

She looked at her husband who still remained quiet, he rubbed his eyes and sighed.

"We have never dealt with a ancient witch from the darker realm" Jace leant back in his chair and stretched his aching muscles.

The two had been working tirelessly for hours and by now it had passed midnight. Jace stood up from the table and came up behind Hadley and kissed her on the top of her head. A sudden urge of love filled Hadley's body and her shoulders slumped as her head tilted to the side. She always loved that gesture, it brought her comfort and reassurance. She tilted her head back and smiled, looking up at Jace. Who brought his head down and softly kissed her on her lips. The thought of witches, witch hunts and being burnt at the stake had left both their minds. Hadley stood up, so she could feel her husbands embrace while their kiss became deeper.

Hadley pulled back and placed her head on his chest looking at all the scattered papers around the study.

"I love you" She whispered to him.

"I love you too my love".

Jace took Hadley by the hand and together they left the witch hunts and the demons in the study.

CHAPTER FOUR

Hadley awoke to a continuous loud banging. Petrified and half dazed she frantically tried to wake up Jace. Eventually, Jace finally mumbled he was awake.

As he sat up, he became aware of the noise which made Hadley sit wide-eyed in their bed. She watched him get out of bed and scan the outside from their bedroom window. Nothing was there, yet the banging continued. Jace pulled on his t-shirt and retrieved a bat from the wardrobe. She watched as he left the room and walk down the stairs. Worried, she also left the bedroom and stood on the landing, wanting to know if Jace would be okay. The banging made Hadley jump every time it came, biting her lower lip, she held her breath as Jace got closer to the front door. She knew her husband was nervous, she knew his hand were sweating as he continuously had to wipe his hands on his shirt. With no peephole, and no light to see out the window in the door, Jace slowly opened the front door.

Hadley was unable to see who was on the other side of the door, but she recognised the voice straight away.

Hadley ran down the stairs as Jace invited in a tormented looking Cindy and a whimpering Marty. After closing the door, Jace took Marty from Cindy who was shaking. Hadley put her arm around Cindy. She felt cold and on closer inspection her eyes were bloodshot and wary. Still holding on to Cindy, Hadley held her up as she led them all to the living room. Jace offered to make them a hot drink, and biscuits for Marty. Cindy only nodded her head, unable to speak through her recurrent sobs of terror.

Hearing Jace ask Marty what his favourite biscuits are, Hadley sat next to Cindy on the big three seater couch. She observed Cindy; her mixed race skin which looked washed out earlier, looked paler than it had just hours before. Her beautiful naturally curled hair was falling out of her bun, damped from sweat. Cindy's body became stiff as she reacted to a creak in the floorboards. Her eyes darted to the lounge door and Hadley saw her body relax as Marty walked in with a plate of biscuits, closely followed by Jace with a steaming green teapot and matching cups on a tray. Marty went up to his mother and handed her a biscuit before sitting beside her. Unable to only muster up a nibble to please her son, she then discarded the rest of the biscuit onto the table. Jace poured all adults their tea and took a seat on the two-seater couch opposite.

"Are you okay to tell us what happened?" Jace sounded sympathetic but also curious when he asked Cindy the question. Hadley picked up her teacup and sipped the warm liquid, waiting for the woman who had run to their house late at night screaming for their help, to explain why.

"I told you we sleep in the pub area now, fewer things happen." Cindy's voice was shaky and would often crack. "But tonight, I don't know what happened. Marty and I were settling in to our makeshift bed, when a chair moved away from one of the tables. Thinking it was just my mind playing tricks on me, I sat up to check, but it started being dragged across the pub. Then more and more started moving, glasses began to be thrown across the bar. Marty.." Cindy stopped talking as a sob caught in her throat.

She put her arm around her son, and closed her eyes. Marty hugged his mother back and whispered something calming, as his head turned more into her embrace. Hadley saw Cindy nod her head, she knew whatever Marty had just said to his mother, had brought her some comfort. Hadley saw Jace looking at her, not wanting to ruin the tender moment between mother and son, he mouthed 'poltergeists'.

Hadley bit down on her bottom lip and shrugged her shoulders. She knew from her years of studying that what Cindy was saying did indicate poltergeists. Noisy ghosts that are known to cause physical disturbances; objects moving or flying across rooms and destroying things.

Hadley had dealt with these types of supernatural beings before, she and Jace had spent a weekend on the Island of Mull in Scotland on a break from their studies. She loved the underrated island and its natural beauty. While they were sitting in a small pub, a family came running in shouting that stones were being thrown at them when they were on the beach. With no sightings of people being the culprit, the parapsychology team at the university were informed and a paranormal investigation was put into full force. However, once the team arrived, Hadley knew from the beginning this was not going to be straight forward. Paranormal historians have written poltergeists are more prone to interact with women over men; so when nothing happened to the men in the group. Scepticism began to form, one gentleman in the group proposed Spontaneous Recurring Psychokinesis, which made Hadley and the other females in the group aggravated.

She remembered Jace trying to be the peacemaker, but failing miserably. She remembered when the press became aware of the investigation, the small island became overpopulated with those wanting to see the stone throwing ghost. Therefore, the university withdrew and the investigation became nothing more than a headline that appeared in newspapers across the United Kingdom.

Hadley suddenly felt a warm rage grow inside her, the failed investigation put a strain on their name as paranormal investigators. However, listening to Cindy made her think this could not be a poltergeist, especially reading the diary.

"I don't think we are dealing with a poltergeist." Hadley voiced "Jace you remember the case in Scotland? Although it was cancelled, we saw and felt a different energy to what we felt when we walked into Cindy's Inn."

She saw Jace ponder on her words and slowly nod in agreement.

"The energy we felt in the Inn was much darker, much more sinister." Jace stopped talking when he saw Marty looking directly at him through his tired eyes and terror washing over his face. Hadley knew this was not a conversation for a young boy to hear, she also knew in her heart she could not let mother and son stay at the Inn until they had controlled the problem.

"Cindy, I am sure Jace would agree with me, you cannot go back there."

She looked over to her husband, she knew he would agree, however, she knew for Cindy's sanity she needed to hear Jace agree. He agreed Cindy and Marty would be their new house guests for the foreseeable future.

"Marty, shall I show you, yours and your mommy's new bedroom? You can sleep on something a lot more comfortable."

Wary but obviously tired Marty agreed, kissed his mom on the cheek and took hold of Hadley's hand.

Hadley knew they would wait for her to return, however, wanting to make Marty feel welcome and safe, she was going to take her time. She noticed Marty paying attention to every detail of the home, the pictures hanging on the wall, the plants on side tables, even the colour of the carpet running up the stairs. She noticed the grip on her hand become tighter when they reached the landing.

Children are more prone to detecting paranormal energies, Hadley worried he could detect something coming from her mothers old room. Walking past her mothers door, she took Marty into one of the double spare rooms. She had tried to make this room, like every other room bar her mothers, warm and welcoming.

Marty's new room still smelt of fresh paint, one focus wall had been papered with gold and white geometric shapes over a black background, the rest of the walls were white. Jace had painted the wooden bed frame black so the gold duvet cover would stand out. Hadley knew the bed was comfortable, she had personally picked out all the mattresses and pillows herself. Marty walked around the room. The room did not resemble a children's room, but he seemed impressed with the style choices.

Hadley moved the extra pillows to the end of the bed, yet she could still sense Marty was still anxious. She knew he would struggle to sleep up here on his own while Cindy sat downstairs. She told Marty to get comfy in the bed while she went and got someone who would love to stay with him.

When she walked back in Marty was already lying down. She sighed a sigh of relief internally, as he was already showing signs of calmness. Marty noticed she was holding something behind her back.

"Tah-Dah!" Hadley sung.

Martys mouth slowly curled into a smile.

"Is that for me?" He asked as he held his arms out ready to take hold of the brown coloured teddy bear. Hadley felt happy with her idea and handed over the teddy to Marty's wanting hands.

"Of course it is, his name is Mr Cuddles, and I am sure he will help protect you and bring you nice dreams."

Marty hugged Mr Cuddles and relaxed further into the comfort of the pillows and soft mattress. Hadley tucked them both in, the bears bowtie was left hanging over the top of the duvet.

"You going to be okay to sleep, until your mommy comes up?" Hadley asked.

Marty nodded his head and checked his new friend was just as comfortable as he was. Hadley saw his forehead crinkle and her concern began to grow again.

"Everything okay?"

Marty didn't answer her, so she carried on.

"You can tell me if something is wrong, maybe I can help find a solution to your problem."

After stroking the bears head Marty finally answered her.

"I'm worried about my friends still there at my home." Marty stopped speaking and Hadley knew he was remembering what had happened earlier at the Inn. Hadley took hold of Marty's hand hoping the gesture would bring him reassurance.

"We will be able to help them I promise. But for now, we need to make sure you get some rest because you have been through a lot."

Hadley could see Marty was still worried, but he nodded his head and cuddled the bear tighter. Before she left the room Hadley asked if he would want the side lamp left on. With a yes, she stood up from the bed, said goodnight to Marty and left the bedroom door ajar.

Walking down the stairs Hadley could hear talk from the living room. She knew Jace would have been comforting Cindy through talks of growing up in Scotland and stories of their very sparse light-hearted investigations. Hearing Cindy chuckle about the time Jace and herself got trapped in an underground bunker. The only thing that made her scream was the huge spiders all over the place.

However, she began to feel more tense as she continued down the stairs knowing as soon as they all discussed the past of the Inn, Cindy would not be as calm. The floorboards creaked again when she reached the hallway, she made a mental note to get Jace to sort them out. Slowly she opened the door and poked in her head, both occupants of the room turned and smiled when they saw her. As Hadley walked into the room, she told Cindy which room her son was in and about the bear which Marty had become immediately attached to. With Jace coming back from the kitchen with more caffeine due to the incredible lateness, they launched into retelling the information they discovered. Hadley made sure to pay attention to Cindy's facial expressions, her body language and the small gasps she made at certain points of the now they called the late night story time.

"Oh my god!" Cindy began hyperventilating, beads of sweat gathered on her forehead and her hands now became too unstable to hold on to the tea cup she was holding.

Hadley quickly took the cup and placed it on the table. She put her arm around Cindy's shoulders and quietly whispered instructions.

Cindy attempted breathing through pursed lips, breathing into her diaphragm rather than her chest. Hadley noticed she looked embarrassed and reassured her that there is nothing to worry about, the news they just told her was shocking, sad and petrifying.

"I knew there was some sort of past, but I did not realise it was so horrifying. They hung a child, that poor, poor child!" Cindy began sobbing.

Hadley knew her mind was playing the brutal last moments of the young girl, like a VHS stuck on one part.

"Marty, talked about his friends a lot when I was putting him into bed. He said he was worried about them." Hadley paused thinking of how concerned the little child looked. Hadley took a gulp of tea, praying some caffeine would get into her system quick. She carried on revealing her train of thoughts.

"I do not think they are harmful, however, I do think they are being kept there. Spirits usually stick around in places they are attached to, like homes they lived in, places loved ones were. So if the children were scarified there, they would have no reason to want to stay there."

Hadley leant on her hand as her elbow perched on the arm of the couch, lost in her thoughts. She looked over to Jace who had been listening to her every word, she saw him scrunch his forehead, which she knew was a sign, his ideas were coming into place. He added,

"You are right, not every spirit is evil, many are just unable to pass on. A harrowing thought if you think about it. But you think that the children are being kept there? They would only be able to be kept there by a very strong, demonic entity."

Hadley widened her eyes, her mouth unintentionally made an O shape.

"The witch, it has to be the witch they burnt; Margaret Yorke. What did she say; you cannot purge pure evil or something."

Hadley began biting her lips, something she did when she was concerned about something.

"This can be the only answer. Obviously when Margaret made the threat to the towns people she wasnae kidding! I would say she is keeping the children's souls there for a purpose. There is much more to find out. But for tonight.." Jace stopped mid-sentence and looked at the clock. He squinted his eyes to make sure he was getting the time correct and continued.

"For tonight, I think we all need rest. Why don't we go and get some sleep? And we can make a plan tomorrow." The women both nodded and Jace began turning off the lights while they walked into the hallway and up the stairs. Hadley got Cindy some pyjamas to sleep in and showed her which room she would be staying in. After they said their goodnights, Hadley made her way back down the stairs and added salt to the bottom of the doorframe. If she was dealing with a witch, she wanted to protect everyone while they slept.

CHAPTER FIVE

Hadley and Jace woke up before their guests, both had never really slept in. Hadley had convinced Jace to go into town and buy something nice for breakfast. When Jace was walking out she shouted, croissants, doughnuts and any other pastries. Hadley then carried on with her normal morning routine, put the coffee maker on, do half an hour of yoga and luckily this time get to read the newspaper first.

Wotton-Under-Edge Halloween Festival Preparations Underway

Hadley raised her eyebrows, the pictures from the previous years' festival filled the page. Children smiling dressed up as witches, vampires and zombies. One boy was dressed as a very impressive werewolf. Groups of families and friends were bobbing for apples, others were eating toffee apples, and a photo of the fair which made its appearance every halloween stood bright and packed with happy Wotton-Under-Edge residents. Hadley was so engrossed in the article she didn't notice Cindy and Marty walk into the kitchen and join her at the table.

"I love fairs!" Marty announced breaking Hadley out of her reading trance.

"Mommy and I go to one every year, don't we mommy? Mommy is scared of the ghost train aren't you? But she loves the toffee apples." Marty looked over to his mom.

Smiling she finally answered for herself, "You feared the ghost train as well, I remember you squeezing my hand very tightly."

Hadley laughed and offered to make Cindy a cup of coffee and Marty and Mr Cuddles a hot chocolate. Marty laughed shaking his head and told Hadley she was silly. Hadley pleased she had been able to make him laugh got up from the table and went to make the drinks.

"Did you both sleep well?" Hadley asked as she waited for the kettle to boil for Marty's drink and poured herself and Cindy a fresh cup of coffee.

"We did, thank you so much for this, I don't know how I can ever repay you."

The kettle whistled and Hadley poured the hot water onto the chocolate powder which was already submerged in milk.

As she brought the drinks over to the table she looked at Cindy.

"Cindy, please do not ever think you need to repay Jace or me. We want to help you and Marty and you are welcome to stay here as long as is needed. It may be a good idea to close the pub while the investigation is in force. I think we angered whatever evil force is living in the Inn when you spoke with us. Therefore, it is not safe for you to go back."

Hadley saw Cindy pondering on her idea of not reopening the pub, she knew it would not be convenient for her, if the pub was shut her income would stop. But she knew going back there would be dangerous for the landlady and her punters.

"I was thinking that last night, but I am worried about not making the little money I already do make. I have to think of our future."

Cindy did the same biting of the lip Hadley usually did when she was anxious or thinking.

"However, you are right, I need to think of the future, but I also need to think of our safety. So, I shall remain closed for at least a couple of days. Nothing really happens in the day, and I am never on my own, not with the locals I always get in there." Cindy said.

Before Hadley could reply…

"BREAKFAST IS HERE!"

Jace walked into the kitchen with a full brown paper bag, branded with the local bakers' logo. Marty recognised the logo straight away and began wooing and cheering about the breakfast he was about to eat. While Jace began emptying the bags items onto the table, Hadley got up and retrieved plates and napkins for them all to use. She also poured a fresh cup of coffee for her husband and mouthed thank you to him through a smile. Hadley was shocked he had taken her request quite literally. The table was now filled with croissants, doughnuts and all sorts of delicious looking pastries.

"Help yourself Marty, take whatever you want." Jace said to a wide-eyed Marty.

Marty went straight for the doughnut with orange and black icing, no doubt the colours were to resemble the halloween fever which was gripping the town.

Breakfast went by uneventful, they all chatted while they ate and drank and made the plans for the day ahead. Cindy was adamant she needed to go back to the Inn and retrieve hers and Marty's belongings. Not wanting her to go alone, Hadley proposed Jace accompany her and for her to not enter alone. That left Hadley, Marty and his new best friend alone for a few hours.

Before leaving, Jace and Cindy both prepared themselves. Salt from Hadley's special jars at the front of the house was scooped up and put into a portable jar.

"Why all this?" Cindy asked.

"Just for extra protection."

Hadley knew that they were walking into an old pagan ritual full of black magic and no bible or crucifix will help them. Hadley came into the study with two limes. Cindy's forehead creased and her brows closed together. With a chuckle, she handed one lime to Jace and Cindy. Jace explained the purpose of this while demonstrating what to do. Amused at watching his mother rub a lime from her head to her toes three times, before cutting it in half and disposing of it. Marty could no longer keep in his curiosity.

"Why does mommy need to do that?" He asked Hadley who had taken a seat besides him.

"It is called lime therapy, it is supposed to distract the evil eyes gaze, which we believe is what the witch possesses." Hadley replied.

"It is much better than some others, when they get back, they will need to put three drops of oil into a pan of fresh water. If the drops remain round, then no evil has linked onto them."

Hadley looked at Jace and Cindy. Jace, upon seeing Cindy's face quickly began reassuring her.

"When we get back we will do a salt shower."

Once they left, Hadley decided to re-salt the corners of the house with Marty and Mr Cuddles in tow. Hadley enjoyed the company, she knew Marty was interested in the job her and Jace did and seemed eager to learn more. After finishing replacing the salt in all corners of the home, the two made their way into the kitchen. Sitting at the table, drinking fresh drinks the conversation quickly fell into how Hadley grew up and past investigations. Replying to Martys question of why she grew up in the church, not wanting to go too in depth about what happened to her mother, Hadley told him, how her mother who was closely connected to the church and when she died of an illness, the church agreed to look after her as they were worried she may have the same illness in her. Assuring Marty she didn't, Hadley went on to tell him, her childhood was filled with learning ancient scripts from the christian faith. However, when she reached a certain age, she knew evil was not just focused on one religion. Therefore, she took it upon herself to learn many religious beliefs and the demonology evil within each one. Not wanting to tell Marty everything, she skipped over that when reading through the scrolls, the books and the stories of what people told her. Hadley believed the demons and the evil was not within just one religion. For centuries humans have used their faith to place comfort on them.

Going back to when the lands were filled with pagans, they used remedies to ward off all evil, not just a specific demon.

Of course, she trained in demonology, she had to, if she wanted to understand her beliefs. Yes, there are "demons" but evil is old, it started at the beginning just as life and pureness did. How could evil be drawn into one religion when religion did not exist at the beginning of time. She remembered what her mother had said before she passed:

"I spit on the book in which your species revels in believing it shall save you. I do not come from the fire pits of hell, but from your depraved nightmares. You cannot summon me away; for when I leave this vessel, I shall find new flesh and blood to curdle and drain."

Hadley knew the priest hadn't saved her mother from the demon, the demon killed her mother and disappeared into the night; or as the church had thought into her.

Heading to the Inn, Jace and Cindy made a plan. Their first stop would be to the florist. Jace wanted to see if he could get any mistletoe. He explained to Cindy that in the Middle Ages people would tack sprigs of mistletoe over the doors of their homes and barns to keep dark witches away. Coming off the main high street Jace came to a halt, a shop smelling of incense and herbs made Jace walk in without telling Cindy. The shop was decorated with halloween decorations, fake spider webs framed the doorway and walls with giant spiders clinging onto their homes, a fireplace took over the room and as Jace walked further into the shop, he realised he had discovered a holistic shop. Little spooky lights hung from the fireplace and pumpkins were scattered around the unusually large shop. The strong smell of incense burning filled Jace's sinuses of wild berry, as the smoke worked its way around the halloween decorations. Cindy had huffed into the shop smacking him on the shoulder for not letting her know he was coming inside. With a sorry, they both continued walking around the surprisingly large interior of this shop. Picking up a round candle to sniff Cindy told Jace she had no idea the town had a shop like this.

"Welcome to Spiritual Healings, my name is Kerry, and I am happy to have you in my shop." A thirty-year-old woman said as she walked closer to the pair.

Her dyed red hair was tied in a high ponytail, her slender figure could be seen from her corset dress which flowed to the ground from the waist. A rich brown colour which complemented her pale skin tone. Cindy put down the candle, shocked from the sudden appearance of Kerry and her calming voice.

"Thank you, I'm Jace and this is Cindy." Jace said with a smile.

Kerry closed her eyes and smiled before saying, "Cindy, you are the one who owns the Inn aren't you? I am happy I finally have the chance to meet you."

Cindy looked at Jace with a look of confusion and curiosity.

"Yeah, I own the Inn, I brought it a couple of months ago my son and I live, well lived there."

Kerry tilted her head to the side in thought, "You don't live there any more?"

Jace could see Cindy was becoming uncomfortable speaking about the Inn. He knew the town admired the Inn but was all sceptical about whether paranormal was really lurking inside or not.

To help her out Jace replied, "No, she is staying with my wife and me at the moment, while the Inn undergoes some renovations."

Cindy mouthed thank you to him and felt she could now speak for herself.

"Yeah, Jace and Hadley are letting us stay with them until it is done. So the whole place is in lockdown until further notice."

Kerry nodded her head with squinted eyes, Jace knew she didn't believe them.

"I must apologise Cindy, I didn't want to drink or stay at your Inn, I have been here a while now, when I first moved here, I wanted to come in. However, when I reached the courtyard, I could not cross. The veil between this realm and the next is extremely thin, and there is a presence within the grounds which I did not want to come in close contact with." Kerry stopped talking.

Her face showed she would rather sit down and tell them her thoughts. She guided the pair to a seating area, away from the main shop floor. Although there was no one else in the shop, all three felt more relaxed in the secluded seating area.

Once sitting down Kerry smoothed out her dress and continued with her statement on why she would not enter the Inn.

"Sorry about that, I would rather have us all feeling comfortable while retelling this. When I arrived I decided to explore the town, I came across your Inn, the building looked beautiful so of course I wanted to see inside. However, when I walked round to the courtyard, I couldn't cross. There was a woman in the window Cindy, first she was a dark figure, but her silhouette formed. Her gaze was fixated on me, I could tell even from the distance. Yet although I was terrified I could not turn away. But then her dark eyes turned into an abyss, her mouth opened and darkness, just darkness showed."

Kerry had put her hand over her mouth, her eyes shut as she remembered her experience at the Inn. Cindy took in a sharp deep breath and Jace dragged his hand through his flowing hair. Once she had composed herself Kerry continued.

"I heard children crying I tried to do a spell to settle the atmosphere, but I couldn't stay, I ran back to the main street and to my shop. I'm sorry". Kerry looked at Jace, "You and your wife, I have heard locals speak about you. You told some drunks about your tattoos."

She pulled her sleeves up and revealed the same symbols both he and Hadley had on their bodies.

"I am like you. You know whatever is in that Inn, is not what we believe. Our ancestors spoke about these phantoms, these ghouls are ancient and from the darkest realm."

Cindy shaken from even more news of the evil which was held within her home said, "Phantoms? I thought we were dealing with witches?"

She looked at both Kerry and Jace with concern and disbelief.

"We are." Jace told her. "Kerry has called it a phantom because these things are not meant to exist; not in this realm anyway. Ghosts and the paranormal are very real, however, beyond the paranormal world is a darker realm. One where black magic and pure evil live. A place we don't fully understand and a place we hope the evil will remain." Jace knew this was something he and Hadley should have realised from the beginning. They had learnt about it while studying, but it was rare, and he didn't think they would be put in this position.

"Cindy I am sorry Hadley and I didn't put all the pieces of the puzzle together, are you sure you want to go back and collect your belongings? This is not going to be easy." Cindy nodded her head.

"Is what you have there, really so important that you want to risk your life? I understand it's your home. But are materialistic things worth your life?" Kerry said. "This thing, I feel knows you have asked Jace and Hadley to help, it probably even sensed their pagan beliefs due to their auras. You have angered it more, and it does not want you or anyone else there, it will try and hurt you". Kerry sounded blunt yet worried about the journey the two were about to take for something so minor.

"I really recommend you stay away, until you figure out, what this thing wants, what it is and how you can banish it." Kerry smiled at Jace. "I can smell lime, I take it you did the lime cleanse at home. Do you have salt and mistletoe? Of course the mistletoe is for your home, but I don't think it would harm if you carried some on you."

Jace pulled out the salt bottles he had in his bag and told Kerry mistletoe was what they had been on the way to get. Kerry stood up and walked to the back of the shop, out of sight from Jace and Cindy.

Cindy collapsed into her hands, Jace let her tears fall as he comforted her while they waited for Kerry to return. Jace thought back to when he and Hadley had first gone to the Inn. He remembered Hadley stopping, eyes wide, staring at a window. He remembered her saying something does not feel right, but he had brushed it off as her being back in her old town. He needed to do more research, this had to be related to the murder of Margaret Yorke. But how and why was her spirit still this strong? What marks were on the last child she sacrificed? She had to have sacrificed more. So many thoughts ran through Jace's mind, and he knew he needed to get Hadley up to date with what Kerry had said.

"Here, please take this. I grow it myself." Kerry had walked in carrying two sprigs of mistletoe, wrapped at the end with black ribbon. She handed them to Jace, who looked at Cindy

"So, are we still going?" He asked. Cindy stood up and hugged Kerry thanking her for her help.

"Yes, its daytime, we should be safe." Cindy hoped.

CHAPTER SIX

The walk to the Inn was not far from Spiritual Healings and Jace went over what needed to happen, to try and make this trip as safe as possible. The plan was to stay together, no wondering off and to avoid falling into a trap of calling out to the witch.

Jace had also told Cindy he wanted to try and find any symbols which may give him and Hadley more of a clue as to how the evil phantom can stay with such a strong presence. He asked Cindy if she had seen any symbols, markings, anything which looked unusual carved within the Inn. Cindy shook her head and told him she had not heard about anything like that when she brought the place, and she had not seen anything while living there.

The Inn looked just as beautifully eerie has it always looked. Seeing a few old men sitting outside the pub area, moaning that their local was not open yet, was not surprising to Cindy.

"A few always come dead on noon. I guess with wives passing, not the best home lives, some people need a place to be." Cindy sighed with a shrug.

She asked if Jace knew what the best thing to say to them was as she knew without a doubt, they would think she was crazy if she told them their favourite place to be was being haunted by a demonic, phantom witch.

"There she is! Oi, isn't this place supposed to be open at 12? It is already quarter to one. We have been waiting here for you to open. Do you not respect your locals anymore Cindy?"

Jace identified the person who had spoken to Cindy in such a rude manner as Mike; the one who had called Hadley and him satanists when they first visited the Inn.

"Oh don't be so rude Mike, I have an announcement to make everyone. I am going to have to remain closed for the time being, a pipe burst last night, which is why Marty and me were not here when you came. The problem is being fixed, however, until further notice the entire building will be shut."

Jace nodded his head in agreement, impressed she could lie so perfectly. A couple of the punters groaned and wondered off, no doubt in look for a replacement until their desired local was back open. Mike however, stood there crossed arms. After a short discussion with Cindy telling Mike to stop being silly and go find somewhere else to drink. Mike walked away mumbling something inaudible to himself.

Jace watched as he walked down the lane and waited until he was out of earshot. When Mike had got to a distance Jace thought was far enough, he turned to Cindy.

"So we ready to go in?"

Cindy had the keys ready in her right hand, her hands were shaking, and she had to take a moment to steady herself before she could unlock the door. After a few deep breaths, the door unlocked and they both walked inside. The pub had a rancid decaying odour, that made Cindy retch and Jace cover his nose with his hand. The lights were out and all the curtains had been closed the pervious night. The only ray of sunlight shone in through a rip in one of the curtains. Cindy told Jace where the light switch was placed, and they made their way over to the bar area.

After searching with fingertips, the lights filled the pub and Cindy gasped when she saw what her home and business had been subjected to. Chairs and bar stools had broken legs, the fabric cushions had been ripped as if an animal had been let loose on the green fabric. Glass glittered the floor and every step ended in a crunch. The crosses Cindy had hung up were now destroyed, a sign they were of no use.

"Okay where is your stuff?" Jace whispered.

Cindy pointed to the area where her and Marty would sleep tucked in the far corner. They both made their way over to the corner, the makeshift bed had been flipped, the clothes they had brought down when they could no longer sleep upstairs, had been thrown and scattered across the area. On closer inspection many of the clothes had been made no longer wearable. Jace helped Cindy quickly pack as much as they could in the spare bags they had brought with them. Once everything was packed, Jace made the decision they should leave. On the way out Jace was on high alert, he wanted to get Cindy out as quickly as possible.

They came back around the bar and Jace noticed something on one of the beams. Paint had been chipped away revealing something that had long been carved into the wood. He whispered to Cindy to stop and Cindy tiptoed back to where Jace was looking and took a closer look at his discovery. He was already stroking his finger over the carving. Cindy struggled to see what it was.

"What is that?" She asked Jace.

Jace had finished moving his finger over the symbol.

"It is a heart and dagger." He replied. He moved over to the next beam which also had paint chipped on a certain spot.

"This one, I don't know what it is, it has a pentacle, but it's not.." Jace moved his hand to a symbol below the unidentified one "The Sacrificial circle".

He tried to speak quietly, but the words came out louder than he wanted them to.

"We need to.." Jace was cut off by the sound of a high pitch laugh; the laugh carried on ringing in their ears. Cindy's bottom lip started to tremble as she looked at Jace, his eyes were darting around the pub. A shadow flickered at the corner of his vision, but was gone as soon as it was spotted. As they were both staring in the direction of the fireplace, the door stating 'do not enter' had begun to close. Both knew the door had originally been shut when they first arrived.

Jace felt a puff of air on his ear lobe, not wanting to frighten Cindy more, he sucked in his breath. His body temperature began to drop, and he could feel Cindy begin to shake with the sudden change in temperature. The lights within the room began to flicker before each light went out with a bang. The surrounding temperature dropped more and Jace moved closer to Cindy, etching her to move closer to the exit. A floorboard creaked by the door that had opened and shut. Cindy inhaled a deep breath, tears forming in the corner of her eyes. She could see each breathe Jace exhaled before realising her breath could be seen. She held on to Jace's arm as they started walking backwards towards the exit door. A rotten smell fell on top of them, as more and more floorboards began to creak. Jace continued to use his body as a shield for Cindy as he pushed her back, hoping they would reach the exit door. He quickly looked behind and past Cindy's head. The exit could be seen, they had agreed to keep the door open for an easier exit. Only a few more feet, and they would be safely out the Inn.

Jace felt it before he could stop it, he felt Cindy lose her footing as she fell backwards like she was a victim of the tabletop game. As she fell down, she took him with her and they both landed on the hard wooden glass filled floor. Before he checked he was okay, he quickly faced Cindy and asked if she was okay.

"Something was behind me Jace, Something felt like it was behind me and I lost my footing, and I am so sorry." Cindy continued crying, her sobs made it hard for Jace to understand everything she was saying. He quickly looked around the pub, unable to find anything which could be the cause of their fall.

Cindy let out a terrifying scream, and pushed her body away from where they had fallen. Jace unprepared for the scream, also jumped, unsure as to what was going on.

"Something just touched me, oh my god, something just brushed up me but there is nothing there!" Cindy screamed again.

Jace looked into Cindy's eyes. Her eyes were wide, and she let out a small cry. Jace moved his eyes to the top of her head, something was moving behind her, but with no electric lights and just the dense light from outside he could only make out that something was moving. Jace squinted his eyes, moving his head more forward to try and get a better look.

"Jace" Cindy whispered petrified.

Cindy's head flung back and she pulled herself back to a sitting position, confused and disoriented. Jace didn't move this time as he watched the hood on Cindy's jacket slowly be pulled up by an unseen force.

'Jace?' Cindy mouthed as she watched him stare behind her with wide eyes.

Cindy's head was flung back again. This time she was unable to sit back upright. Her tiny frame was pulled backwards as she let out a terrifying scream calling for Jace to help her.

Jace pulled himself up and ran in the direction Cindy's screams were coming from. Cindy had come to a stop, still screaming but this time, screaming for something or someone to get off her. Jace couldn't see anyone on top of her, but she was kicking and trying to protect her face from something. Jace called out Cindy's name, letting her know he was on his way to help. When he came to where she was lying he began to kneel so he could help her up. But the air was sucked out of him as he was thrown by a unbeknown force back to the other side of the pub. Jace landed on tables and rolled onto the floor, groaning in pain as tried to get a hold of his breathing.

"Jace, please help me!" Cindy pleaded to him.

Jace stood on his unsteady feet, the laughter arose from the darkness once again, more sinister than before. Struggling to breathe he ran towards where Cindy was still lying, pleading for the thing on top of her to get off. Jace made it to Cindy and pulled her up right. If anything was on her, he did not feel anything trying to push her back down. They both heard another creak coming from the area Jace had been thrown in. The lights flickered and came back on, although the temperature still remained cold. Cindy could see Jace was struggling to stand upright, wincing in pain from the rib area. Jace took a glance at Cindy, although nothing that he could see or feel was on top of her, he could see blood leaking from fresh scratches on her face. A floorboard creaked again before the sound of someone running towards them began. Cindy screamed and began to run for the door. Jace didn't bother looking for the source of the sound and bolted to the exit with Cindy. The faster they ran, the faster and louder the steps behind them became. Jace shouted to Cindy to run faster and keep looking straight ahead, the daylight from the exit was showing, but the running footsteps and the creaking of floorboards never stopped.

Cindy made it out the door first, closely followed by Jace who felt more safe in the last rays of the autumn daylight sunshine. Panting for breath he moved Cindy further Into the courtyard away from the door to the pub.

CHAPTER SEVEN

During the day Marty had asked Hadley if he could learn. Unsure of what he wanted to learn, Hadley laughed and followed Marty into the study. She watched as he scanned every book, eyes wide as he began pulling them off the shelves, revealing the front covers. Hadley walked over and took the books he had picked to the table. Settling into the chairs, Marty pointed to the one with a Pentacle on the cover. Hadley raised her eyebrows.

"Ah, you want to learn about this do you?" She said to Marty. "This on the cover is a Pentacle. Have you ever heard of it before?"

Marty shook his head.

"Well, the Pentagram is used by many religions. When I was taken in by the church after my mother died, I had to learn lots about Christianity, I spent a lot of my time in the church library. One book said in ancient times, the Pentagram was a Christian Symbol of the five wounds of Christ. They also say if the Pentagram is reversed," Hadley spun the book around, showing Marty what she meant, "See the two points are now facing up? Well, this is a symbol of the satanic faith. For a while, the reverse Pentagram has been used in black magic and voodoo. But when the five pointed upright star is placed in a circle like the one on this cover, it is called a pentacle. The five points represent each element, fire, earth, water, air and spirit. And the circle is the universe in which these elements are kept."

"Magic? Like the witch I heard you speaking to mommy about, like at my house?" Marty hugged the bear Hadley had given to him. Hadley did not even notice him carrying the bear around the house.

"No, well, yes. But Marty, the witch at the Inn is not of Pagan Wiccan. She is of black magic, ancient magic which resembles the evil eye. She is not from this realm."

"Realm, what is a realm?" Marty asked.

"Well, we have the realm you and I live on called Midgard. The realm where Goddess Hel rules is Helheim, there she decides how your soul will carry on in the kingdom of the dead, if you didn't make it to Summer-Land. Then we have the darkest of the darkest, I remember reading about what Christians call hell. And I think this is what they mean, however, it is not underneath us."

Hadley stopped when she remembered the necklace Marty had tucked under his t-shirt.

"I'm sorry Marty, do you want to learn something else?"

Marty squeezed Mr Cuddles and sighed shaking his head.

"No it's okay Hadley, I like to listen to stories. When mommy reads me my bedtime story, it is my favourite part of the day."

Hadley loved the innocence of the little boy, she knew he had seen evil just like she had. Even worse, he was younger than she had been.

"Okay," Hadley continued "Well as I was saying the pentacle is used in Wicca for spells. This books information dates back centuries. Telling us all about Wiccan rituals, and about the gods and goddesses. It was someone's book of shadows. They must have died and never passed it on to their coven or someone they trusted. Luckily, Jace and me got our hands on it." She began turning the pages, showing Marty the scribbles and doodles that once belonged to a white witch.

"Freya is mother earth born of Nerthus. She is the goddess of love, a mother, a protectress of children and of women in childbirth. The story goes she was sleeping peacefully and Loki the Prankster, the mischief-maker of the gods became fixated on the glimmering Brosingamene. The Brosingamene is a gorgeous necklace which lay on Freya's Snow White neck. You see Goddess Freya can be quite vain and only wants those things which are above beautiful. However, no longer able to control his obsession, Loki removed the silver cricket from her neck.

But Freya awoke from her sleep and sensed the loss and that is when she caught a glimpse of Loki before he swiftly passed from sight into the barrow that leads to Dreum. Not able to overcome her loss, Freya descended into complete darkness, all light, all life, all creatures joined in her doom. All searchers were sent to find the mischief maker, yet they would never find him, as who would be foolish enough to descend into Dreum. Still weak from grief Freya elected herself to descend searching for her Brosingamene. But mischief Loki left no trail and those she asked said Loki carried no such jewel."

Marty gasped, eyes wide as he listened to Hadley.

"Did she get it back?"

"Well, Hearhden the mighty smith of the gods arose from his rest to find the cause of the sorrow. Striding from his smithy, he saw the silver cricket where Loki had laid it. Loki had laid it upon the rock before his door. Because who would be silly enough to go into Dreum after him.

When Hearhden took hold of Brosingamene, Loki appeared, his face wild with rage. Yet Loki would not attack the mighty smith. He tried with tricks and whiles to get his hands back on the necklace, unable to sway the smith. Tiring of the fight Hearhden raised his mighty club, sending Loki on his way. So great with joy was Freya with the Hearhden, he placed the Brosingamene back onto her snow-white neck." Hadley finished.

"She got it back!" Marty smiled upon hearing the end.

"Is there only the girl god?"

"Oh no there are many gods and goddesses. Woden is the all father god of war, Eir is the goddess of healing, Borr is the father of Woden, Thor is god of thunder and battle. He has a wife named Sif who is goddess of the harvest. There are many more. Lets look at another book shall we?" Hadley shut the book of shadows and reached for a blue leather-bound book. The title was carved into the leather, which no longer had that new leather smell. Marty had an attempt to read the title of the book, but could not get the words out.

"Ancient Egyptian Demonology: Studies on The Boundaries Between The Demonic and The Divine in Egyptian Magic" Hadley read aloud.

They spent the next few hours going through books, looking at pictures, and Hadley answered any questions Marty asked. Before they started their next activity Hadley made lunch for them both. Marty picked sandwiches, ham and cheese which he said were his favourite. They both made their way to the kitchen, a few pastries were left from the morning, which Marty insisted he was going to eat for a lunch pudding. Hadley asked if his mother would be happy with this much sugar, but she didn't know how to say no to a child.

When lunch was prepared Hadley made her way over to the table with cans of diet cola and the sandwiches Marty had asked for. Hadley reached over to the paper, which she was unable to finish skimming through that same morning. She reached the ad section when she was on her last few bites of the sandwich.

"Oh wow, look Hadley, puppies!" Marty pointed to the add which displayed five chocolate coloured Labrador puppies.

"They are so cute, you should get one, you have a massive house and garden." Marty continued.

Hadley nodded her head and agreed she and Jace did have a big house. Hadley looked at the ad and smiled at Marty.

"I think we may need to convince Jace."

Hadley was beginning to get worried. Jace and Cindy had been gone the whole day. The sun had already passed the horizon and dinner was almost done. Hadley had let Marty choose the meal for them all, as he had been getting anxious waiting for his mother to return.

"They will be back soon Marty, why don't we finish getting the table set while we wait for the food to finish cooking. The spaghetti should be done soon."

Hadley hadn't cooked spaghetti bolognese in a long time and was unsure whether they had the ingredients when Marty suggested it. However, when they went looking for ingredients, they found fresh mince, vegetables and more all stored in the fridge.

"I guess Jace was hinting he eventually wanted your choice as well." Hadley said to Marty as they got the ingredients all together.

Happy his choice of cuisine was on offer, Marty helped Hadley prepare the meat and watched as she fried the mince to a light brown.

"Do you want to pour the sauce in?" She asked Marty who happily agreed. She pulled a chair up to the stove and helped him stand before the pan. She handed over the jar, and he carefully tipped it, watching as the contents sloshed onto the mince. By now the mince was cooked, the spaghetti was ready to be drained and the table was set. Marty suggested lighting some candles, as he told Hadley his mother liked candles. Hadley drained the spaghetti and they both heard the key unlock the front door. Marty already sitting at the table with his bear, quickly pushed his chair back and ran to the door as Jace and Cindy were walking in.

Hadley could hear Marty ask his mother what was wrong with her face and he sounded upset. Hadley left the food in the drainer and quickly walked to the hall to see what was wrong. A gasp broke from her when she saw Jace and Cindy. Shaking she walked over to Jace and hugged him.

"I was so worried about you, I love you are you okay?"

This was not a conversation for Marty to hear, so Hadley proposed the two quickly shower and clean up, they would tend to their wounds, and then they would eat dinner before Marty went to bed. With Marty telling Cindy he had cooked her their favourite meal, she smiled and agreed on the plan.

"Jace?" Hadley said as she took Marty from Cindy's arms, "Why don't you tell Cindy how to cleanse in the shower with salt while Marty and I finish getting dinner ready. Cindy, when you come back, I will care for the wounds on your face."

Hadley walked back into the kitchen and heard Jace take Cindy over to the salt jars and refill the jars they had in their bags.

"Why are they going to have salt in the shower with them Hadley? And what is wrong with mommy's face?"

Hadley could sense Marty wanted to cry as he spoke to her. She carried him back to the table and handed him Mr Cuddles, who he squeezed very tightly. As she took the spaghetti from the drainer and placed into a deep bowl she tried to speak as softly and as carefully as she could. "Your mommy and Jace have been to a bad place, the salt will cleanse them of any evil which may have tried to cling its self onto them. After the shower they will be safe just like you and me are."

She brought the bowl over to the table and continued, "Your mommy has some cuts on her face, but don't worry, we will take care of her."

Marty nodded burying his chin into the bears head. Hadley continued getting the rest of the food onto the table, finishing with the garlic bread that they had almost forgotten about. Hadley had chosen white candles to burn while they ate, to add another barrier of protection to them around the table.

While lighting the last candle Cindy made her way back to the dining area. Slowly walking hunched over behind her was Jace. Hadley ran and put his arm around her shoulders helping him to the dinner table. Wincing she helped him sit down and took a look at Cindy's face. Most of the scratches had already begun to clot. However, one on her cheek was deep and blood was continuing to seep through the tissue Cindy held on her face.

"While Jace and Marty begin eating, why don't we put something on that cut, so you can eat." She said to Cindy. Marty was staring at her with wide eyes.

"Good idea." Cindy agreed.

As the two walked into the downstairs bathroom, they could hear Marty proudly announcing he had helped Hadley cook the dinner.

In the bathroom Hadley got Cindy to sit on the toilet after she put the lid down. The first aid box was under the sink and once Hadley started rummaging through, she found antibiotic ointment and asked Cindy to move the tissue away. The cut had slowed down, however, not stopped, so she couldn't put the ointment on. Instead, Hadley cleaned the wound as much as she could before placing three skin sutures strips over, then placed a gauze dressing over the strips. Happy that Cindy would be able to eat without blood dripping down her face, Hadley announced she was all done.

Cindy thanked her and walked over to the mirror, her face told a thousand words and Hadley hugged her telling her it was all going to be okay. Wiping away her tears Cindy nodded thanking Hadley again. Hadley smiled.

"It's okay Cindy, we are here to help you, now lets go get something to eat before them two leave use with crumbs of garlic bread."

Cindy laughed as they both walked back to the dining area. When they reached the table, Marty was tucking into his food, which had made its way onto his face as well as his lap.

After swallowing a mouth full he smiled when he saw Cindy sit beside him.

"Are you okay now mommy?"

She kissed the top of his head, "Yes baby, now let me try your amazing cooking. It smells delicious!"

Happy with the answer Marty went back to eating his food.

Hadley sat next to Jace who was struggling to eat due to his pain. Hadley kissed his arm and mouthed 'you okay?' to him. Jace closed his eyes and smiled before nodding his head. She knew he was lying, but the conversation about what happened at the Inn was not dinner conversation. They spent the rest of dinner listening to Marty tell them about his and Hadley's day. Giddy with excitement, Marty couldn't wait to show his mom and Jace the fort that he and Hadley had built in the living room.

They all wanted to keep the evening as light and pleasant as they could for Marty. Hadley offered to clean the dishes while Marty dragged Cindy and Jace into the living room. She could hear the wow's and oh's as they walked round the living room with castellan Marty; proudly showing off the fort he and Hadley spent the afternoon making.

When Hadley finished in the kitchen she joined the others in the lounge with a fresh pot of tea and a soft drink for Marty. After a while Cindy noticed Marty had begun to grow tired and offered to take him to bed with his bear. Nodding he asked for a bedtime story. Happily agreeing Cindy went to find her backpack that she took to the Inn with her and pulled out a fairytale book, showing it to Marty who seemed overjoyed about having his bedtime storybook back. He hugged Hadley and Jace goodnight and walked upstairs with his mother.

"What happened? How did you get so badly injured and what the hell happened?" Hadley blurted out. "Please tell me, what happened."

"You've asked that question 3 times now, where do I start?" Jace replied.

"Start at the Inn, I do not care about anything except for what happened at the Inn." Hadley said.

Jace gripped Hadley's hand tighter.

"The pub area was a wreck, I am not surprised Cindy grabbed Marty and ran. This is an almighty force; I was thrown across the pub and Cindy was attacked and held down by something."

Hadley looked at her husband with shocked eyes.

"I should have been there with you." She uttered.

"There would have been nothing you could have done, I would have hated you to get hurt. Besides I felt your protection spell when I walked towards the house."

Hadley kissed him gently.

"When we got there the smell was overpowering, rotten and musky. I found old symbols carved into the wooden beams. I couldn't think of the book at the time but.." Jace stopped and titled his head up in thought.

"Hadley, help me to the study."

Surprised, Hadley helped him up and got him steady him on his feet. She put his arm around her shoulders and they both walked to the study. Jace dropped his arm from her shoulder and continued walking to one of the bookshelves. Hadley, worried he might lose his balance followed him to the bookshelves.

"Dammit, where is it?" Jace moaned.

Hadley watched as he went to another shelf and once again skim the binders of each book.

"Got it!" Jace announced as he pulled out a black leather book. Hadley caught up with him and helped him to the table. When he placed the book onto the table, Hadley scrunched her forehead and looked at him. Confused, she opened the cover:

"The Black Caterwaul Owl." Hadley's eyes widened "Grimoires." Hadley thought out loud "Okay, what did you see in that place?"

Jace sat down and began flipping through the pages.

"On the beams I saw these markings, no, symbols even. Here is one."

Hadley looked to where his finger was pointing.

"Heart and dagger and, and the dagger was in the heart." Hadley looked at Jace who nodded his head solemnly.

"What does it mean if the dagger is in the heart?" Cindy said. Jace and Hadley turned their heads to the door.

"Have you found something?" She continued speaking as she joined them at the table.

"Yes, to one of the symbols we found. The heart and dagger is voodoo, it symbolises Erzulie Dantor; she represents vengeance. They would put the dagger into the heart if they were suffering from heartbreak or had been betrayed. Literally symbolising that someone stabbed them in the heart." Jace said.

Hadley remembered hearing about other witches who had attempted to turn to voodoo for its more black, demonic powers. But these witches never succeeded in the voodoo gods and goddesses. No, they brought up things from the darker realm.

"Care to share your thoughts?" Hadley was snapped out of her thoughts by Jace. She soon realised Cindy and Jace were staring at her.

"Oh, I did it again didn't I, sorry. I was just thinking about something I read years ago, about a white witch whose lover was hung by a towns council, and she swore vengeance. However, it didn't work because she was using a different type of magic. You guys keep looking for the other symbol and I will search for the book."

Hadley got up from the table and began searching the bookshelves, while Cindy and Jace searched for the other symbol.

"I remember you said sacrifice circle." Cindy said.

Hadley walked back to the table clutching a book close to her chest. She placed it down on the table and took in a deep breath.

"If the sacrifice circle was there, then this is far more darker than we could have ever imagined." Hadley said while sitting back down and opening the book. Hadley began looking for the fable her and Jace heard while growing up.

"What is that book Hadley?" Cindy asked.

Hadley looked at her and smiled, she knew Cindy wanted to figure out what was ruining her livelihood, but she also knew Cindy was becoming more interested in learning about the other side of life.

"It is a collection of old fables and stories of Witches and Warlocks who tried to do black magic and found the cruelest of consequences." Hadley replied.

After flipping through the pages, Hadley finally announced she had found the specific story she was looking for.

"The Witch Who Wanted Her Vengeance." Hadley said as she slid the book over to Jace and Cindy.

Cindy pulled the book closer to them, so they could both read the short story. Hadley watched as Cindy lipped read the words to herself, she could see her facial expressions change as she went further into the story. As they were reading Hadley pulled the other book closer to her and looked at the page Jace had been reading. At the top of the page there was the sacrifice circle, Hadley learnt about the symbols while at university. She had seen it used many times in abandoned buildings, but none were drawn correctly. She knew the one at the Inn would have been drawn right, she also knew if Margaret had summoned more than one demon before she died, the markings indicated sacrificing and murder had been going on in the Inn for centuries.

Hadley's mind was racing as she tried to piece Margarets life together. She thought if Margaret's sister was murdered that was when she would have turned to the black magic of Wicca and Voodoo. If she summoned Erzulie Dantor straight after, that would not explain the human sacrifices, or the massive amount of dark power which still lurked around today. No, Hadley thought, Margaret must have summoned something even more sinister, something that did not want to leave and Margaret allowed to tarnish her dying soul.

"So her partner was hung, and she tried to bring him back. But, it went wrong, and he came back a Draugar instead. What is a Draugar?" Cindy asked.

"A Draugar is a mythological creature, bit like a zombie because its stinkin' and dead, sometimes they even come back up from their graves or ashes to wreak havoc on folk who tormented them when they were still alive! Although it killed the man who wronged him, the witch cast the spell wrong and the Draugar turned on its maker killing her without a thought." Jace replied. "But Margaret called upon a Voodoo entity. What does this story have to do with what we are looking into?"

"This witch was trying to invoke Erzulie Dantor at her lovers grave, however, she was not as strong as she thought, she got Wicca black magic and Voodoo completely mixed up. Margaret must have found out how to do it properly, therefore, showing us she was already more powerful than we first thought. But Erzulie Dantor cannot be the only demon she summoned. After feeling the power and black magic can give her, I do not think she ever looked back. Certain demons require an unforgivable offering, human sacrifice even child sacrifice."

Hadley looked at Jace, "Remember the diary? Near the end, the author wrote the townspeople had found a child on a slabbed table covered in blood with symbols carved into his body. I think Margaret succeeded in her summoning when her body was burnt. I don't think it mattered, whatever possessed her body came in at the last minute and kept her soul here.

CHAPTER EIGHT

Hadley left Jace to sleep in the following morning, she noticed it had taken him a while to get comfortable and fall asleep during the night. Hadley had helped as much as she could, she propped pillows on either side of him, so he could sleep in the upright position. She knew he would be cranky, and she felt guilty being able to sleep in a more comfortable position.

Before she headed downstairs, she poked her head around Cindy's door wanting to check they had slept okay and for some reason to make sure they were still there. With her craving for coffee becoming more intense she quietly shut the door and walked downstairs. Once in the kitchen she got the coffee machine working and wondered into the study. They had left the room as it was last night, books scattered, coffee cups and wine glasses still on the table. As she opened the curtains, her eyes were not prepared for the autumn sunlight. Once they had adjusted Hadley walked back to the table and began collecting the glasses and mugs.

"Hadley, what is that?" Marty said as he walked into the study and went over to the window. Hadley hadn't heard him come in and jumped when she heard the boys voice. Composing herself, she put the glasses back onto the table and walked over to join Marty. Hadley didn't see anything, and she asked Marty to point out what he saw. She followed his finger which ended up pointing at one of the flowerbeds just a few feet away from the house.

"Marty move away from the window." Hadley whispered as she ushered him away as quickly as she could; careful not to push him over.

"Stay in the house and go wake your mommy up okay. Do not come outside, it might not be safe." Hadley pleaded with Marty.

Marty nodded his head and ran up the stairs to wake his mother. Hadley nervously walked into the hall and put her trainers and a coat on before she opened the front door. Her bare legs felt the sudden chill in the air as she made her way around the house to where the specific flowerbed was. Hadley's breathing started to become more rapid. She hoped what she saw was a prank, she hoped that what was in or near the flower bed was not real. Her only comfort was that she was in the daylight. When she got closer, her footsteps came to an abrupt stop. Her hand automatically went to her mouth to cover a scream, her rapid breathing suddenly stopped, and she took a couple more steps forward.

Hadley was staring at a female body. She suddenly realised how young the victim was and fell to her knees and checked for any signs of life.

She couldn't see the chest moving and the body looked like a dummy. But she knew it was human, and she looked no older than fourteen.

'What was you doing out here baby girl?' Hadley thought to herself. She quickly scanned the body, aware to not get her fingerprints anywhere on the body. The girls face was smudged in blood, one line went from the middle

of her forehead down to her chest. Blood had been used to draw around her eyes and the sides of her mouth had been sewn shut. Her chest had been carved with symbols and Hadley made a mental note of each one. The girl was wearing a vest top and shorts, to Hadley they appeared to be night wear and again Hadley wondered what was she doing out here alone and who could have done this.

    She noticed blood had soaked through the light pink vest top which meant this girl had suffered even more mutilation in the hands of her murderer. Hadley needed to see what was under the vest and pulled out a glove from one of her pockets. She put the glove on; grateful she wore leather gloves and carefully lifted the bottom of the vest to reveal the girls stomach. The symbol was the same one that Jace had described the night before, etched deep into the skin, a circle within a circle with an X covering the pentacle inside and a perfect cross at the bottom. Hadley shook her head, how can this be the same symbol, who else was aware of it?

    Hadley placed the vest back down, she wanted to cover the body. Hadley took one last look at the girls face when she suddenly opened her eyes, and sat upright. A whistle of a scream left the girls half sewn mouth before blood began to flow out. Petrified Hadley scrambled back, as shock and terror overcame her. She watched as the girl fell back, gargling on the blood still leaving her mouth. Her eyes clouded over and remained open, staring up to the sky showing no reflection.

    "Hadley?"

She heard someone call her name and she turned her head in the direction the voice came from. Through watery eyes she could make out Cindy's silhouette running towards her.

"What, what is that?" Cindy screamed as she came closer.

Cindy ran to Hadley and helped her stand up. Hadley's bare legs were covered in leaves and twigs. As soon as Hadley stood up and looked at Cindy her breathing calmed down, and she started pulling Cindy away from the body. Cindy didn't make any protest in being pulled away and eventually the two women began running back to the house. Marty was standing on the porch hugging Mr cuddles, trying to stretch his neck as much as he could to see what his mother and Hadley were running from. Cindy picked him up and carried him into the house with Hadley close behind her. When Hadley made it over the protection line she shut the door and ran to the telephone.

After waking Jace and informing him on what she had discovered in the garden, they all waited in the living room for the police to arrive. The coroner had already been and gone, so the only comfort Hadley felt with that was that the young girls body was now somewhere less public. Seeing his wife still severely shaken, Jace went and opened the door on hearing the doorbell. Clutching a cup of coffee, Hadley refused to stand up and greet the two police officers as they entered the room. Tears had not stopped falling from her eyes since she put the phone down.

Cindy siting on the three seater sofa let go of Marty and stood to shake the new guests hands with a measly smile. Jace asked for them to sit on the two-seater and he walked over to the armchair so he could offer Hadley some support. Being as professional as they could, they asked Hadley to tell them exactly what happened from the moment she woke up. Retracing her steps in her mind, Hadley retold the police officers everything she could remember from the moment she woke up to the moment she phoned them.

She noticed one of the officers was staring blankly at her, his eyes baring into hers and lifting his eyebrow when Hadley started crying again. He seemed old and tired of his job, doubtful of anything she told them. His brown ageing hair sticking out from under his hat.

The other officer was also male but seemed much younger, a rookie to the profession. His ginger hair was tucked neatly under his hat and his skin began growing paler as he listened and made notes on Hadley's statement. Once Hadley finished telling them everything that had happened, the two officers looked at each other. Hadley noticed the young officer nod at the older one as if they had been speaking in code through their stares.

The older officer cleared his throat before he spoke. "Mrs Fernsby, you have to see from our point of view, we are in a very unfamiliar situation. The victim, a fourteen-year-old girl was found on your property with markings all over her body. Markings which look a little similar to yours." He said as he waved his hand in the air to where she was sitting.

"More of your type is coming into the area and complaints are coming in every day of people being scared or concerned about devil worshipping cults."

Hadley choked on her coffee as she listened to the officer call herself and Jace devil worshippers and implied they were part of a cult.

"I am sorry to inform you officer," Hadley snapped. "My husband and I do not worship any devils and neither of us are in a cult. Someone has killed a young girl, and you seem to be implying we are the culprits who mutilated her body."

Hadley was beginning to feel her anger boil.

"I have told you everything I know, therefore, I will be excusing myself." She said as she stood up and walked out the room.

Hadley walked into the kitchen and poured herself another cup of coffee before splashing her face with cold water from the kitchen tap. She could hear the officers asking Jace questions and she told herself she would not go back in to the living room. Taking another gulp of coffee she walked into the study and stared out of the window Marty had discovered the body through. She continued looking out the window, by this time the sun had gone behind a thick mount of black cloud and raindrops began to appear on the window.

Hadley could not believe what was happening.

She dealt with the paranormal, the crimes and mysteries that came from things not on this realm. Yet, now a child was found dead right outside her home. The way the body suddenly sat upright when Hadley was certain the child had been dead was a thought which kept replaying in her mind. Behind her, she heard Cindy and Marty leave the living room and make their way upstairs. Jace was still answering questions about their life before moving into the house. Hadley could picture the symbol on the girls stomach and searched her brain for any kind of explanation.

The symbol looked familiar, she knew she had seen it in a book before, and she knew the book was not part of their collection. Hadley eventually shut the curtain, not wanting to look at the crime scene for the rest of the day. As she was walking out the study she heard Jace say goodbye to the officers and watched as they walked out the front door. Hadley stayed in the doorway of the study and watched as Jace closed the door and stood there for just a minute.

Jace turned and noticed Hadley staring at him, her eyes were still stinging and she still felt the odd tear fall out. Hadley did a half smile and walked over to him ready for his embrace. Still holding on to her cup of coffee she leant forward onto his chest as his arms wrapped around her. Hadley was exhausted, but she knew they needed to debrief and Jace still had information to tell her about his and Cindy's trip yesterday. Jace suggested before they got into all of that they all shower and clean up. Hadley was happy with the suggestion, her body still felt cold and dirt still covered her legs.

Hadley let the warm water consume her as she stood in the shower. She let the water loosen her muscles and scrubbed her body to rid of any stench of the dead child she believed still clung to her skin. Once out she quickly changed into her comfy clothes and towel dried her hair. She wanted to check on Cindy and Marty and once again she poked her head around their bedroom door. Hadley saw them both asleep on the bed, the television still on playing an episode of Scooby-Doo. Hadley didn't want to wake them, Marty had pointed out the body, but she was unsure whether he saw anything. Hadley wanted to keep him away from this part of their investigation. She closed the door and walked back down the stairs, hearing the shower turn back on and the bathroom door close. While she waited for Jace, she wanted to think of anything except what they were going through at the moment. She noticed Jace must have brought the newspaper in, so she poured herself another cup of coffee and started reading the mundane news the local newspaper held.

Most of the news were a repeat from the previous day, Hadley shuddered thinking what tomorrow's morning news would bring, but she pushed the thought back. She knew no one in the house was responsible, and she knew they would find justice for the child. She began getting bored by the towns 'tabloid' news and flicked through to the daily horoscopes. Hadley wanted to read if any good news would come her way, although she knew whoever wrote these probably wrote the fortune cookie slips for the local takeaways.

'Optimism and opportunities fill your interactions today.'

Hadley scoffed as she read the one sentence out loud. She was amazed at how little effort they put into the writing which some people love and follow. After reading the horoscope for Jace and simply shaking her head, she moved onto the next page. Another page full of the halloween town fair which was a now only one week and a couple of days away. She looked at the date of the fair and read 'open Sunday 30th October 3pm.' As Hadley was staring at the pictures and sipping her coffee the thought of the girls body flashed through her mind.

The symbols, her cloudy eyes, the blood flowing out of her mouth, that scream which would have been piercing if she could open her mouth fully. Hadley put down her cup and snapped back to the present. She knew these thoughts would not go away from her mind anytime soon. Shaking her head, Hadley turned to the next page, again the advert for the puppies stood out to her. She wanted to speak to Jace, she knew her protection spell stopped the killer putting the body closer to their home.

As Hadley was deep in thought looking at the picture of the puppies, Jace walked into the kitchen and walked over to her to see what she was so invested in.

"You want a puppy?" He asked as he read the paper and took Hadley's last sip of cold coffee. Hadley lightly tapped his arm for drinking her coffee.

"I mean, I don't think it is a bad idea. I have always loved having animals and," Hadley stopped replying. She did not want to tell Jace the real reason as to why she wanted a four legged fur ball in the house. But she was sure he had already guessed

"I know sweetheart, why don't we go and look at them. I think it might be a good idea." Jace bent down and kissed her on the top of her head. Hadley was shocked.

"I mean, your protection spell obviously worked last night, but if we had a dog around we might find out who it was if they come back."

Hadley was taken aback even more, he had just said everything she was thinking of only a couple of minutes before. Hadley smiled and stood up to hug Jace.

"We should leave a note for the others, I will just tell them we went to the shops." Hadley suggested. She kissed Jace and went to find some plain paper to write the note for Cindy.

After leaving the house, Hadley began to feel anxious she knew the town may have already heard about the murder. She also knew a few people in the town would be

thinking the same as the police officers. Jace continued to reassure her that they had not done anything wrong. Hadley asked Jace to tell her about Kerry and the shop he and Cindy went into before making their way to the Inn yesterday. Although Jace was still in pain, he knew he had to try and do whatever he could to help Hadley, he squeezed her hand and continued to tell her about Kerry and her shop. He told her of what Kerry knew and thought about the Inn, and that she also had the same faith as her.

"Really?" Hadley asked surprised another Wiccan had moved into the town. Jace nodded his head and winced slightly when a shooting pain came from his rib cage. Hadley stopped and checked on her husband.

"We shouldn't have come, you need more rest." She said unable to hide her worry. Jace shook his head and began leading her into the town centre. Hadley was not convinced and decided they needed to rest for a bit before continuing on.

Hadley had been giving Jace herbal healing tea since last night and although he was beginning to stand up straight, she knew he still had pain. Not wanting to do a healing spell in front of people in a café, she decided to take him to Kerry's shop and ask if they could rest there until he felt more able to carry on.

Spiritual Healings was open to Hadley's relief and after getting a few stares from some people in town Hadley suddenly felt safe when they entered the shop. Kerry was busy speaking to a customer when they arrived and Hadley not wanting to interrupt, asked Jace if there was anywhere they could sit. Jace told her about the seating area Kerry had taken Cindy and him to the previous day and Hadley helped him round the shop.

She sat Jace down on one of the sofas and pulled out the healing herbs she had been using every time Jace showed any sign of pain. She listened to what Kerry was saying to her only customer; they were speaking about incense and what would best be used for a calming effect. After a while she heard Kerry walking towards where they were sitting, concern crossing her face.

Hadley stood up when Kerry got closer and put her hand out ready to introduce herself. Kerry disregarded the hand and went straight in for a hug. Hadley was surprised she found herself hugging her back.

"It is so lovely to meet you Hadley, Jace told me we should meet. However, I didn't think it would be so soon."

Hadley smiled at Kerry's kind-hearted welcome. She explained to her why they had dropped in so suddenly and asked if Kerry would be able to help. With no persuading at all, Kerry simply nodded her head and wandered off behind a curtain behind the till area. Jace had found a comfortable position and refused to move until he had his tea. Hadley decided to walk around and discover what was being sold.

"Hadley?" someone said from behind her, Hadley had reached the crystal section and quickly spun around when she heard her name. Shocked, Hadley was taken aback at who was standing in front of her.

"Evelyn!" Hadley felt a sense of love and regret creep up on her as Evelyn hugged her.

"I am so sorry I haven't had a chance to come and see you yet, please forgive me." Hadley said as she hugged the woman back.

With a laugh, she let Hadley go.

"Do not apologise child, I know it must have been an adjustment moving back here. My husband told me you went to the library the other day and took out a number of books about the town. May I ask what for?"

To Hadley Evelyn may have grown older, but her personality had not changed. She was still the nosey caregiver who had brought her up when she was taken in by the church.

Husband? Hadley thought.

When she was growing up Evelyn was a single woman, working for the church, and offered to be one of Hadley's main carers. Now her blonde hair had turned white and was neatly kept in short tight curls. Her eyesight had fallen with age as she wore big round glasses and her fashion sense had changed from long dresses and cardigans, to sweatshirts over blouses and slacks.

"You have a husband, I am so happy for you, please let me introduce you to my other half." Hadley pointed in the direction Jace was sitting and led Evelyn to the seating area. Hadley noticed Jace trying to stand up, but Evelyn got there before her.

"Please, no need to stand. It is lovely to meet the man who won our Hadley's heart."

Hadley smiled when she heard Evelyn say 'our Hadley' and went to sit next to Jace as the woman took one of the armchairs next to them. Kerry walked out from behind the curtain carrying a dark blue tea pot with kittens dancing around the sides.

She looked surprised to see her customer sitting with Jace and Hadley as she placed the tray on the table and took a seat in the other armchair.

"Thank you." Hadley said as she moved closer to the table and took a cup from the stack. Opening the bag of herbs Hadley took a pinch of crushed dandelion root and dropped it into the empty cup. As she picked up the tea pot and began to pour in the hot water she recited;

"Goddess Eir, I call upon you for your healing powers. May you charge this water for healing. May it purge the body of illness, and restore the drinker to new strengths."

Hadley finished the spell by stirring the water and letting the water consume the dandelion root. When she opened her eyes, she noticed Jace and Kerry had also closed their eyes and opened them not long after she opened her own. Evelyn had just watched with curiosity and simply nodded her head at Hadley when she handed over the cup and saucer to Jace. She watched as Jace took the first sip and could tell his body was again beginning to feel normal. Happy with her work, she took teabags out of a shallow dish and placed three into individual cups and made tea for the others.

"I always knew you would go back to your true roots Hadley." Evelyn finally broke the peaceful silence which had fallen on the group.

"Do not think I didn't know you were not only reading about Christianity when we took you in."

Hadley stopped sipping her tea and looked at Evelyn dead in the eyes. Her face started to burn, and she knew she was turning red.

"I. I'm sorry." Hadley began, but Evelyn waved her hand stopping her from speaking further.

"Hadley, when the church took you in, me and a few others knew you had not renounced your faith. We also knew Laurie would never do the same. Your mother and I came up with the idea, when she still had control of the demon inside her. She knew she was not going to get out alive, and so we made a plan for when she was no longer the driver of her body and mind. I was to ask father Andrews to step in and tell him your mother wishes to be helped by the church. Unlike father Andrews, we knew the demon would not be released without killing your mother. We also knew the demon would play on this idea. The thought of you being placed in a home was something Laurie could not accept. So, the only way I could take care of you, was if father Andrews believed you had both converted to Christianity."

Evelyn looked relieved to have finally told the truth about why the church took Hadley in. Guilt filled Hadley's body as she thought of Evelyn going behind Father Andrews back and lying just to help her. Hadley was unable to speak, she felt a lump in her throat and could only give a weak but meaningful smile at the woman who went behind her faith to save her and give her a better life.

Hadley felt Jace put his hand on hers, and she finally caught her breath.

"I am forever grateful Evelyn, thank you so much." Hadley expressed.

Kerry shifted in her chair and put her tea cup back on the table and poured herself another cup. A look Hadley couldn't work out went across Kerry's face.

"Is everything okay Kerry?" Hadley asked.

Kerry looked embarrassed on realising her poker face was not great.

"I don't mean to ruin the special moment because it really is special. But I heard about what happened, well, not heard. I had two police officers come round this morning asking me questions about my whereabouts, my beliefs and if I was involved in a cult."

Hadley suddenly felt angry, she should have known she and Jace wouldn't be the only suspects. The police were going to be going to anyone who seemed and looked odd and out of place in a small town like this.

"I was shocked, and saddened to hear it was a child who had had to go through such a horrific ordeal. They didn't tell me all the details, I suspected they wanted to see if I knew something only the person who did the crime would know." Kerry disclosed.

"Yes the church was also informed of the crime as soon as the body was taken. However, we were told of what the murderer carved into Sarahs skin."

Everyone looked at Evelyn after she said the girls name and Evelyn took this as a sign to continue.

"She was a good girl, her mother regularly attends church services. However, Sarah stopped coming with her mother when she started attending high school. It was well known she started being the rebellious teen. But she would never do anything illegal or join something like a cult." Evelyn said.

"Sarah was not killed by a cult, there is no cult here in Wotton-Under-Edge. The mark that was cut into Sarahs stomach is the same mark Jace found carved into the beams of the Ramm Inn." Hadley voiced.

Kerry quickly got up from the table and went over to the counter and retrieved a paper and pen.

"Here." She said as she handed the pen and paper to Hadley.

"Please show us the symbol."

Hadley took the pen and paper and began drawing the symbol exactly as she remembered, two circles, one inside the other. Inside the middle circle was a pentacle with an X going through it and the cross at the bottom. She passed it to Kerry.

"This is something I have not seen before." Kerry announced with deep concern.

"And you say it was carved on the beams in the Inn?"

Jace nodded "Yes, as well as the heart and dagger and the sacrifice circle."

"Voodoo." Kerry gasped. Hadley saw Evelyn take everything in but remain quiet.

"I do not think voodoo has been used for hundreds of years round here. Jace and I found articles in the library talking about the Inns past and one spoke of three women who were accused of witchcraft and murdered. But then it goes on to speak about another woman named Margaret who was the sister of the first woman tried and killed. She was a witch, but I am certain she turned dark when her sister was killed. That's when she used voodoo to invoke Erzulie Dantor." Hadley stated.

"She invoked Erzulie to avenge her sister." Kerry spoke her thoughts out loud.

"That is what we believe, however, Erzulie would not stay on this plane. Therefore, we think once she went to black magic it consumed her. She went onto perform rituals which involved human sacrifice, and it opened a gateway for something of pure darkness to enter which she allowed to enter her physical form before she was killed. Keeping her spiritual entity filled with darkness here." Hadley claimed.

"Where did you get this information Hadley, an article did you say?"

Hadley suddenly felt uncomfortable with Evelyn's question and did not want to tell her about the diary her and Jace had found.

"Erm yes, we took a lot of old articles and such. Evelyn, this thing is stronger than whatever took over my mother, but is from the same place. This is no Pagan, no Christian and nothing to do with a cult. This is something we can only hope to rid of." Hadley finished as she spoke directly to Evelyn.

Evelyn took the paper which was on the table.

"The church and I already know, you are not to blame for Sarahs death Hadley. And neither is Jace nor Kerry. I shall do all I can, but we have always known there was something within the Inn. Father Andrews did an exorcism on the Inn many years ago and the town believe it removed whatever evil was within. I will do my best to conceal what you have told me, I believe it is safer than ruining many peoples faiths."

Evelyn stood and said her goodbyes, Hadley stood and hugged her thanking her for everything she had told her. With a kiss on the check Evelyn told Hadley to never apologise for something she wanted to do. Kerry also stood to hug her and told Evelyn she could take the incense as a gift. With that, Hadley walked Evelyn out the store.

Hadley joined Kerry and Jace back round the table, Jace was informing Kerry of how strong the entity was within the Inn.

"She couldn't have just called upon Vali for her revenge." Kerry sighed.

Jace laughed and nodded in agreement. Hadley took the drawing off the table and stared at it.

"I have seen this somewhere I know I have." Hadley dug deeper into her memories to try and find the answer she was looking for. As she was searching her brain, Hadley saw Jace was looking more peaceful and in less pain. "Maybe it was something at uni? You did spend a lot of time in the library." Jace suggested.

Hadley thought Jace's words over, "Maybe you're right." Hadley said biting her bottom lip in thought.

"When we get home later I will phone Sandra." Hadley looked at Kerry. "You need to protect yourself. I would hate for something to happen to you Kerry." Hadley said.

Kerry smiled, "I shall call upon Goddess Hlin and do a protection spell on my shop and home." Kerry reassured Hadley, "But please do not hesitate to come for my help, our gods and goddesses can help us, but we are still much stronger together."

Hadley thanked Kerry for her kind words and gave her a hug.

"But now we must go look at a puppy." She smiled and turned to Jace who was already beginning to stand up. She went over to help, although she knew the spell was working, she knew he still needed time to heal. When he was up, he walked round to where Kerry was standing and hugged her goodbye.

Leaving Kerry's shop, Hadley felt more relaxed in the knowledge that people knew they had not committed the crime which found its way into their garden. Hadley took hold of her husbands hand and they both made their way to the address listed on the add.

"I can't wait to see them! I hope one will like us." Hadley squealed with excitement.

CHAPTER NINE

Hadley had told Jace to go to the nearest pet shop and get supplies for their new family member. On the walk home Jace was carrying two bags full of toys, food, bedding and puppy pads. Hadley couldn't stop smiling, as she carried her new baby to their home. She could not wait to see Martys face when they walked in.

As soon as she saw him she felt love and knew they had to take him home. The original owners seemed shocked when she and Jace showed up to their door. Hadley was certain they must have thought they had something to do with Sarahs death. But they did not say anything, and soon they were all chatting and laughing. Hadley believed their impressions had changed as they offered drinks and allowed them to take one of their puppies.

When Hadley and Jace reached the path to their home, she could see the lights were on and the curtains had already been drawn. As soon as Hadley reached the porch she felt the power of her protection spell and kissed the puppy on the head.

"Welcome to your new home little one." She whispered. Jace unlocked the door and Marty came running into the hallway.

"Mommy look! Look what Hadley is holding!" Marty was unable to control himself as he and Mr Cuddles came running up to Hadley. Hadley heard Cindy messing around with pots before she walked into the hallway. A smile crossed her face as she noticed the brown Labrador in Hadley's arms.

"Marty come away, let them come into the house."
"Dinner smells amazing, what are we having?" Jace asked as he closed the front door.

Hadley made her way over to Cindy with a smile and moved some blanket away from the puppies head, so he could finally see his surroundings.

Cindy scuffled his fur and smiled. "It is bangers and mash with onion gravy, Marty thought you would like it Jace." Cindy replied.

Jace made a yum sound and looked at Marty before picking him up and flinging him over his shoulder. "You sure were right there."

Hadley walked into the kitchen and a sudden urge of anxiousness filled her. What if her new baby doesn't like it here? What if didn't like them? These thoughts had been running through her mind since Jace said they could get a dog.

"It is just because of what happened today my love, it has thrown you off." Jace said as he came up behind her reading her mind. Hadley sat on the kitchen floor next to where Jace had placed the supplies. Marty had joined her and began speaking to the dog in a high baby voice.

Hadley knew Jace was right, the day had started off traumatic, they had discovered a dead child and on top of that, they needed to discover what demon possessed a fallen witch. Cindy had gone back to finishing dinner and without realising it, Hadley finally noticed her diet of just caffeine for the day was not making the cut.

"What is he called?" Marty asked.

Hadley shrugged her shoulders. "I have no idea, what do you think we should call him?"

Marty looked focused and serious for a second, keeping his eyes fixated on the dog.

"Well, he likes to chew his new toys a lot, I think we should call him Chewy." Marty said looking hopeful at Hadley.

"I like it." Hadley said agreeing on Marty's choice.

"I like it too," Cindy chipped in "and even more good news, dinner is ready."

During dinner Jace and Hadley told Cindy about the meeting they had with Kerry and Evelyn.

"So we are not suspects?" Cindy asked after listening intensely to the conversation.

"Hopefully, I mean the church has always had a strong voice in this town, but of course, they cannot overturn the police. However, we know we aren't involved and this murder has something to do with the Inn. However, I got a strange feeling from Evelyn when she asked how we knew so much about the Inns past. Anyway, I need to phone Sandra."

Hadley excused herself from the table and went into the study to find her old lecturers phone number. After a long search Hadley could hear the ringback tone. Finally, the line connected and Hadley heard the strong Scottish accent.

"Hello, Sandra speaking how can I help you?"

"Hey Sandra, its Hadley I hope this isn't a bad time?"

"Hadley! It's so lovely to hear from you. No, this isn't a bad time at all is there something you wanted help with?" Hadley knew Sandra would always agree to help if Hadley asked. They had spent four years working together, building more than just a teacher student relationship.

"It is lovely to hear your voice as well, I wanted to call you because Jace and me have come across a case which, well, you know my past. The entity is stronger, more sinister than that. We believe it possessed the body right before death and was able to still stay in this realm."

Sandra didn't reply.

"Yeah….. and the symbol which I know I have seen before, but I cannot find it anywhere. I was hoping you could help me find it." Hadley could hear Sandra take a deep breath.

"Tell me about the symbol and I can see if I can help." Sandra eventually said. Hadley explained the symbol, describing each specific part she had seen.

"There is another thing." She added. "This morning a dead body of a young girl was found in our garden, her body was mutilated and the symbol was sketched into her stomach." She held back tears as her mind raced back to the morning.

Hadley could hear Sandra mumbling to herself. She knew Sandra would be in her huge study and would be frantically looking through her extensive collection of one of a kind books. Sandra had been quiet for a while and

Hadley was unsure whether the line had cut off or if something bad had happened.

"Sandra, is everything alright?"

More silence followed until she heard Sandra clearing her throat.

"Yes sorry Hadley, it took me a while to locate the book I required. You said there has been a murder already?" Hadley suddenly began to feel hot. She could already tell there was something wrong by the tone in Sandras voice. Her tone had become stern, her speech had become slower and was no longer high-pitched as it was when the phone call started.

"Yes, one murder so far."

"You were right to phone me, the symbol you saw is something you would be familiar with, and I am petrified for you." Sandra voiced. "Do you remember one summer when you and I took the time to put each demon into a category? Witch, vampire, incubus, banshee."

Hadley nodded her head, forgetting Sandra would not be able to see her gesture. Hadley did remember that summer, it had taken them months to finish as a side job due to others at the university scoffing at the idea of such beings. Hadley remembered trying to explain to those cynics that vampires are not as they are in books. The small group she had been involved with discovered vampires were demons from the darkest of realms who possessed someone's body, if summoned. They did need blood to survive within the shell they possessed, but they could not change someone. The only vampire to change someone from a bite was from the Vampire king himself.

"Yes I remember." Hadley responded.

"Orera. That is the name of the type of demon you are trying to find. They prefer to possess the body of a witch as they can become more powerful. However, just like any demon who takes over a body they need fuel." Sandra uncovered.

"They need a sacrifice."

"Not just one sacrifice Hadley, the Orera needs three. As long as the last one is done on the thirtieth. Who is to say when the others will be? However, since you already have one, I would not be surprised if you have another one very soon. These demons are extremely difficult to invoke, there has only ever been one documented coming into this realm, as far as we know. The notes on this are minimal, if the Orera possesses a living witch, they can move about freely. However, this one you say had taken on the form of a dying witch. Not to mention how far back it happened."

Hadley could hear the fear and confusion in Sandras voice, which brought no comfort .

"Wait, so you are saying, the Orera needs a living body to be able to wonder about? She is wandering around the Inn though".

"Yes, this is very interesting, yet confusing. From the one case that had been reported it says they need a living body to move about. But I wonder if she possessed the witches body at the place she was killed then maybe she can move about there. But that is just me guessing."

Hadley began jotting down notes on a spare piece of paper on the table, she knew if she didn't, she would not remember much when she had to retell all this to Jace and Cindy.

"But how is this Orera sacrificing when she can not leave the Inn?" Hadley pointed out.

"That is yet another interesting question and I suppose we have no real answer except the one we can rationalise ourselves. If I took a wild guess, I would say this one has been here for so long, it can manipulate and telepathically get someone else to do the sacrifices for them. As long as her symbol is displayed, she would technically be the one doing the sacrifice by controlling the poor vessel she chose. But of course, this is just a theory." Sandra expressed.

"A theory is all we have." Hadley sighed "How long do we have since the first sacrifice is complete?"

Hadley closed her eyes as the thought of another two children could be found at anytime.

"It says the final ritual needs to be on the thirtieth of October, just over a week away. There is no other information to tell you. If I find more I will call straight away, I hope I have helped." Sandra said her goodbyes and hung up the phone.

Hadley sat for a few minutes in silence rereading her notes while tapping the pen on the table. As she was coming back into the now after the phone call and her thoughts, she started hearing the chatting and laughing from the living room. She left the note in the study and went to join everyone; Marty was sitting on the floor playing with Chewy. While Jace and Cindy were watching them play from the sofas.

"You get hold of Sandra?" Jace asked as Hadley took a seat next to him.

"Yeah, we discussed a lot, which I will tell you two all about when.." Hadley pointed in Martys direction "goes to bed."

Cindy mouthed thank you to Hadley, who smiled and winked back.

"So is my baby fitting in?" Hadley asked Marty as she moved onto the floor. Chewy noticing her crawled onto her lap and began licking her face.

"Oh I think he is!" As she began laughing along with Marty. They spent the rest of the evening watching telly and discussing Marty and Cindy's day. When it reached eight pm Cindy announced it was time for Marty to say his goodnights. Hadley had begun liking Cindy and Marty being in their home, she loved having another girl to chat with over the morning coffee when Jace decided to sleep in, and she loved the goodnights when Marty would hug them all. After giving Chewy an enormous number of goodnight kisses, Marty finally went upstairs with Cindy for his bedtime story.

Hadley began retelling the information her and Sandra had discussed on the phone when Cindy and Kerry had joined them. Jace had come up with the idea that having Kerry involved may help, incase she knew more of the demon once she was told the name. Hadley felt her words flowing out her mouth like vomit.

"Orera." Cindy said trying to pronounce the word exactly like Hadley did. "So this demon is the one who resides in my Inn. How do we get rid of it?" Cindy said with hope in her voice.

Hadley looked at Jace, pleading for him to say something.

"Cindy, we have never dealt with this demon before, and Sandra told Hadley there is little to no information on this demon." Jace said.

Hadley could see Cindy's face fall.

"That is not to say there is no way we can't defeat this, there is just little help we can use. Remember Sandra said it needed to fuel its self by the 30th October." Hadley tried to reassure her.

"The day of the Halloween fair." Kerry announced.

"If the Orera is controlling someone to do her sacrificing than the fair will be the perfect place for her to choose someone." Jace added to the conversation.

Hadley bit her lip, a sense of concern and doom filled her insides. "We need to find out more about the Orera. There has to be more, how do we banish, defeat whatever we have to do, if we have no idea how to?"

Cindy looked flustered, Hadley knew she wanted to take Marty to the fair when it opened. Hadley put her hand on Cindy's arm.

"It will be okay, we are not going to let anything happen to Marty, I promise you."

Hadley looked at Jace and Kerry pleading with them through her eyes for support.

"Right, nothing is going to harm him." Jace agreed. "Absolutely nothing will happen, you have us." Kerry chipped in.

"But he wants to go to the fair, I promised him I would take him. God, why did I have to buy that awful Inn, why did I think I could do this on my own? I have no magical powers, I have no idea what I am doing except putting my son in constant danger."

Hadley passed the box tissues to Cindy and sat beside her. Hadley knew putting her arms around Cindy would make her cry more, but she could not let her friend feel alone in a room full of people.

When Cindy finally settled and all tears had left her body Kerry came back from the kitchen with a cup of tea for her. Hadley raised her eyebrow, only for Kerry to wink back.

"Here" Kerry said as she handed the cup to Cindy. Cindy mumbled a thank you and took a gulp, before finishing the rest. Cindy yawned as her eyelids began to close, Jace and Hadley watched with Kerry as they saw Cindy's body relax more.

"Cindy why don't I help you to bed?" Hadley whispered so not to spook her. Cindy mumbled and Hadley took it as yes. She helped Cindy stand and guided her to the bedroom. Marty was already fast asleep when Hadley and Cindy entered the room. Hadley could see Mr Cuddles head peeping out the covers and hear the slight snore coming from Marty. She silently helped Cindy walk around the bed and got her comfortable under the covers.

"So magic tea." Hadley said with a smile when she walked back into the study.

"Oh just a simple little spell." Kerry expressed "Pour boiling water into a cup, add a teaspoon of mugwort and as you stir say mugwort bring peace to the one who needs peace. Let them slumber in softness till morning light. So mote it be. I am just pleased you had mugwort. If you run out you know where to get your supplies from now."Hadley smiled and nodded her head .

"Of course, we would not want to go anywhere else, we brought all these supplies with us from Scotland."

Hadley looked at the time. "Jace, it's time for your tea again. Kerry can I get you a drink, tea, coffee, hot chocolate?" Kerry's eyes lit up when she heard the words hot chocolate.

"Hot chocolate please." Kerry replied.

As Hadley left the study to go make the drinks, she could hear Jace and Kerry talking about Scotland. When she reached the Kitchen it was only the odd bits she could hear. But she knew she heard Killiecrankie and not long after she heard a gruesome floating head. Hadley remembered Jace loving that paranormal investigation with the university. It was one of their first investigations together. Before then, they were always put into separate groups. Hadley remembered walking round the gorge with Jace and the high-tech equipment the university lent out to students. Jace wanted to hear the footsteps of the governments' army as they marched to their doom. She remembered they had to stay an extra night there as the anniversary was on the twenty-seventh of July, and they got there the twenty-sixth. Hadley added marshmallows to the hot chocolates and a pinch of crushed dandelion root before she stirred the tea for Jace she chanted her spell.

"Goddess Eir, I call upon you for your healing powers. May you charge this water for healing. May it purge the body of illness, and restore the drinker to new strengths."

She placed all the drinks on a tray and steadily walked back into the study.
"And that investigation was when I knew I would eventually marry that woman there." Jace said as Hadley walked in.
Hadley smiled as she placed the tray onto the table and walked over to Jace to kiss him on the lips.
"I'm certain if you did not make us get there a day early, which meant we needed to camp in makeshift tents, I would have thought the same about you." Hadley

remarked she passed Jace his tea and Kerry her hot chocolate.

"I have been thinking since Cindy and I left the Inn." Jace expressed. Hadley and Kerry both looked at Jace waiting for him to continue.

"Cindy said after she tripped, something had brushed up against her. And the scratches on her face, they looked like an animal did it." Jace stopped talking as Chewy came up to him and he picked the puppy up and let him lay on his lap. Kerry watched Jace as he stroked the puppy with one hand and pick up his tea with the other.

"A familiar?" Kerry questioned.

Hadley tilted her head as considered Kerry's proposal. "That could possibly be an explanation, I am going to take a gamble and say the Orera needs a familiar. They seem very medieval in their witchcraft. I read in one of the books that Alice had a cat. If the Orera took on Margarets body just before death, maybe she was able to get the cat into the Inn and slaughter it there, ready for the familiar to go into the cats dying body."

Hadley saw Jace and Kerry nod in agreement. She knew this was becoming more serious and more dangerous. Hadley got a new piece of paper and started jotting down notes on what they all needed to figure out before the thirtieth of October. The most important thing was saving two innocent children from being the Orera's next sacrificial meal. The second was finding out how important the familiar was for the Orera. And the third was getting rid of the demon who lived in the Inn.

CHAPTER TEN

Hadley awoke the next morning next to a sleeping Jace, she had heard him wince in pain during the night and she didn't want to wake him. She knew he refused to go see a doctor, but she also knew her tea would not completely heal him. Quietly she tipped toed out the bedroom and made her way down the stairs to the kitchen. The house felt cold, and she shivered as she tied her hair into a high ponytail and smiled as she saw Kerry starting up the coffee machine.

"Morning, did you sleep okay?" Hadley asked.

She had told Kerry to stay the night as they had been up late and after what the household woken up to that morning, she could not deny her uncomfortable unease of letting Kerry leave the house at night.

"Morning, I did thank you and thanks for letting me stay last night. Do you want a coffee?"

"Yes please and oh no, please, after everything that is going on, I just didn't want you to leave the house after dark." Hadley said. "I am just going to check outside the house, make sure everything is fine, and then I will start breakfast."

Hadley left the kitchen and walked down the hallway, she spotted one of Jace's jumpers on the sofa and pulled it over her head before making her way to the front door. The air felt damp due to the fog, but she could not see any bodies, any evil, nothing to show something happened on their land while they all slept. Hadley gave a sigh of relief as she felt her protection spell still strong around the house. She picked up the newspaper before going back inside and was met by Marty running down the stairs with Chewy next to him.

"I think he needs the toilet Hadley." Marty said as he reached the bottom of the stairs. Hadley nodded her head with a serious face.

"Right you are, captain. Can you take him out the back while I start breakfast?"

Marty quickly realised the game and gleefully joined in. "Sir, yes sir!" He replied while giving a salute.

Hadley stood back and gave a salute to match his before he and Chewy ran to the kitchen and out the back door.

"There was something in that tea last night wasn't there?" Cindy said from the middle of the stairs, her arms crossed and her right hip sticking out. Hadley realised she still had her hand up in a salute and slowly put it down.

"Cindy!" Hadley said in a high pitch.

Cindy cocked an eyebrow keeping a stern look on her face as her hands moved to her hips. Hadley pursed her lips together.

"Well, it was just some mugwort." Hadley began.

"With a hint of spell?" Cindy questioned.

Hadley closed her eyes and took a deep breath while she thought of a way to explain herself.

"Hadley don't look so worried, I was joking. Thank you so much whatever it was. I really needed that sleep." Cindy broke her seriousness as she made her way down the stairs and gave Hadley a hug.

"Do not do that to me again!" Hadley said with a laugh as she squeezed Cindy back. "However, you have Kerry to thank for that good nights sleep."

Hadley heard the back door open, and she took that as hers and Cindy's queue to go see the muddy damage the children had brought back in with them.

"Kerry, can I have a hot chocolate?" Marty asked.

Hadley saw Kerry look in their direction as they entered the kitchen.

"Maybe you should ask your mother little Marty? I can make you one if she says yes." Kerry replied but aiming the question towards Cindy.

"Of course you can but first we need to clean up, look at all that mud." Hadley looked at Marty and Chewy, the damage wasn't as bad as she thought it would be, she could see it was mainly wet with bits of grass and mud. Hadley went and fetched towels from a cupboard on the landing and wiped down Chewy.

"Cindy, would you mind starting breakfast while I phone the doctors? I want them to make a house call. Jace was in pain last night and if he is too stubborn to ask for medical help, well, I will do it for him." Hadley announced as she folded up the towel and placed it somewhere she could use it next time Chewy went outside.

Cindy agreed and Hadley went into the study to find the yellow pages and get the number for the local doctors. The call lasted a while. Jace had not even registered with the doctors, so she spent twenty minutes, giving them Jace's name, his previous doctor and all his medical history. Hadley put down the phone to the smell of bacon, realising she was more hungry than she thought. Quickly she made her way to the kitchen and took a slice of bacon before plating up breakfast for Jace.

"I will be right back".

Hadley could hear Jace stirring as she pushed open the door with her hip.

"Don't say anything, but I have breakfast for you and the doctor is coming in a few hours to check on you. But look bacon and pancakes. I think Cindy put vanilla in because it smells amazing and…" Hadley rushed the middle part, hoping Jace caught what she said. But she also hoped the bacon and vanilla pancakes would make him less annoyed. Jace fell back into his pillow with a grunt and muttered something under his breath.

"Pancakes and bacon my love!" Hadley said again with more enthusiasm than she knew she needed to. She placed the tray onto his lap and perched herself onto the bed next to him.

"Hadley, thank-you for the breakfast, but why did you call the doctors? You know I will have to stay in bed, and we have a lot of work to do." Jace moaned as he ate a fork full of bacon. Hadley was prepared for him to be annoyed at her, but still deep down she felt upset.

"Don't be annoyed at me, my love. I just want you to get better." Hadley felt Jace take her hand and saw him coming in closer for a kiss.

"I didn't mean to upset you." Jace said as he kissed Hadley on the lips.

Hadley stayed with him until she could no longer hear him over her stomach rumbling.

When she returned to the kitchen, the others were still sitting round the table, with Chewy dribbling close by. Hadley walked straight to the coffee machine before putting bacon and pancakes on a plate.

"Oh and no spells to 'calm' him down." Hadley added while emphasising the word calm. Hadley saw both women roll their eyes and laughed.

"Yep, typical stubborn man."

After breakfast Kerry said her goodbyes before heading home and Hadley changed and decided to read the newspaper.

She knew what the headline would be, and Hadley felt her stomach turn when she saw a photo of her home and a smiling face of the girl she found in her garden. A lot of the article was placed on how there were no suspects at present but devil worshippers and those involved in the occult were who the police had as their prime suspects. The part of the article which interested Hadley knew more about Sarah.

She skimmed through the occult part, uninterested in reading how the reporters knew very little about the truth and how little they knew about the occult. Sarah Yates was fourteen years old, she went to the Katharine Lady Berkeley's School and was a high achiever. Hadley read

Sarah had a younger brother and lived with her mother and father.

The next page consisted of a collage filled with Sarahs beautiful innocent face. One photo Hadley could not keep her eyes off was the one where Sarah was with her family holding ice creams all smiling standing on a pier. Hadley was unable to look away, all she could see was Sarahs sewn up mouth, the blood on her face and the blackness of her aura.

Hadley was interrupted by Chewy. She felt grateful for the distraction. Her heart was breaking as she knew if they were unable to find a way to rid the Orera, there would be two more articles just like the one she was reading. Hadley knew Chewy couldn't respond, but she found comfort in telling him her fears and worries. While she was explaining what they believe an Orera was, a knock on the front door made her stop mid-sentence.

Chewy was already in the hallway, tail wagging ready to greet the visitor. Hadley checked the time and was shocked an hour had already passed. She knew the visitor would be the doctor she had booked for Jace. Before she answered the door, Hadley checked she looked presentable in the hallway mirror. Her face looked paler than it usually did, and she looked solemnly at her reflection. Once the dog had been put under control as best she could. She stood up straighter and opened the door.

"Hey, thank you so much for coming. I'm Hadley." Hadley said as he held out her hand.

"Nice to meet you Hadley. I'm Doctor Richardson." He took her offer for a handshake, and Hadley invited him into the hall.

"What a beautiful dog." The doctor remarked as Chewy sniffed his shoes.

"Thank you, we got him yesterday." Hadley proudly said. "Let me take you to Jace, he has stayed in bed today." Hadley gestured for the doctor to follow her up the stairs with Chewy closely following behind. Hadley heard Cindy tell Marty they must stay in their bedroom while the doctor is here checking on Jace. Chewy must have heard her as well as he walked to their bedroom door and began begging to enter. Marty opened the door in no time at all, gleefully cheering Chewy's name before inviting him into the bedroom to join him and his mother watch telly.

Hadley noticed the doctor look down the hallway to where the dog wondered to but did not bother asking who else was in the home. Gently Hadley tapped on the bedroom door and heard Jace call come in.

When they entered the room, Jace was in an upright position, still trying to do complete the crossword which was in the previous days' newspaper.

"Good afternoon Jace, I am Doctor Richardson. Your wife has filled me in on what she believes the problem is. She said you have injured your ribs falling off the ladder while doing some renovations in the attic."

Jace looked at Hadley who was nodding and smiling, urging for him to go along with the cover story.

"Nice to meet you, yeah I had a fall I'm no sure what I've done. Think its bruised ribs." Jace said to the doctor who had already put a blood pressure cuff on his upper arm.

Hadley sat on the bed next to Jace and watched as the doctor began writing down notes on the paperwork he had brought a long with him. Hadley hadn't paid much attention to the doctors' appearance since he entered the home. But now she could see he was around mid-fifty, thick brown hair with bushy eyebrows and wore a small pair of glasses which were perched on the end of his nose. His suit was clean and crisp which Hadley thought looked expensive. He wore a striped shirt with a neatly done bowtie, the only thing that looked old and used was the briefcase he carried with him. The leather was worn and shredding and Hadley wondered if the briefcase was sentimental to him which meant he could not part ways with it.

After examining Jace, Richardson confirmed he had bruised ribs and needed to spend a few days resting, to recover without any other complications.

Hadley was certain no complications would happen, but she nodded her head and agreed she would make sure Jace stayed on bed rest.

"I am surprised by how well your pain threshold is, many patients are unable to talk through the pain of an injury such as yours. However, I will prescribe you with some extra strong painkillers." The doctor turned to Hadley who was standing near the bedroom door.

"You can pick them up from the pharmacy today." Hadley told him that wouldn't be a problem and the doctor nodded his head once before saying goodbye to Jace.

"No need to walk me out, here is the prescription. I believe the pharmacy is open until half five tonight. Please do not hesitate to contact me if you have any questions" The doctor shook Hadley's hand and made his way down to the front door and left the home. Hadley looked at the prescription the doctor had handed her, and walked over to Jace to show him.

"I will make you more tea, but I think it will be a good idea to take these as well. The tea can only help so much. But one thing you are definitely going to do is follow the doctors orders of staying in bed." Hadley kissed Jace before he could protest. Hadley knew Jace would know what she was doing, and she felt him break the kiss.

"We have too much to do for me to stay in bed." Jace said "I can't just sit here."

Hadley gave him a peck on the cheek.

"I know my love, but you are no good injured. Besides, all we are going to do today is research. I will get Cindy to stay here with Marty and Chewy while I go to the pharmacy and pick up your prescription. I will also pop in and speak to Kerry and see if she has any more thoughts on the Orera and it's familiar. Can I get you something before I leave?"

Hadley went into Cindy and Marty's room and retold her what the doctor had said, she also asked if she would be okay with the plan she had come up with. With no hesitation Cindy agreed to the plan and Hadley knew it was because Cindy felt safe in the home. Hadley asked Marty if he would like to be in charge of looking after Chewy and smiled when he saluted her his answer.

"I won't be too long!" Hadley shouted from the hallway as she put on her boots and coat. She heard three different goodbyes and left the house knowing everything and everyone would be safe.

By the time Hadley got to the pharmacy a light drizzle had begun to fall from the ever darkening sky. Hadley felt a shiver go through her body as she entered the store, the warm blast of air made the hairs on her arms stand in formation. The store smelt of disinfection and the faintest smell of tobacco smoke. She made her way past the sparse customers waiting for their prescriptions and stood on the waiting cross. She could see from a few stares, the odd townspeople still had their doubts on whether her and Jace were responsible for Sarahs death. But she knew Evelyn and the church had convinced the majority, as she received nods and sympathetic smiles from the rest.

After Hadley handed over her prescription she took a seat next to an elderly woman, whose hair was curled too tight and neatly pinned under a flower headscarf. Her trench coat was wrapped tightly around her thin frame, covering her pure white blouse and khaki ankle length skirt. Hadley sat on the plastic chair half daydreaming, half taking in her surroundings.

The store was selling plastic halloween decorations, a hanging Frankenstein and a wall plastic covering with a werewolf and a vampire in a fierce battle. The one decoration Hadley became fixated on was the tiny witch figurines that shook when you tapped them with your finger. Their faces matched the same green as the Frankenstein and their bright orange hair was moulded into curls under their very pointed black hats. She chuckled and picked up four of the witch figurines and one hanging Frankenstein. With no line she quickly paid and went back to the same seat to wait for her prescription once again.

She counted how many people were before her, the elderly lady next to her and a young mother holding her toddler on her hip. The pharmacist called out Patrick Ford and the young mother moved her son to the other hip and took the small paper bag off the counter and left the store. When the elderly woman name was called Hadley overheard the pharmacist asking if the woman knew how to take her medication; statins, beta blockers and blood thinners. She watched as the pharmacist exchanged hushed conversations before wishing her well and going back to collect the next prescription.

Hadley took a right on the high street after leaving the pharmacy and smelt the incense a second later. She had told the others she would drop into Spiritual Healings and see Kerry. She was hoping Kerry would have found some new information.

Although the information on the Orera was scarce she knew Kerry knew elders and other Wiccans who may have some knowledge. When she entered the shop, she was greeted again by the spooky but tasteful halloween decorations Kerry had put out. She could hear Kerry talking to a customer about crystal balls, Hadley remembered her mother teaching her about scrying when she was younger. Her mother would spend hours telling her stories of witches using them.

She remembered her mother telling her of a witch, who was used for her powers by those in power. Every day those in power would make the witch use crystallomancy. They would twist and manipulate what she had foreseen to gain more leverage against their fight to the top. When she first heard the story her mother had stopped at that part. Telling her the rest of the story did not end well. But she had begged and begged until her mother gave in. She remembered getting more comfortable in bed and invited her mother to get under the duvet with her. When they were both warm in bed, her mother continued the story and recalled of how the witch became filled with sickness and guilt knowing her visions were being used to put her captors lives above others. How she could hear the souls of those who had been tortured and put to death because of her. She purposely bled to try and rid her body of her power, unable to live a sane life with the sadness which consumed her. Hadley remembered hugging her mother tight, feeling sorry for the witch as she imagined her hands in chains, waiting to be called upon for something her captors knew nothing about.

The witch knew for her soul to arrive in Summer-land, there was only one thing the she could do. If her power could not leave her body, the witch knew her soul would have to be freed. So with a brave heart, when her captors called for her, she looked into her crystal ball and lied. Lied with a deceptive smile knowing her fate had been set. When the captors began losing their power, with no one to blame but the witch they burnt her at the stake.

As the flames became to grow and her body began to burn, the witch saw a raven watching her, ready to take her home. No screams left her lungs, no more power would she give them. For her soul was on its way to Summer-land, thanks to the sacrifice she made.

Hadley walked round the shop and saw Kerry was speaking to two teenage girls dressed in long black dresses. Who were reading a booklet Kerry had given them while listening intently to how to use the crystal ball.

"But remember young ones, your greatest power is what you give back when all else is lost."

Kerry must have been told the story as a child as well, Hadley thought.

The girls both nodded their head, unsure of what Kerry meant. But took her words seriously has they paid for the crystal ball and left whispering to each other.

"They want to be witches." Kerry said with a smile "But I could not talk them out of buying something so advanced.

They have been watching Bewitched." Kerry finished with a giggle. Hadley watched as the two girls left the shop.

"Want or already are?" Hadley asked as she joined in with Kerry.

Hadley saw Kerry think about her question, her brain overthinking yet not able to produce a quick answer.

"I think they will do well, this is the only store around, therefore, I can keep an eye on what magic they intend to do."

Hadley nodded her head, like Kerry she was happy minors were interested in the craft.

"Don't worry, we can both keep an eye on them." Kerry reassured her as if reading Hadley's mind. "By the way I have some things to tell you. Let me go get the stuff, I will join you in the seating area in a minute." Kerry said and walked behind the curtain.

CHAPTER ELEVEN

Hadley watched as Kerry came over to the seating area with a tray of tea and an old book. Kerry put the tray on the table and poured two cups of tea and passed one to Hadley. She sat down and Hadley filled her in with how Jace was getting on. After a while of gossiping and sipping on their tea Hadley asked if Kerry had found anything new about the Orera.

"I had a delivery of some books and found some pretty interesting things in this one." Kerry said as she held up a brown leather book. The book looked tattered which made it unsellable, however, it was still readable.

"Yeah." Kerry added as she saw Hadley staring at the book "I can't sell it, but I wouldn't sell it anyway. It is one of a kind and I would have kept it for myself."

Hadley nodded understanding there must be something about the darker realm in the book. Hadley took the book from Kerry to look at the cover. Plain brown with the title faded 'The mystery's of the Darker Realm'.

"Wow." Hadley gasped, "I will have to let Sarah at the university know about this."

Kerry nodded in agreement.

"This must be the only copy, it is fascinating." Kerry added. Kerry took back the book from Hadley and began slowly turning the pages. Every page was filled with demon drawings and descriptions, blood hounds, vampires, werewolves, the common known demons which were not afraid to make themselves known. Kerry continued turning the pages, more demons only a handful of people are known to have seen or experienced began showing themselves. The Jagmizag who aimed to possess those in power, their true form showed sharp teeth, grey jagged skin, a malnourished figure and a long tail.

The Brelam, the Tharkon, the Zilgtoton, the book continued to show more and more disturbing demons which would terrify the nightmares of anyone. Hadley stopped reading and looked at Kerry who was staring at her.

"You are looking for the demon which took your mother aren't you?" Kerry asked as she placed a comforting hand on Hadley's arm.

"I know we are looking for the Orera, but if this book has any answers, I want to know." Hadley responded.

"Are you sure it wasn't the Orera demon? Your mother was a witch."

Hadley thought about what Kerry said as she turned the page to the next demon.

"I did think that, but it doesn't feel right. The demon which took over my mother appeared when she.." Hadley stopped speaking. Her mind began piecing together the pieces of her mothers downfall.

"When she helped Evelyn and the church with something." Hadley thought for a moment and silently grieved for her mother once more.

"The Orras." Hadley read a page which took her attention.

"The Orras is a demon which first became known in the seventeenth century. Born from the same area within the darker realm as the Orera. The Orras will possess the body of a witch but cannot perform magic. The only power they have is being able to burn the witches body it possesses from the inside. In true form they represent a beautiful woman with long lilac hair. Although beautiful, they hold the trademark of every demonic being, the black as night abyss eyes."

Hadley wiped away a tear from her cheek.

"I'm sorry Hadley." Kerry said.

"We can stop today if you want, and you can read about the Orera another day."

Hadley shook her head.

"No, it's fine. I'm fine honestly. That was the past and there is no way of going back into the past to save her. In the present, we have a new demon to deal with." Hadley said back as she took a tissue from the box Kerry handed her.

Kerry went and made a fresh pot of tea as Hadley composed herself and once again began turning the pages seeing more pictures of the demons in the darker realm. Hadley paid no attention to the demons on the pages, she continued to turn the pages until she saw the Orera. She glanced at the page amazed at how much information had been written on the demon Sarah and the university knew very little about. The picture showed a hunched female form, the trademark pitch-black eyes, long dark purple hair and a face that showed immortal withering old age.

"Not the most beautiful of demons is she?" Kerry said as she walked back with the fresh pot of tea.

"Hideous for sure." Hadley agreed.

Kerry placed the tray back onto the table and poured the tea.

"The Orera is best known to possess witches who call upon them." Hadley began. "They are the oldest form of demonic witch and are believed to have evolved from the Orras. The Orera needs to feed every year and feeds ofF the souls of those who are sacrificed resembling specific symbols attached to the demon. The more they fed the stronger the Orera will become." Hadley stopped and looked at Kerry.

"The more they fed the stronger they become? This demon has been here centuries. Every year three children are killed and everyone just turns a blind eye!" Kerry scowled.

"This can't be right, how can this go unnoticed?" Hadley enquired. Kerry shook her head, anger brewing in her expression.

"Carry on reading."

"The Orera will come to this realm with a number of abilities, these include: dream manipulation, telekinesis and memory manipulation. Every one hundred years the bones of the last sacrifices need to be buried near to where the Orera familiars body is buried."

Kerry took the book from Hadley.

"The Orera has three nights in which the sacrifice needs to be performed. The first two are unknown, but it has been documented that the final sacrifice is always on the thirtieth."

Hadley sat back in the chair and closed her eyes and pinched the bridge of her nose.

"Sarah was killed on the twenty-second. There is no way we can determine the second date. All we have is the final date."

Hadley began making notes on everything they had discussed.

"I know one thing we are going to do." Hadley announced once she put the pen down. "We are going to find Evelyn and speak to the church as to why this has been going on for so long."

Kerry agreed to the decision and collected the keys ready to close shop. Hadley was unsure how they were going to defeat the Orera. But one thing she did know, the church and others who lived in this town had some explaining to do.

The drizzle which Hadley walked in earlier had now turned into a heavy downpour. Hadley and Kerry huddled under the umbrella Kerry brought with her and quickly made their way to the church meeting hall. Hadley began to feel her body tremble with anxiety, sickness began to fill her stomach. The church meeting hall was a simple building behind the church just outside the graveyard plot. The graveyard was well-kept, grass was cut regularly and flowers were always placed for the newly deceased occupants. The priests house was just off the church land but could still be seen from the low fences and neatly kept bushes.

Hadley remembered spending winter afternoons there with Evelyn as they helped the priest prepare the Christmas nativity play. The church hall was a place Hadley never liked going, yet her childhood was filled with memories from within them walls.

As Hadley and Kerry made their way past the unattended reception desk, the smell of hot dust, floor polish and endless cups of tea filled their senses. The walls were an off-white, illuminated by industrial lights which hung from the dropped ceiling. Hadley took in every detail of the interior, nothing had changed since her mother had died.

After her mother was taken away, she was brought to the church hall and told to sit on the wooden bench, which was still by the office door as the church council decided what would happen to her. Hadley hated this place, there was no warmth, just eerie silence until the hall would be rented out for a holiday fair or a kids' birthday. The reception area had one hallway which had a small tea and coffee room at the end. The shutter was up and tea cups and coffee mugs were placed on the counter ready to be set out in the main hall. Hadley looked through the dark wooden framed double door, chairs had been set for what Hadley assumed was going to be a town meeting.

"Where is everyone?" Kerry asked as she joined Hadley looking through the glass into the main hall.

"It looks like they should be setting up for something." Hadley replied with a furrowed brow. "Lets check the office."

The two walked up the corridor only a few feet from the main hall double door and saw shadows in the frosted glass. Hadley looked at Kerry who raised her eyebrows with suspiciousness and knocked on the door. Hadley saw the shadows move about the office and heard hushed voices, she knocked again this time more forceful, not accepting a non answer again.

"Just open the door, why are we even giving them an option." Kerry uttered.

Hadley gave a quick nod and turned the doorknob without hesitation. She knew Kerry was right, with the current situation, why should they pay respect to those who may be hiding what happens within the church.

Hadley stood in the doorway, her eyes rested on those who were huddled in the office. Father Richardson, Evelyn, Doctor Anderson and two other woman Hadley was unfamiliar with were sat around a desk.

"Hadley, I did not expect you to lose your manners. However, Evelyn here was expecting you to come by at some point." Father Richardson said.

Hadley sensed his tone was verging into sarcasm but ignored the bluntness of his words. She and Kerry moved more into the office, their facial expressions showing nothing but seriousness and anger.

"Hadley, Kerry, please sit down." Evelyn said as she stood up.

"We are okay standing." Hadley responded keeping her eyes on the doctor who had been in her home not too long ago.

Hadley wondered if Kerry was thinking the same thing as her, why would the doctor be here and did he tell them about the injury Jace had been left with?

"We want to know what is going on in this town, why every year three children are being sacrificed and no one seems to bat an eye?" Kerry reeled off on a tundra of pure anger.

Hadley could see all the eyes of those in the office look to the floor.

"Why are you not answering her?" Hadley argued until each pair of eyes were focused back onto them. "Evelyn was everything you told us the other day a lie. Because what we have found out, it is sickening. You knew the powers of this demon, and you lied to us pretending you and the church had no idea what was going on. Even worse a dead child ended up outside my home!" Hadley could feel herself losing control of her emotions. She felt Kerry put a hand on her arm as a sign to reel in her emotions. Hadley took a step back.

"I think we are going to need some answers, and believe me, we will not leave until we do." Kerry said.

"We will not be threatened by magic young lady. You have no idea what you are dealing with. Our ancestors have passed down how we handle these couple of weeks, yes there are sacrifices, but we deal with them as they come." Richardson blurted with anger. Hadley and Kerry looked at each other, fury brewing between them.

"Threatening you with magic!" Kerry shouted as Hadley held her back from stepping towards the doctor.

"Everyone, please calm down." Evelyn finally said. "Benjamin, these two would never use magic against the innocent, and you should know better than to accuse two Wiccans of such things."

Hadley could feel Kerry tense and release her muscles as Evelyn spoke.

Hadley was unable to know if Evelyn was being genuine or not and hated the fact she was unsure of the woman who took on the role of raising her. The two women who had not spoken a word since she and Kerry entered the room were staring at them with judgemental piercing eyes.

"Is there something you would like to add ladies? Or are you just here for the gossip?" Hadley knew her sarcasm was not going to be met with appreciation but Kerry and herself had been accused of threatening magic, so she no longer cared. One of the women twitched in her chair making her pencil skirt ruffle up past her knees showing a ladder in her tights.

"We knew the moment you came back trouble would stir and so right we were. Have you really not thought of why we let Cindy and her family move into the Inn?"

Hadley gasped at the woman's comment.

"You gave the Orera her sacrifices. You are nothing but monsters." Hadley argued, knowing Kerry was no longer going to hold her back.

"If Jace and I did not come here, you would have let Marty be sacrificed!" Hadley began to cry, she suddenly realised that the beautiful town she had moved back to was just as bad as the darker realm the Orera came from.

"Cindy only has one child though, how would you have picked the other two?" Hadley asked through quiet sobs.

"I don't understand why you are letting them explain themselves to you, Hadley. I suppose members of the police are also involved in this, how else would you be able to get away this for so long?" Kerry snarled.

"What you two ladies are not understanding is, if we do not do this, if we do not bow down to Margaret. Her threats to this town will be enforced. Therefore, we allow outsiders to come and take over the Inn, many are families who have nothing, and they saw the Inn as a new start. Of course, we usually get families with many children. But Cindy was very persistent on letting us allow her to run the Inn." Father Anderson voiced.

Hadley hated how he spoke with such calmness, no crack in his voice when he spoke of the children they had sacrificed throughout the years.

"You knew about this?" Hadley asked directing her question to Evelyn. Hadley looked at Evelyn with nothing but disappointment.

"There is nothing we can say Hadley to make this any better. This is the way we have to live, it has been this way for centuries. We have done everything we can to try and get rid of what did you call it? Orera? We tried an exorcism, we tried to use." Evelyn stopped speaking.

Hadley knew what she was going to say, "I was right wasn't I? You asked my mother to use a spell which could never be done by one witch alone. You knew that place was sitting on lay-lines and because of you an Orras could pass through and take over her body." Hadley wanted to collapse, her legs begin to feel weak and numb.

"So what?" Hadley continued not wanting to show any more weakness to the monstrosities she was speaking to. "You want us to just leave and let Cindy move back into the Inn and have Marty be sacrificed?"

Evelyn shook her head as a tear formed and fell down her cheek.

"You can cry all you want Evelyn, all of you have blood on your hands. Centuries of blood." Kerry said.

"We know this. Don't assume we do not know the sins our souls bare." Father Anderson voiced.

"We are unsure of how Sarah was sacrificed. This is why we were meeting this afternoon. But we do not need your help. This is the churches' problem as it has been since the fifteenth century. We have seen your so-called witch magic, and it has no place here." Father Anderson told Hadley and Kerry as he walked to the door gesturing for them to leave.

Hadley could see Kerrys stance change.

"Kerry, don't." Hadley warned as she put her hand on Kerrys shoulder.

"They won't tell us much more. Come on, we need to get back to the house." Hadley whispered as she began guiding Kerry out the office door.

"This is not over." Kerry snarled as she let Hadley pull her out the room.

CHAPTER TWELVE

Hadley and Kerry made eye contact knowing they had not come to a decision on how they would tell Cindy the truth. When they entered the house Hadley and Kerry were greeted with smiles and barks. Hadley gave Marty and Chewy a hug before excusing herself upstairs to go and speak with Jace. Hadley could feel her heart breaking as she walked up the stairs holding tightly onto the banister. She feared if she let go she would not be able to make it to the top.

"Hey Had's. Glad you are back, I was just deciding what to do for dinner." Cindy cheerfully announced from the top of the stairs. Hadley looked up.

"Hey lovely." Hadley said back as she put her arms out to hug her friend. "Why don't we order something? We can arrange it when I come back down, I just want to go see Jace. Kerry is downstairs I think she is being overtaken by the troublesome twosome." Hadley found herself being able to pull of a fake laugh.

She watched as Cindy walked down the stairs and go into the lounge. Hadley heard Jace call her name, but she couldn't make her feet go to the bedroom. Instead, she found herself shutting the bathroom door behind her and the faint click as she locked the door. Hadley knew she was about to crumble, as she felt her body slide down the door until she was sitting on the bathroom floor. Hadley let out a silent scream as her tears ran down producing puddles on the floor.

"Let me in please darling!" Hadley heard Jace whisper from the other side of the door. Hadley didn't respond, she just felt her hand reach up behind her and unlock the door. She moved across the bathroom to lean on the wall next to the sink as Jace walked in.

"You shouldn't be out of bed." Hadley said as her husband struggled to sit next to her on the floor.

"I am not staying in bed while I can hear my wife crying in the bathroom." Jace took Hadley's hand and pulled her closer to him. Hadley lent her head onto his shoulder and took in his smell for comfort.

"Jace, I don't know what we are going to. Kerry and I have found out something horrible. I have no idea how we are meant to tell her."

Hadley retold Jace everything that had happened since she left the house to get his prescription. When Hadley finished she looked at Jace who was staring off into the distance with a look of shock and horror plastered onto his face.

"You need to be straight with Cindy. Its not gonna be easy to tell her, but she has to know! You don't have to do this alone Hadley, you've got Kerry and me to help you… but she needs to know."

After helping Jace up off the floor and him refusing to go back to bed, Hadley and Jace walked down the stairs and made their way into the lounge to join the others.

"I hope you don't mind, but I ordered pizza, it should be here soon." Cindy said as the two entered the room.

Dinner went by faster than Hadley had hoped, she had taken Cindy to one side and told her that they needed to speak with her without Marty. Hadley knew Cindy could pick up on her tone that something was wrong, so quickly convinced Marty to go to bed earlier than normal with the promise Chewy could join him.

By seven pm Marty had taken Chewy outside for his nighttime toilet run and was being led up to bed by Cindy. Hadley's anger had reappeared in full force as she, Jace and Kerry made their way into the study to wait for Cindy to come back down.

Hadley took her head out of her hands to see Kerry pacing the study while swearing under her breath and Jace was sitting on the couch with nothing but a grim expression. Hadley began role-playing how she would start the conversation with Cindy once she joined them.

Every scenario Hadley came up with left a sour taste in her mouth which could not be washed away with sips of beer. Hadley heard a floorboard on the stairs' creek and they all turned their heads towards the doorway.

Hadley found herself sitting up straight and began taking deep breaths. As Hadley watched Cindy walk into the study, she knew Cindy had seen her wipe the sweat which had collected on her forehead. Hadley was unable to stop herself from biting her bottom lip as Cindy examined everyone in the study. Kerry had sat in the nearest chair to try and control her fidgeting. Hadley noticed only Jace could put on a brave face as his shoulders were now in the correct position, but she noticed he kept his hands between his thighs.

"I know you have found out something, you all look like nervous wrecks." Cindy said finally breaking the silence. Hadley stood up and moved to a seat nearer to Cindy, she knew she had to tell her somehow, but she refused to tell her while sitting opposite her like a police interrogation.

"Cindy, this is going to be hard to hear, but I want you to know, that we all love you and care for you and we will not let anything happen to you or Marty." Hadley began.

Cindy nodded her head, her mouth became a thin line unable to produce any sounds.

"Kerry and I found out about the Orera. What it does and how it survives outside the darker realm." Hadley gulped as she tried to control the pace of her sentences. "We went to find more answers from those involved in the church, and they told us this happens every year and every year they allow families with three or more children to move into the Inn. Those children are to be the sacrifices for the Orera. But they decided to allow you to move in with only one child and would, I guess figure out how to get the other two sacrifices." Hadley choked on her words. She felt annoyed at herself for not getting an explanation to how they would find two more innocent victims. She presumed they had no idea how they would solve that problem themselves. Hadley took hold of Cindy's hand unsure whether her friend was going into catatonic shock.

"Cindy I promise you, none of us are going to let them take Marty. We have you safe here with us, nothing supernatural or demonic can get inside these walls. And Marty will not leave this house without someone right next to him." Hadley said doing her best to reassure Cindy who was staring straight through her.

Hadley saw Jace and Kerry begin to move until they were all huddled around Cindy who had not even blinked since Hadley began to speak.

"Cindy we can't begin to imagine how you must be feeling inside. But what we do know is nothing is going to happen to Marty or to you. I promise you nothing will happen to either of you." Jace said as he placed his hand on Cindy's forearm "But we need to know you are okay, so can you say something?".

Hadley thought Jace was thinking the same thing she was, had Cindy gone into catatonic shock. Kerry put her arm around Cindy and began whispering 'it will be okay' continuously into her ear. Hadley walked into the kitchen, she thought sugar would be a good thing in case Cindy was also suffering with hypoglycaemia. As she opened the fridge to get a can of coke out, she noticed her hands were trembling. Unsure whether she was going to be able to pick up the can, Hadley tried to gain control of her body once again. *'Get a hold of yourself Hadley, Cindy needs you.'* She sighed to herself as she picked up the coke can.

"Sweetheart, she is coming round." Jace said as Hadley closed the fridge door.

"Cindy have some sips of this." Hadley said as she walked back into the study and handed over the can "The sugar will help with the shock."

Hadley felt relieved that Cindy took the can from her, her motor functions were showing signs of coming back into motion. Hadley felt the whole room sigh with relief as they watched Cindy take small sips. Her colour started coming back into her skin.

"Cindy do you want to talk about it? Say whatever you want to get it out your system." Kerry said as she saw Cindy open and close her mouth not letting any sounds escape. They all watched as Cindy composed herself, her insides falling apart as she reprocessed every word Hadley had just told her.

"They were going to let my son be sacrificed to that demon?"

Hadley and Kerry both nodded their head, their eyes refusing to meet Cindy's.

"Yes they were. But they are not going to get anywhere near him now." Jace informed her. "They cannot get into this house, and neither can anything the Orera sends here. This house is protected by strong magic, and you have two amazing witches here. Hadley and Kerry will do everything they can."

Hadley looked at Jace. "Jace is right, Kerry and I are strong. And Jace has always found ways to stop the destruction the paranormal cause in this realm. Even those that are more uncommon from the darker realm. You are safe with us and I promise Marty is not going to be the Orera's sacrificial dinner." Hadley promised. Her eyes focusing on her husband as she felt a surge of love pump from her heart.

"Thank you." Cindy responded. "This is all too much, if you hadn't had come when you did, Marty would probably already be dead." Cindy finally let the tears fall from her eyes as Hadley noticed the hug from Kerry tighten.

"If they couldn't give her Marty, how are they getting these victims? It is obvious that the Orera cannot leave my Inn. Otherwise she would have followed Marty and me here, and got Jace and I when we escaped the other day." Hadley was surprised by Cindy's words, after everything she had just been told, she could still rationally think and analyse the situation.

"That is what I have been wondering most of the evening. I keep going back to the powers the Orera has and how strong they must be having spent centuries here. I speculate she can manipulate those who were in the meeting room Hadley and Kerry went to today." Jace alleged.

"That could be true, since we have found out she can control minds and dreams. Those who have been giving up those innocent children to her have left themselves vulnerable. It was clear they belong to the families who have always be responsible." Kerry asseverated.

Hadley nodded in agreement, she was starting to understand how this could be happening, but they needed proof.

"Why don't you try and get into one of their dreams?" Cindy proposed.

Hadley, Jace and Kerry all looked at Cindy with wide eyes.

"Dream hop." Kerry said "That is risky, I know what needs to be done, but I have never performed it. Hadley?"

"No, I mean I have read about it. But it can go wrong easily and the one who is dream hopping can be lost forever." Hadley said.

"What do you mean lost forever?" Cindy asked.

"There are stories of witches who attempted to dream hop, but they were unable to make it back to their bodies in full. Their soul was split into two, half stayed in the persons dream and simply disappeared when the person woke up. The other half that made it back couldn't function, making the witch wither, unable to leave her bed until they simply passed away." Hadley licked her dry lips not wanting to finish retelling the stories she had heard.

"Cindy if we do this and do not come back whole, we won't make it to Summer-land. You have to understand we believe that when we die, only the body dies. The soul lives on and goes to a nonphysical realm which is much denser than ours. Our souls coexist with the greatest energies; Woden and Freya. There, without judgement an incarnation review happens, the lessons we learned or ignored are brought to light. Then when the conditions on earth are correct, the soul is reincarnated and life can begin again. But without a full soul, the soul cannot be reviewed, it cannot be reincarnated back to life." Hadley watched Cindy take in the information she had just told her and hoped she understood the downfall of the plan.

"I understand, I really do, But does that mean you won't attempt it? If you don't try what is the point in even trying to stop the Orera? Jace said you are both powerful witches, if you don't try two more innocent children will be slaughtered." Cindy pleaded.

"You are right." Hadley said rubbing her eyes and turning to Kerry. "I will do it Kerry. If you are here, I think we will be able to make sure I come back."

Kerry bit her nails but nodded solemnly.

"If you trust me enough to make the potion, then we can try." Kerry said, "Jace can you prepare the bedroom? Hadley and me will prepare the potion. Cindy if you don't mind, maybe check in on Marty and then help Jace."

Once in the kitchen, Kerry and Hadley began preparing the spell.

"Hadley, I'm worried. What if you don't come back?" Kerry said as she began putting herbs into the mortar. Hadley passed her a pinch of lotus, watercress, water lily and seaweed and watched as Kerry began mixing them together.

"I'm worried as well. But if we don't try, we may never find the answers we are looking for."

Kerry nodded her head with a look of complete terror plastered her face.

"Okay we have the herbs done, now we need water." Kerry said.

"Wait, lets use moon water." Hadley suggested as she took a pewter cup to the walk in pantry.

Arriving back to the counter Hadley handed the pewter back to Kerry and she stirred in the herbs.

"This is going to taste horrible, but you don't need to drink it all, just half. We need to keep the rest next to you." Kerry told Hadley. The two finished preparing the potion and made their way upstairs.

"It looks perfect, thank you." Hadley said as she walked in the room. Jace had shut the curtains and was lighting the last candle. He had moved the bed into the middle of the room, so a candle could be placed on each quarter. Cindy had poured salt in a circle on the floor, making sure not to close the circle until Hadley had entered.

"Right." Kerry said. "Take this fluorite and place it under the pillow, it is going to help your concentration and get you mentally focused." She told Hadley.

"I love you. Make sure you come back to me." Jace said kissing Hadley before she entered the circle.

"I love you too my love. I promise I will come back." Hadley said back.

"Thank you for doing this." Cindy said as she took Hadley into a tight embrace.

"We've got this okay?" Kerry said as she hugged Hadley. "Remember when you enter the circle put the crystal under the pillow, drink half the potion and we will call the corners before we recite the spell. I will count to three after you lie down, and we will recite it together." Kerry let go of the hug first and held Hadley at arms length "One more thing, keep this in your hand." Kerry handed another crystal to Hadley. Hadley looked at the crystal.

"Heliotrope?"

"Yes, the crystal for courage for those who are called to give themselves for the good of others." Kerry responded and kissed Hadley on the cheek. Hadley took a deep breath and entered the circle, Cindy followed close behind, carefully closing the circle behind Hadley. Hadley walked to the bed and placed the fluorite under her pillow. Clutching the heliotrope she gulped half of the potion which was in the pewter cup. Together they both called upon the circles.

"Okay now place the cup onto the table and lie down." Kerry instructed her as she lit the opium scented incense. Hadley did as she was told and made herself comfortable above the sheets.

"Good. Now on the count of three we will recite the spell and invoke the Goddess." Hadley listened as Kerry spoke, her breaths became shallow, and she gripped the crystal tighter.

"Okay. One, two, three."
'Goddess Nott, Daughter of Jotun,
Goddess of sleep and dreams, Let the dream be with clear vision,
May I ride on your chariot across the night sky,
Originator of the nights energies,
Insight and questions that are often wondered, may the dream provide messages
Throughout the slumber
Let me use your powers to hop from dream to dream.
By the power of three
So mote it be.'

Hadley felt herself sink deeper into the bed, darkness consumed her mind. Hadley saw nothing but stars, as she sank deeper into another realm. The stars began to dwindle, slowly turning into street lamps. Hadley blinked as she realised she was sitting on a cold pavement. Looking up, she noticed the street lamps were further apart than normal. The street she found herself on was deserted, her senses were numb, there were no people to be seen, no sounds to be heard and no smells to be smelt.

'Where am I?' Hadley spoke to the empty street, Hadley knew three things. She needed to know where she was, she needed to know whose dream this was, and she needed to know why she was allowed to enter this dream.

Still sitting on the floor, Hadley pulled herself up and looked around. The place looked familiar, but the street lights were further apart. She began walking towards the nearest building. The closer she came to the building, the more her relief changed to dread. Hadley found herself at the entrance of the Ramm Inn, the courtyard was deserted, but the lights inside were on. She was unsure what she was supposed to do, she knew nothing could hurt her in someones dream. But she also knew no-one had dream hopped when dealing with an Orera. Hadley decided not to go near the Inn and chose to crouch behind a hedge which was just outside the Inns' courtyard entrance.

Not wanting the Orera to have any chance of detecting her in someone's dream; which she suspected the demon was controlling. She stayed silent and immobilised until she heard the Inn door open. Peering out of the hedge, Hadley could make out a male figure walking across the courtyard, the door to the Inn was still open, so Hadley stayed still until she heard the door slam and the male figure pass her by.

When she was sure she would be able to follow the male with no detection from the Inn or the male himself, she quietly moved from behind the hedge and began following him down the lane. Now knowing where she was Hadley was aware she would be going onto the high street. She decided to start making a mental note, of everything that seemed unusual to her. The street lamps were still one, she made a note of how the sky was not black, but a deep dark blue which let no stars shine through. She also noted how fog was apparent on the high street; but it only existed on the ground and came just below her knees. When she reached the entrance to the high street, the man was already a few feet ahead. Still to Hadley's relief he was unaware of her presence. Not wanting to be seen in full she kept up a pace in the shadows of the shops, occasionally looking behind her to make sure no one else was here. Hadley came to a halt when the man stopped unexpectedly and lifted his head up to the sky.

Hadley refused to move, and crouched down to cover herself more in the darkness. She watched as he began sniffing the air and held her breath. But the man kept his head upwards and went right. With no one else showing themselves, Hadley began moving in the direction the man took. Peering round the corner, she saw the man had stopped again and was staring into the darkness of the road. Still unable to make out the features, Hadley grew more concerned on who she was following.

Feeling a rush of cold air sweep past, Hadley looked behind her. She began to feel her legs buckle underneath her and held on to the wall of the building to stop herself from collapsing. Nothing appeared on the high street behind her and taking back control of her breathing she looked back round the corner.

To Hadley's surprise the man she had been following was nowhere to be seen. With him not in sight, she walked round the corner and to the area she had last seen the man standing. All that was left was the fog and the silence. *'The hell am I meant to do now?'* she said to herself and turned to face a shop window. She could faintly see pumpkins in the window smiling from the street lamp which stood on the curb-side. Hadley realised this was Kerrys store and this was where the man had been standing, staring before he disappeared.

'Why did he stop here and what has this got to do with Kerrys store?' Hadley thought.

"Do not make me drag you child!"

Hadley spun on her heels, her heart began racing, and she knew that voice must have been the man coming back here. She knew she only had moments to hide somewhere, if she was found now, the Orera would know what she was doing.

"Hurry now, there is not much time left."

Hadley knew there was nowhere to hide, she would never make it back to the corner she had been peering round. She spun and saw her reflection in the Spiritual Healings window. Her only hope was whoever this dream belonged to; they were not too concerned about having shop doors locked. With no time to think of a new plan, she took hold of the door handle and with a sigh of relief she heard a click. With no time to think, she opened the door and crept inside. Carefully shutting it behind her. The shop which normally had a strong scent of incense, smelt of mould and rot. A shadow crept up into the shop from the window. Time was up.

She knew the man was now outside. Crouching down she crept closer to the store window. Knowing her position was going to cause pain to her knees she placed her hand on the window display board for more support. Hadley quickly pulled away as she felt her hand sink into a thick liquid. Unable to see what it was, she nervously sniffed her hand, hoping she would not smell metal.

'Rotten pumpkin' she sighed with relief.

Now aware no crime had been committed in Kerrys window display, Hadley went back to paying attention to the man outside. Luckily, he was still unaware she was boycotting his dream. She knew this would be the perfect opportunity to finally see who the man was.

The view was limited, the lack of the already dim light and the awkward angle she found herself in, meant she had to strain her neck to get a good view. The man had short grey hair with no signs of balding, he looked elderly maybe in his mid to late seventies. His black straight trousers covered the tops of his loafers and he wore a dark-coloured jumper over a button-up shirt which she assumed was tucked into his trousers.

"Do not cry child. This has to be done."

The stern voice shocked Hadley to the core, now she was closer the voice became more recognisable. Shaking her head in disbelief she moved closer to get a different view and confirm her suspicions. With a new position but still hiding in the darkness of the window display, she gasped as she saw the clerical collar sitting neatly around his neck. She finally realised she was in Father Andersons dream. A new question came to Hadley's mind, why was Father Anderson outside Kerrys shop with what she assumed was a child? She was still unable to see from the angle she was in.

Looking round, Hadley planned to move into a position she knew she would be able to see who the Father was speaking to. Quietly she moved position again, pausing every few shuffles to check she was not being watched by the Father.

When she was in the new position, aware she was putting herself more at risk of being seen, she put her attention onto what was happening outside the shop. Hadley put her hand over her mouth to stop a scream escaping.

Horrified she watched as the Father ripped open the young boys night top and began carving the same symbols she saw on Sarahs stomach. Small sobs began to leave Hadley's body as she watched the boys eyes widen with horror. A pleading scream left his child sized lungs. Hadley was unable to do anything except cry and watch as he used the boys own blood to draw the bloodline down his tiny face. Everything that was on Sarahs body was being carved and mutilated onto the innocent boys body.

She felt bile began to rise from her stomach as she noticed no emotion was showing on Father Andersons face. She felt her body become weak as she watched as the boys mouth was stitched up the same way Sarahs had been. She placed her hand on the window, she could feel her heartbreaking as she watched the child being sacrificed. The boys frightened eyes were wide, as a number two was drawn onto his forehead with his blood.

His sleeping clothes which were covered in dinosaurs were now soaking in blood. Sweat had made his blonde hair stick to his face, parts also covered in thick dark red blood. His innocent blue eyes were showing he was slowly losing his life. Hadley still had her hand on the window and the other covering her mouth.

Forcing her body to stay hidden was becoming more difficult, she could feel her body begin to shake as she watched tears fall down the young boys cheek. A small cry finally left her as the boy made eye contact with her. She noticed he lifted his hand as if he was trying to reach her hand which was now stuck onto the window.

The window was becoming foggy due to the heat and sweat producing off her body. She kept eye contact with the boy removing her hand from her mouth to announce she was sorry. Unsure whether the child saw what she mouthed to him, his eyes were already back onto Father Anderson as he tried to scream when a knife was being put onto his neck. Hadley quickly darted her eyes to what the boy was staring at. She watched as Father Anderson sliced the boys neck open. Blood poured out like a waterfall drowning the boys body with blood.

Unable to hold in the sobs any longer Hadley let out a terrifying scream as the blade finished slicing through his skin. Hadley froze, aware she had blown her cover but still unable to stop her cries. Father Anderson still holding the knife turned to face the window. She flew backwards as black eyes stared into her. She knew those eyes, the trademark eyes that she had faced many times before. Scuttling backwards Hadley began screaming as Father Anderson kicked open the shop door. Unable to stand she began crawling away as fast as she could, until she felt a tight grip around her ankle. In an instant she felt her body being pulled back, her nails scrapping on the hard floor of the shop. Without warning she was flipped over, so she was facing the ceiling. Screaming for Kerry to bring her back, she felt Father Anderson straddle her, his face inches away from hers. Hadley did nothing but scream to be pulled back to her body, as she felt Father Anderson lick her tears from her cheeks. Hadley could feel her body go stiff, she looked into the black abyss eyes until darkness consumed her.

CHAPTER THIRTEEN

'Goddess Nott, Daughter of Jotun,
Goddess of sleep and dreams, Let the dream be with clear vision,
May she ride on your chariot across the night sky,
Originator of the nights energies,
Insight and questions that are often wondered, may the dream provide messages
Throughout the slumber
Let her use your powers to hop from dream to dream.
By the power of three
So mote it be'

Kerry watched as Hadley gasped for air before falling into a deep sleep. Kerry shut her eyes to connect with the energy flowing off Hadley and stayed still until she felt Hadley's soul completely leave the room.

"Thank you Goddess Nott." She said as she opened her eyes. "The spell worked, she has been allowed to cross." She told Jace and Cindy. Kerry looked at them both and noticed Cindy was frozen.

"It's okay Cindy, we will be able to get her back." Kerry assured her as she walked over and put her arm around her shoulders. "Jace, why don't you go and make some coffee? We need to stay vigilant while Hadley is not here."

Jace nodded his head, unable to take his eyes off his wife.

"Yeah sure." He agreed as he ran his fingers through his hair. Kerry and Cindy watched as Jace left the room with his head low. Kerry sat on the floor with her legs crossed and stretched her back with a satisfying click. She could see Cindy looked stressed through the candlelight and asked her to come and sit with her.

"I don't know how you guys do this. But I am grateful." Cindy sighed as she made her way to the floor. Kerry laughed, a dry wooden laughter which she did not mean to produce.

"As witches we don't necessarily assume we will be trying to defeat beings from the darker plane. If I am completely honest, I came to this small town because I thought it would be a quiet life. Be able to feel more connected to the earth and nature. But I know I was meant to be here, just like Hadley and Jace knew they needed to come back." Kerry said pondering on her thoughts.

Cindy pursed her lips into a weak smile and looked at Hadley lying on the bed.

"When her soul comes back will she be okay?" Cindy asked. Kerry bit her lip not wanting to lie.

"There are certain rules we have to follow, if you stay in someone else's dream too long it can tarnish your soul. But I guess the main problem many people would consider with dream hopping is the ethical one. I mean you wouldn't go into someone's home without being asked and here we are invading someone's mind." Kerry replied.

Without making a sound Jace entered the room holding a tray with a pot of coffee and three mugs. With a slight wince, he placed the tray in front of the two girls and sat next to them.

"You are still in pain." Kerry noted to Jace. Jace refused to look at her as he poured the coffee into the first mug.

"I am fine." Jace snorted back, a sense of unease and annoyance in his tone.

"Hadley needs to know if you are not healing right. I am in no way trying to stress you out Jace, but we all need you to be in your best health." Kerry continued ignoring his instant change in tone.

"Have you taken your medication tonight?" Cindy asked with a look of concern after listening to the others' conversation.

Kerry saw Jace sigh and shake his head, rolling her eyes she tilted her head to Cindy who got up and walked down the stairs to collect his pills.

"I haven't been able to focus on medication and looking after myself when Hadley is putting herself in danger. If i lost her.." Jace admitted as a small sob formed in his throat.

"You love her Jace, of course you are going to be anxious about this." Kerry said to him "She is very lucky to have found you."

Jace wiped away a tear which had escaped his eyes and passed Kerry her mug of coffee.

"Here, take them now. At least you won't be in pain when Hadley comes back." Cindy said as she reappeared with a box of tablets. Without arguing Jace took the box and popped two big capsules into his mouth with a gulp of coffee.

Kerry saw Hadley's body twitch and began quickly going round everything to make sure nothing had gone wrong.

"What's happening? Is something wrong?" Cindy said as she quickly got up to check on Hadley.

"Cindy be careful of the circle." Kerry asserted with force. "Everything is fine from what I can sense and see, the incense has just run out." Kerry then calmly pointed out as she lit a match to start a new stick.

"I'm sorry, this is just making my nerves go crazy." Cindy voiced as she wiped sweat from her face.

Kerry looked at her with a smile and nodded, reassuring her she was not alone in her emotions. Kerry stared at Hadley to reassure herself that the only problem was the incense running out. Happy that Hadley was now settled and relaxed again, Kerry went and sat back with Jace and Cindy.

"Why don't you do spells and magic stuff Jace?" Cindy asked wanting to distract them from their haunting thoughts.

"My family have never been Wiccan, we follow the Anglo-Saxon beliefs, but we do not involve magic into it. Hadley was the first witch I came across when we met at university." Jace replied smiling at the thoughts of the past. "Of course I had heard of them, many of us do growing up with stories being passed down. But I never felt the calling to turn to witchcraft. I am happy believing in my Gods and knowing I shall be drinking with them one day in Summerland."

Kerry laughed.

"Why do all men assume they are going to just drink when their souls pass over?"

Jace pretended to be offended as he gulped down his coffee. "You ladies can have your visions of what Summerland will look like. Running round in flowing dresses on fields of bright-green grass. But not me, I shall be sitting at Woden's table with a nice glass of something." Jace said.

Kerry shook her head in amusement and noticed Cindy looked lost in the conversation.

"What about you Cind? What do you believe happens after we pass on?" She asked wanting to involve Cindy in the conversation. Kerry saw Jace look at her with an eyebrow raised.

"I don't really know any more." Cindy confessed. "I never really believed in magic, curses, demons, witches or religion." She said with a shrug. "Growing up my parents took my siblings and me to church but when we reached a certain age we were allowed to decide if we still wanted to go. Only my sister kept going, my brothers and I chose not to."

"When Hadley and I came into the Inn we saw crosses hung on the beams and Marty wears a silver cross on his necklace. Did you try and go back to your faith?" Jace asked Cindy with interest.

"Again I don't know. I guess when you get scared of something you try and find anything to help. I don't think I wanted God to save me, I was more concerned in the feeling of safeness the cross brought to me as a child. Does that make any sense?"

Kerry thought about the reply. She noticed Cindy seemed embarrassed with her attachment to the cross.

"Why do you look ashamed of saying the cross brings you a feeling of safeness?" Kerry asked, a look of confusion on her face.

"Because you guys are Pagans and Wiccans and I guess I felt you would laugh at me for believing differently to you. You have these powers and your demonologists…"

Kerry put her hand up to stop Cindy from finishing her sentence.

"We would never laugh at you for your beliefs. If you want to believe in the Christian faith, then believe in the Christian faith. If you don't, but you feel an attachment to the cross or crucifix then that's fine as well. The objects and the spells we use do not have powers unless we believe they do. The crystal in Hadley's hand does represent certain powers. However, if she doesn't believe in them powers, then it is simply just a pretty rock." Kerry explained.

Cindy nodded her head. "So keeping the necklace round Martys neck is not a bad idea." Cindy wondered out loud.

"I think it is a good idea he keeps the necklace on him." Kerry agreed.

Jace who had been listening to the conversation while staring at Hadley, turned to the two women with a questioning look.

"Cindy? Why do you think you needed powers to be a demonologist?" He asked.

Cindy shuffled uncomfortably. "Oh, erm I guess I thought you needed to be powerful to fight demons." She replied as she saw Jace and Kerry smile.

"Was that a stupid thought?" Cindy said as she felt a warm feeling rise to her cheeks.

"No of course not." Jace reassured her. "Being a demonologist does not require you to have these powers. You just need knowledge and courage. I believe there are many demonologists in the world without qualifications. You do not need a piece of paper, you just need the will to want to help others. Hadley and myself just got lucky to be given a place on the parapsychology course."

Hours passed with no movement from Hadley, Kerry lit another incense to keep the scent present within the room.

"She has been there a long time." Kerry told the others as they were all standing around the circle. "I am going to start calling her back."

"What if she hasn't found out what she needed?"

Kerry looked at Cindy with an intense stare.

"Cindy she has been in there hours, if she hasn't found her answer, then she never will, and I do not care any more. If we want her back. All of her back then we need to get her back now." Kerry put her palms out.

'Goddess Nott, Daughter of Jotun,

> Goddess of sleep and dreams, may the dream she
> entered be as clear as she hoped,
> Bring her back to her body,
> May her soul return whole.'

As Kerry began reciting the spell to help bring Hadley back, her body began convulsing uncontrollably. Kerry saw Jace take a step forward, determination on his face to run to his wife and hold her body still.

"Jace, no." Kerry shouted "If you cross that circle she is never coming back."

Kerry could see the look on his face, unsure as whether to believe the words she was saying.

He took another step forward when Hadley's body sat upright before falling back down.

"Don't be foolish Jace. Stepping into that circle will be the death of her. Do you want to be the reason her soul is lost?" Kerry knew she was being harsh, she could see his face twist with pain as he considered her words.

"What's happening? Oh my god Hadley. Kerry call her back." Cindy cried moving away from the circle.

Kerry began to recite the spell again:

> 'Goddess Nott,
> Daughter of Jotun,
> Goddess of sleep and dreams, may the
> dream she entered be as clear as she hoped,
> Bring her back to her body,
> May her soul return whole,

from your forceful powers,
Bring Hadley back now,
By the power of three,
So mote it be.'

Kerry watched as Hadley's body continued to twist and turn showing no signs of her returning back to her body. Sweat began drenching the sheets underneath her body, her mouth opened to scream, but no sound filled the room.

"Something is going wrong." Kerry said panicked. "Hadley. Hadley, follow my voice. You are strong, you can come back now. Jace, Cindy, call for her. Something is happening, and she is losing focus on where she is." she ordered the other two.

Jace and Cindy both began calling out Hadley's name, pleading with her to return to her body. Kerry's breathing began to turn heavy, her legs twitched and as she felt a warm trickle run onto her lips. She put her hand to her face and wiped. Blood began running from her nose. Her heart stopped as she looked back over to Hadley and saw her nose begin to bleed. Kerry was unable to stop the blood flow as it dripped onto her lips leaving a metal taste in her mouth. Knowing her nosebleed was not going to stop until Hadley returned, Kerry continued to encourage Jace and Cindy to keep calling her back.

Kerry felt a weight fall on to her as her legs gave way and she fell to the floor. From her knees she felt her body be pushed back and landed with a hard thump onto the floor. Shouting for the others to continue calling Hadley back, she focused on what was happening to her. She felt her body fill with terror, her blood turning to thick black tar. Slowly as the tar filled her body her limbs became paralysed. She saw Jace and Cindy frantically shouting at the bed for Hadley to come back and turning their heads back to where she lay. Sweat drained from her pores as she felt a sensation on her cheek and a pressure on her chest. Kerry began to be consumed by the darkness, she knew what was happening to her must be what was happening to Hadley. Kerry pushed everything she had left into not falling into the darkness.

"Hadley come back to me darling, do not leave me." Kerry heard Jace cry to his wife. She could hear the desperation in his voice. She knew he must have seen the blood coming from her nose and the strain which showed on her face.

'Jace please don't cross the circle.' She tried to shout but discovered her mouth could not open. Thoughts ran through her mind, maybe she should let Jace cross the circle.

She hated herself for thinking it, but she knew what was happening. She was dying and so was Hadley. Her life was ending and she had no idea how to stop it from happening.

Kerry felt her lungs collapse under the pressure which was still being put onto her chest. Losing consciousness Kerry began to see black spots. The spots started blurring her vision and her Cheyne-Stokes breathing began. Kerry heard a gasp from the bed.

CHAPTER FOURTEEN

Hadley felt a rush of air enter her body as the weight on her chest suddenly vanished. Not feeling truly connected to her body she was unable to see where she was through her blurred vision. She was unsure whether she was back in her home or if she had been taken somewhere by Father Anderson.

"Hadley?" She heard a male voice say. Unable to see who the voice belonged to, she stayed in an upright position.

"We……go……see……alright".

Jace felt his heart break as he looked at his wife.

"I don't think she can see or understand us." he alleged to Cindy.

Behind them Kerry was sitting in the same upright position as Hadley was but seemed more connected to her environment.

"Kerry!" Cindy said running over to help her up. "Are you okay? What the hell just happened?"

Kerry still shaken took Cindy's hand and let her help her up off the floor. Her chest was still heavy, and she was certain a bruise forming.

"I'm okay, we need to finish the spell so we can break the circle." She gasped wiping blood from her face. After composing herself to stand tall and powerful Kerry began closing the circle.

'Thank you Goddess Nott for blessing us with your power,
Thank you, spirit of the North for joining us and lending us the power of Earth
Thank you, spirit of the East for joining us and lending us the power of Air
Thank you, spirit of the west for joining us and lending us the power of water
Thank you, spirit of the south for lending us the power of Fire.'

Petrified and unable to feel and connect to anything around her, Hadley saw the face of the boy before his neck was split open. She felt her heart began to race again as she remembered screaming while the child was being killed in front of her. His cries for his mother, the blood covering the dinosaurs on his night clothes, the colour of his hair stained red. The image of Father Anderson running at her as she tried to get away but unable to stand up. The black abyss eyes staring into her and the feeling of his tongue on her cheek.

Hadley couldn't stop thinking of everything she had seen, the boy, the blood, the Father. The boy, the blood, the Father. Hadley let out a terrifying scream which made Jace, Kerry and Cindy take a few steps back. Kerry knew she needed to finish the spell before anyone crossed the circle. She stopped and looked at Jace.

"No Jace." She shouted over the screams coming from Hadley. "We need to finish the spell." Quickly Kerry repeated the first five lines and continued with the rest.

'Stay if you will, go if you must.
Farewell Goddess Nott, and so mote it be.'

Kerry knelt down and made an opening in the salt circle.

"You may enter now." She said to Jace.

In no time at all, Hadley was being cradled by Jace as he tried to calm her down. Cindy and Kerry both joined them on the bed as the screams began to die down.

"Your safe now Had's. You are home." Cindy assured her as she put her hand on Hadley's leg. Kerry took the heliotrope from Hadley's hand and placed it on the table next to them.

"Cindy and I will go make tea and get something sugary for you to eat." Kerry told Hadley.

Cindy placed a kiss on Hadley's forehead before getting off the bed to join Kerry downstairs. When the two left Jace began pulling the damp sheets off the bed, so Hadley would feel more comfortable. Instead of taking them downstairs he threw them in the corner and joined Hadley on the bed, taking her into his arms, making her his little spoon. Hadley was still calming herself down, forcing herself to keep down the bile which wanted to escape.

"Where'd you get off to darling?" Jace whispered into Hadley's ear.

Hadley moved closer to Jace and squeezed his arms to wrap them more tightly around her.

"If you aren't ready to speak about it when they come back up, you don't need to. But I need you to eat and drink whatever they bring up." Jace said.

Hadley nodded her head, unsure if Jace would understand the nod was to say yes to both statements. Jace placed a kiss onto his wife and continued to lay there until Kerry and Cindy walked back into the room.

"It's just tea with a lot of sugar in and cookies to dunk." Kerry said as she placed the tray on the mattress.

Hadley slowly made her way into an upright sitting position with the help from Jace and took the unusually large cup of tea from Kerry with a weak but meaningful smile.

"Thank you." Hadley finally struggled to say as her throat felt raw.

For the next ten minutes, Hadley felt everyone's eyes on her, and they didn't leave until she took her first bite of a cookie. Hadley felt the sugar from the tea and the cookie fill her body with much-needed energy.

"What happened Had's?" Cindy asked as she handed Hadley another cookie. Hadley ate two more cookies before finishing her tea.

"I don't even know where to begin." Hadley replied. "Why don't you start by telling us where you were?" Jace suggested.

Hadley took another cookie and nodded her head before she recounted everything that happened.

"Father Anderson." Jace swore "That son of a.."

"Jace" Hadley interrupted tapping him on the leg. Hadley saw Kerry and Cindy stare at her, both of their faces were of amused surprise.

"I Just don't like that sort of language in my house." Hadley admitted.

She watched as all three lips curled up in amusement for just a tiny second until the realisation of what she saw came back to them.

"I need to leave." Kerry announced "I need to go check."

"Is that a good idea?" Jace asked as he watched Kerry stand from the bed and walk towards the door.

"What do you mean, do you think it is a good idea? Hadley just told us she saw a child being brutally killed outside my shop. And you expect me to stand here and do nothing?" Kerry snapped back.

"She's right my love. What if I wasn't in a dream but at an actual event? We need to check, there may be a dead child lying outside Kerrys shop." Hadley said as she felt a lump in her throat form.

"You all go, I will stay with Marty and Chewy." Cindy suggested.

Hadley asked Jace if he was in pain and if he was, he should stay with Cindy.

"I'm fine. I will drive." Jace replied as he noticed Kerry staring at him remembering their conversation from earlier on. Hadley had already got off the bed and began quickly looking for a change of clothes.

"I'm just going to change." She told the others as she headed towards the bathroom, relieved to be getting out of her damp clothes.

Hadley struggled to get her feet out of her jeans and resorted to sitting on the floor and angrily pulling them off, taking her socks off at the same time. Deciding to stay on the floor to put the new pair she had brought with her on, she jiggled on the floor to pull them up over her thighs. Standing up she quickly threw her top onto the floor and replaced it with a tatty black jumper. Looking in the cabinet mirror to tie her crisp dried hair up she noticed her skin was paler than she had ever seen it. The circles around her eyes had darkened immensely making them look sunken and tired.

'I could have died tonight.' She thought to herself as she turned on the cold tap letting it run for a few seconds.

"You ready?" Kerry asked knocking on the door. Hadley dropped the water she had caught in her hands as she jumped from the knock on the door.

'Get a grip Hadley!' She said to herself as she rubbed her temples.

"Hadley you okay in there?" Kerry asked again.

"Yeah I'm fine I'll be out in a second." Hadley replied as she recollected water in her hands and splashed the cold water onto her face.

As she left the bathroom and headed down the stairs, she grabbed one of her coats off the hanger. She made sure the zip went right to her throat.

"I'm ready." She shouted, unsure whether the others were in the living room or kitchen as all the lights were on downstairs.

"Is Marty and Chewy okay?" Hadley asked Cindy who had joined her in the hall.

"Yeah they were both fast asleep when I popped my head round the door." Cindy reassured her with a warm smile.

"Okay." Jace said with a nod of the head "Ready to go?" He rattled the keys in his right hand and took a step towards the door. Hadley and Kerry followed behind him after receiving a good luck hug from Cindy.

The grey Ford Escort was cold and smelt unused after not being driven since the day they moved into the house. Hadley took shotgun while Kerry plugged the seat belt in on one of the back seats. The walk would take no longer twenty minutes. But Hadley knew Jace wanted to go in the car in case something happened and the group needed a quick getaway. The drive went by in silence, parts were in complete darkness until they passed a residential part. Hadley sat staring at her lap too afraid to look out the car window.

As they drove into the centre of the village, Hadley could feel her heart beating against her chest. Jace took her hand and gave it a reassuring squeeze. To their surprise there were more people out in the town than usual given the time of night.

"This is not a good sign." Kerry said as she stared out the window already undoing her seat belt. "Just park here." She told Jace desperate to get out the car.

Jace pulled the car up to the kerb, and they all exited the vehicle in synch. Kerry took the lead and began to pick up speed as she headed towards her shop. Hadley made sure her zip was still pulled up to the top as she tried to keep up. She took in the surrounding environment. The areas which were consumed with darkness were now filled with light from the lampposts. The fog no longer covered the road and the stars shined on their black background. Jace caught up with her after struggling to lock the car and wrapped his arm round her waist to keep her moving forward. Kerry had already turned the corner, but Hadley could already see the blue flashing lights coming from their destination. She looked up at Jace before hanging her head low in defeat.

As Hadley and Jace walked onto the street, Kerry ran up to them tears falling from her eyes.

"We were too late."

She cried as Hadley looked round her to see police taping off the area, a body covered with a sheet lying on the floor. Hadley was unable to say anything except walk past Kerry towards the crime scene. The display window had been smashed from the inside. Causing a crunch sound every time someone entered the taped off area. Hadley closed her eyes as tears began to fall when she heard a scream only a mother could make when something terrible happens to their child.

She felt Jace pull her back as a woman came running through the tape and falling onto her knees. Before anyone could stop her, she pulled the sheet back and let out a wail which made everyone present at the scene to stop. All eyes were on the boy and his mother as she cradled him in her arms. Hadley noticed no one stopped her touching the crime scene. No one had the nerve to tell her to stop and move away from her deceased son.

Time stood still until the coroner arrived and whispered something to the mother. His words got her to stand up and allow her to be walked to a car. As soon as the car door shut action on the scene proceeded. The coroner began the pathological testing before arranging for the body to be removed from the scene. More people began moving around and Hadley noticed the older policeman who came to her house the morning Sarahs body was found.

"Miss Knight?" the officer asked Kerry as Hadley made her way over to her.

"Yes?" Kerry replied.

"Miss knight this is your shop isn't it?" He asked, watching as Kerry nodded her head.

"Where have you been tonight?"

"I was at the Fernsbys all-night sir."

"You two, the officer said wagging his finger towards Hadley and Jace, "You can testify this can you?"

Jace and Hadley both confirmed Kerry had been at theirs all night.

"Bit of a coincidence the first body was discovered outside your home and now this one outside Miss Knights shop."

Hadley began to feel uncomfortable, she knew he did not believe their first story of innocence, and he was not believing them again.

"Officer are you implying we have something to do with this?" Kerry deemed. Her posture becoming more defensive with every stare the officer gave to the group.

"This is my shop." She argued "This is my shop and a child was killed in front of it. Of course, I am going to be asking questions."

The officer clicked his pen against his notepad. "Just a little suspicious don't you think? We will need to take statements from all three of you. So do not wander off far."

They watched as the officer walked away without looking back to go speak to someone else.

Hadley found an officer which was willing to speak to them when they told her Kerry was the shop owner. The officer told them they had no idea who could be responsible, but the case will be linked in with the murder of Sarah. All turned their heads when they heard a whistle. The first officer who had spoken with them was whistling for them to come over to where he stood.

"We are not dogs." Jace whispered angrily.

"Right, I will need you all to make your way to the police station where I can then take your statements." He barked at them.

"We will make our own way there. We aren't criminals, so we won't be getting in your police car like we are." Jace remarked.

"Suit yourself." The officer sneered while slamming the back of the car door shut.

"But if you don't get there I will have to hold all three of you in custody." He said, a smile appearing on his face. Without saying a word the three turned away and began walking to where they had parked.

"I'll catch up. I want to know what is happening with my shop." Kerry shouted. As she ran towards the woman officer they had previously been speaking to.

Hadley pulled down the zip of her coat only to pull it back up again. She presumed it was her way of making sure the zip was right at the top.

"We are the prime suspects again." Hadley whispered to Jace as they walked past the new group of spectators who had arrived at the scene.

"But we know we haven't done anything." Jace whispered back. "All they are going to be doing is asking us questions. Instead of saying we helped you dream hop, we will just tell them we were watching telly, studying, anything except the truth."

Hadley knew Jace would be calm through this. Dealing with the police had never been an issue for him. Throughout their career they had dealt with police numerous times and Jace had always remained calm, chatty and positive.

"We were watching telly all night right?" Kerry questioned as she caught up to Hadley and Jace.

"Yeah that's what Jace recommended." Hadley answered as she opened the car door.

"What's happening with the shop?" Jace asked as he inserted the key and the engine came alive.

"They are going to get someone to board up the window, but I am not allowed to enter the shop without an official with me while the investigation is on going." Kerry replied. "Which means I am not allowed to enter my home." Her tone becoming filled with annoyance. "Where am I going to live and what am I going to do with my cat?"

"Chewy is only a puppy, bring the cat with you to ours. I would feel more safe knowing you were staying with us." Hadley said.

"Really are you sure?" Kerry questioned. "Jace are you okay with that?"

"Ye fine, you have been a brilliant asset to our investigation. I mean the more of us there, the safer Cindy and Marty will feel." Jace said as he drove round a corner and parked outside the police station. "Remember we were watching telly." He reminded them before they all left the car.

The three left the station at midnight with the older police officer watching them as they walked back to their car.

"He still thinks we are involved in this somehow." Hadley said as she stared out the car window.

"At least he is allowing me to enter my home, so I can collect my things." Kerry said as the car drove away from the station.

When they arrived back at the shop an officer was already waiting outside to take Kerry in and collect her belongings. Hadley and Jace waited behind the crime tape, watching as the last of the crowd left to go back home.

"Hadley?" A woman's voice called to her from up the street. Hadley and Jace turned round to see Evelyn walking towards them.

"I can't believe this has happened. Father Anderson has been informed and will be here tomorrow." She told them.

"Why are you here?" Hadley asked as she folded her arms across her chest.

"I heard another child was murdered, Father Anderson sent me to come and see what was going on." Evelyn replied.

"How considerate of the Father." Jace snarled.

Evelyn's face turned into confusion as she looked at the couple. Kerry could be heard inside her shop indicating she was ready to leave.

"Instead of you all coming here tomorrow, you and the others need to come to my house in the daytime. There are things we need to discuss." Hadley said not wanting to discuss anything in earshot of the police.

"Lets go." Kerry said ignoring Evelyn as she approached the others.

"Hadley?" Evelyn protested not wanting them to leave. Hadley, Jace and Kerry began walking towards to the car.

"Tomorrow Evelyn." Hadley voiced without looking behind her.

CHAPTER FIFTEEN

With only a few hours of sleep between them all, all adults were in the kitchen discussing over coffee what had taken place the following night.

"Do you really think they have no idea that they are the ones doing the sacrifices?" Cindy asked.

"If they do, Evelyn was playing oblivious to it." Jace remarked.

"Maybe if the Orera is controlling them she is also blocking out their memories?" Cindy asked again.

"That is probably true. But there is no excuse, they are still slaying innocent children." Hadley mumbled.

"Well she only has one more sacrifice to go," Kerry put forward.

"Less than a week from what we read." Hadley poured herself another cup of coffee after realising her eyes were becoming heavier.

"I think the last victim will be picked at the Halloween fare." She said.

"The perfect location to pick a child of your choice." Kerry agreed.

Hadley no longer able to handle the chill which kept running down her spine, got up to sit on the floor with Chewy. Hoping giving the puppy some comfort would bring her some.

"Jace why don't you go get something for breakfast before Marty wakes up?" Hadley suggested. Jace agreed and with a number of suggestions thrown at him, he kissed Hadley and left to go pick something up.

"I am so glad Chewy is okay with your cat Kez." Hadley said as the puppy laid his head onto her legs.

"So am I. Nugget usually spends all his time sleeping, so we probably won't see him much." Kerry told them.

"The names you two pick for your pets is comical." Cindy laughed.

"Excuse me, Marty picked my baby's name, so blame him for that!" Hadley protested while joining in with the laughter. They waited for Jace to return with the same strange atmosphere. The discussion would turn serious before turning light-hearted, Hadley guessed it was so they could make it through the events happening around them.

"I don't think Jace will be much longer. I will go see if Marty is ready to get up." Cindy announced as she excused herself from the table.

"Come on boy, lets go wake up Marty." She said in a baby voice to the puppy. Chewy lifted his head and his tail began wagging to Marty's name; he quickly got up and followed Cindy up the stairs.

Hadley got onto her knees and stretched, opening her chest before standing up and rolling her neck to the left and then to the right, feeling relief in her muscles.

"Do you think the gods and goddess are testing us?" Kerry asked as she watched Hadley make unusual shapes with her body. Hadley stopped and looked at Kerry surprised at her questions.

"What do you mean?" Hadley asked interested in Kerrys train of thoughts.

"I don't actually know. I am scared about what we are doing, I have never dealt with something like this."

Hadley could see the look of terror on Kerrys face and went to sit next to her.

"I think that's why you are questioning it. But once it is over, maybe you will find the answer, if not maybe its just something that you were meant to come across. All I Know is when we get to Woden and Freya, we better be praised." Hadley said with a smile. Kerry still looked uneasy but agreed.

"Morning Hadley. Morning Kerry." Marty happily said as he strode into the kitchen in his striped pyjamas.

"Where is Jace?" He asked as he sat down on one of the kitchen chairs.

"He has gone to get a nice breakfast for us all." Hadley replied as she smiled at Martys messy bed hair. Martys face showed excitement as Cindy brought him over a glass of apple juice.

"Mommy can we get my Halloween costume today?" Marty asked. Hadley knew Marty didn't know the truth, she knew Cindy would never tell him what was going on. They had all done a good job hiding the truth and keeping him safe from what the church crusade had planned for him. But Hadley knew he was excited about Halloween. This would be his first time going to the towns Halloween fair, the first time he would experience getting to pick a costume and go trick or treating in a town that went all out for the holiday. Cindy looked at Hadley wondering what to say. Hadley shrugged her shoulders unsure of what she could tell her son.

"We have some people coming round soon. But if we cannot go today we can all go tomorrow." Cindy suggested as she kissed Marty on the top of his head. Happy with the answer Marty leaned on the table with his forearms.

"Did you catch the demon?" He asked so matter-of-factly. Kerry suppressed a laugh from the tone in his voice before realising his innocence to the question.

"No Marty, we haven't caught the demon yet. But we will don't you worry about that."

"Maybe it's because Halloween is coming up that the demon is here." Marty voiced his thoughts.

"Maybe" Hadley agreed.

"The demon in the picture book looks like what my friends said she looks like."

All three women stared at Marty who was messing with his teddies bow tie.

"Marty, you looked at the book with the demon in?" Cindy asked shocked.

"Yes."

"When?" Cindy asked again.

"Yesterday when I was playing with Chewy. He ran into the study, so I followed him and saw the book. I'm sorry mommy I didn't know I wasn't suppose to." Marty said after looking at his mothers face.

"It's okay, just next time try and divert your eyes from anything like that." Cindy reassured her son.

Hadley pulled an uncomfortable expression before mouthing sorry to Cindy. Cindy smiled mouthed back it is okay.

When Jace arrived back, he had brought just as much food as he had the last time.

"Not just pastries this time." Jace boomed, smiling as he began emptying the bags. "I also got bacon sandwiches, sausage sandwiches and scrambled egg on the side."

"Wow!" Marty squealed as he took a bacon sandwich from the pile. Hadley brought plates and glasses to the table and the apple and orange juice out of the fridge. When everyone's plates and glasses were full, they all ate breakfast as a family.

"Can I give Chewy a sausage?" Marty asked after seeing Chewy staring up at the table.

"Just one, and then we will take him outside for a bit." Hadley said. She watched as Marty tried to get Chewy to sit with the sausage in his hand. Martys voice began to go higher as the puppy ignored his commands. Giving up he threw the sausage and went to get his shoes and coat on. Hadley waited by the back door until a happy wrapped up Marty joined her.

"Come on chewy." Marty called as Hadley held open the door for them to go into the garden.

"What time do you think they will get here?" Jace asked Kerry and Cindy.

"I have no idea, I have been trying to think of how Hadley can even start this conversation with them." Kerry replied. "And that's not even thinking about the aftermath.

How are we going to stop them from committing the last sacrifice? Do we have to physically tie them up, how are we going to stop this?" Kerry wondered.

"She is right Jace. How do we stop this? This has been going on for centuries, I think we are in way over our heads." Cindy added as she began to help Kerry clean up the plates and left over food. Jace slid his chair back from the table and picked up a couple of the glasses.

"I know." He sighed. "Hadley is not sleeping well, I don't think she slept at all last night." He told them as he placed the glasses next to the sink.

"You all anxious as well?" Hadley said as she reentered the house.

"You heard our conversation?" Jace asked as he turned towards her. Hadley held open the door as Marty and Chewy walked in and sighed as she shut the door.

"Only the last bit." She admitted. She walked to Jace and let his warmth warm her cold body from his embrace.

"Are we all going to speak to them?" Cindy asked as she picked up Marty and kissed him on the tip of his nose.

"Speak to who?" Marty giggled as he leant back playfully to avoid another kiss from his mother.

"Mommy and the others have some important things to discuss with some people. When they come you are in charge of looking after Chewy and Nugget if that is okay with you?" Cindy asked Marty while pretending to take offence to his resilience to her kisses. Marty nodded his head showing he was happy to be put in charge of the animals.

"Thank you. Now lets go get you out of your pyjamas." Cindy told him and took him upstairs.

By noon all four were in the study anxiously waiting for the visitors to arrive.

"They are taking their time aren't they not?" Jace expressed as he stood by the window. Hadley was not shocked, those high in the church were extremely egoistic. The smell of sandalwood filled the downstairs and Hadley took in two deep breaths to let the scent calm her.

"They're here." Jace announced.

Everyone looked at each other as the atmosphere turned darker.

"I'll get the door." Kerry said as she quickly stood up and disappeared into the hallway. Jace joined the circle which they had made round the table with extra chairs from the kitchen.

"They are in here." Kerry announced to the group of visitors who had just entered the house. She strode in confidently behind them and stood by the window, her expression serious.

Hadley watched as Evelyn made her self comfortable on one of the wooden chairs and noticed Father Anderson look at the bookshelves as he passed.

"Interesting collection you have here Hadley." He muttered when he finally made his way to the group. Hadley lifted her eyebrows and curled her lips not willing to make small talk with the man she saw murder a child.

"Evelyn said you wanted us to come round last night." Father Anderson stated "Well, here we are."

Hadley was unsure whether he was being sarcastic or just his usual arrogant self. But to keep her composure, she ignored everything.

"Yes" Hadley begun, "I did invite you all here, please help yourself to tea." Hadley said as she gestured to the coffee table. A fresh tea pot with tea cups and saucers had been placed on a tray before the guests had arrived.

"Thank you, Hadley." Evelyn said as she moved to pour herself a cup of tea.

"Do not touch that!" Father Anderson roared.

Evelyn turned to the father with a confused look and Hadley and the others were all taken aback by the abrupt outburst.

"Why can I not pour myself tea Father?" Evelyn asked as she turned back to face Hadley.

"You know why." He replied with a stern commanding growl. Hadley lifted a suspicious eyebrow before sighing.

"Oh you fool Father." She said laughing. "You think we have done something to the tea, the biscuits as well I suppose?" Hadley tilted the plate of biscuits to show they were there. "We are not the medieval witches you are taught to fear. You do not need to fear the tea we have prepared, or the biscuits we brought from the shop."

Hadley said as she rolled her eyes and poured herself a cup of tea. "See. No evil magic tea." She took a gulp from the cup. "Now let's continue shall we? I called you here because we have some horrific leads into who is committing the sacrifices for the Orera." Hadley knew she had all their attention now and could see Father Anderson beginning to twitch.

"That is great news." Evelyn responded "How did you come about these leads? Have you gone to the police?" She asked.

"We have not gone to the police, yet." Hadley explained. She stopped talking and looked at the people who raised her. "Last night, Kerry and me did a spell which allowed me to dream hop into one of your dreams. There I followed one of you from the Inn to Kerrys shop." Hadley made eye contact with all of them. "That is when I saw one of you sacrifice the child." Hadley watched as their expressions turned grave with disbelief and shock.

"So." Jace scowled, "You are not just an accomplice to these acts."

"Preposterous!" Benjamin growled standing up with his fists clenched. Jace followed Benjamins movements and stood up too, his body trembling with anger.

"Jace." Hadley warned as she placed her hand on his arm. "Doctor Richardson, Benjamin. I suggest you sit down. You are in my house and there will be no fighting here."

Jace sat back down, his eyes never leaving the doctor who continued to stand.

"Ben sit down." Evelyn demanded dryly. Doctor Richardson slowly sat back down with a huff. Kerry continued to stand by the window her arms folded across her chest, not wanting to interact with the guests.

"How do we know you are speaking the truth?" One of the women asked

"Do you have any proof?" She let out a small laugh, but her eyes stayed somber. "No proof. Yet you accuse us, the ones who have protected this village for years with no proof of the crime only this hocus pocus. I must say I am disappointed."

Hadley saw Kerry flinch from the corner of her eye and felt Jace tense up with the sarcastic tone of her voice.

"I'm sorry, I don't think we have been properly introduced to you and.." Hadley nodded her head to the other woman whose face looked bored and unbothered.

"Of course you would not remember us Hadley, but we remember you. We asked for you not to attend our Sunday school sessions given your true faith." The unbothered woman muttered.

"We told Evelyn we do not have devil worshippers in our class. But if you truly don't remember who we are it's Annie and Jane Stuart." Annie remarked.

Hadley shrugged her shoulders

"Not that it matters anymore. I called you here to tell you what I saw. One of you are responsible for Sarahs death and the young boys last night."

"So whether you want to believe us or not, you will be responsible for the final death." Kerry snarled finishing Hadley's sentence.

Hadley nodded in agreement as she watched all their expressions and body language.

"Even if you don't believe us, you vile people are still guilty of murder. Letting all them families move into the Inn, so their children could be victims. You and your ancestors are all guilty sinners. No better than the demon you feed." Cindy vociferated.

Hadley's eyes widened, as she stared at Cindy in admiration. Jace and Kerry broke their stern look to smile at her words.

"How dare you use such blasphemy!" Father Anderson began to shout as he quickly left his seat and walked over to Cindy lifting his hand. Understanding where the situation was turning, Jace stood and grabbed Father Andersons forearm before he could bring it down onto Cindy.

"Father!" Evelyn screamed, shocked by his actions.

"You never hit a woman, and you especially never hit someone in my house." Jace tightened his grip "Do you understand me?"

Cindy who had cowered deeper into the chair had regained her composure and stared directly at the Father.

"I think it is best you sit down don't you?" Jace said brusquely.

"Guilt can do crazy things to a man." Kerry sneered as she watched him sit down with a grunt.

"There has already been enough violence Father, we do not need anymore." Hadley calmly said. "Now are you going to take what we say as truth or are you going to continue accusing us of lying? Because come the thirtieth one of you will spill blood for the Orera again and then what? We watch another family be tormented until it's time for her feeding again?" Hadley attested. "We will put an end to this, and then you will all pay for the crimes you and your families have committed for centuries."

"Hadley you don't understand, this had to be done for the greater good." Evelyn pleaded tears forming in her eyes.

"What you have done is barbaric. You helped a demon by feeding it life, there is no good in that." Hadley argued. Hadley shook her head as she stared at the people in front of her. She wondered how they were unable to understand their own logic or reasoning to the crimes they had committed.

"What is the plan for the day of the fair?" Cindy asked as she turned her head to look at Hadley. Hadley looked at Kerry and nodded in agreement.

"On the day of the halloween fair, you will all be here." Kerry announced, her voice stern.

"What?" Benjamin barked, but Kerry put her hand up in protest and ignored him.

"Yes, you will be here. This house is protected under our magic. That should stop the Orera being able to control you. We, of course will take more precautions and we will perform binding spells and put all of you into a slight daze." Hadley could see all their faces twitch while listening to Kerry.

"Any objection, and we will use force." Hadley shrugged when no one spoke once Kerry had finished.

"You are threatening us with magic?" Annie argued.

"We would rather not threaten you. But if you comply with what we are asking of you, then you may take it as a threat." Jace calmly said. "One more thing. When we are finished here, you will escort Cindy and me to the villages private records."

"We will do no such thing!" Father Anderson spat.

"There is no argument in this. We told you we will end this. You will pay for your crimes and the records are what will make sure it happens." Jace told him.

Father Anderson stared, his lips formed a straight line as his breathing turned into a continuous grunt.

"You will not be able to beat this demon." Benjamin commented. "Do you think we or our ancestors wanted to do this?" Everyone turned to Benjamin who had kept quiet since his last protest.

"Even if you didn't. You still need to be held responsible for what you have done. You have blood on your hands and that can not just be washed off." Hadley said.

"How pathetic. Trying to be the victim of all of this when you have sent innocent children to the slaughter house." Kerry chimed in.

"Face it your time is up." Cindy smiled as she stood up. "Jace are you ready to be escorted? Because I know I am."

Jace breathed in tightly as he stood up not wanting to show he was still in pain. The others followed and began walking out the study with their hands hanging to the floor.

CHAPTER SIXTEEN

Marty joined Hadley and Kerry in the kitchen after hearing the front door shut and people shouting goodbye. Hadley took Chewy outside while Kerry got Marty a can of coke and slid it to him over the table.

"Is mommy coming back soon?" He asked Kerry who was opening her drink.

"Yes and don't worry she is with Jace, so she will be okay." Kerry reassured him. "Do you have any idea what you want for dinner tonight?" She asked, wanting to keep the conversation light hearted.

Marty shrugged with a smile and continued sipping on his drink. "How's Nugget?" She asked as the cat ran back into his bedroom. She tried again only for him to nod his head. "Marty, what's wrong?" Kerry saw a look cross his face as his mouth dropped into a frown.

"I keep hearing everyone talking and I heard my name but no one will let me listen. But I have listened." He mumbled as he tipped the coke can on the table and took a sip.

"We just want to protect you, you understand that right? And knowing everything is not always the best thing."

"But how am I meant to be a demon killer like you Hadley and Jace if I'm not allowed to help?"

His sentence took Kerry by surprise, and she let out a little laugh

"You want to be a demon killer do you?" Marty nodded with a sheepish smile "Well." Kerry said, "That requires you to be at least level 18. What level are you now?" Kerry noticed him become interested in the conversation and raised her eyebrows in amusement.

"Level? I am a level now?" He asked.

"Yes. So how old are you?"

"Five." He responded as he raised his hand to show four fingers and a thumb .

"Wow, so you are level 5 now. But you will be level eighteen one day lil man." Kerry sipped her drink as she saw Marty trying to work out how long that one day would be.

Marty walked out the kitchen into the living room with Chewy to go watch cartoons after Hadley made him some popcorn and told him he could watch what ever he wanted.

"How do you think it went?" Kerry asked Hadley as she joined her in the study. The murmur of the telly could be heard through the walls as Hadley closed her eyes and sighed.

"Better than expected. But not entirely the best." Hadley replied wiping her hand down her face. "When Jace and Cindy return we have the end to those involved. But we still need to figure out how to defeat the one that will get us to that end." Hadley saw Kerry put her head in her hands and groan. "There has to be a way. There is always a way to kill a demon." Hadley announced with frustration. Kerry looked up and nodded unable to hide the doubt on her face. "Where is my book?" Kerry said standing up. Hadley pointed to the bookshelf and watched Kerry quickly make her way to the shelf.

"Maybe we missed something." Kerry began flipping through the pages, her eyes skimming every page for something that could help them.

"The Orera has to have a weakness. Everything has a weakness. Vampires weakness is their heart, a banshee's weakness is gold, a wendigo's weakness is fire. They all have weaknesses, we just need to find her weakness." Hadley could see the determination in Kerrys eyes as she spoke.

"The familiar?" Hadley asked "The Orera is medieval, they depend on their familiar. The familiar is the weakness." Kerry stopped flipping the pages and looked up to Hadley.

"You could be right" she agreed "look."

Hadley looked at the page Kerry had stopped on, her eyebrow raised.

The page showed a drawing of a mummified animal lying inside a wooden coffin. Hadley and Kerry looked at each other.

"From what I can remember, Margaret or her sister had a cat." Hadley said as the front door unlocked. The two women heard a strong Scottish accent shout 'honey we're home!' and both walked to the hallway. Marty came running out of the lounge, puppy right beside him, both excited to see Cindy and Jace arrive back. Hadley walked up to Jace to give him a kiss before asking if everything went okay. Jace lifted a bag in the air, "Aye, we have it all." He beamed.

"Yeah, but it took us a while. They did not want to give it over to us." Cindy scoffed as she remembered the last couple of hours.

"At least we have it." Hadley said as she hugged Jace round the waist. He kissed the top of her head as he whispered *'we are going to do this'* only for Hadley to hear. Hadley looked up at Jace and gave a slight nod.

"Kerry and I found some things, we think we know the Oreras weakness." She told Jace "But we still need to make a plan."

Jace nodded and walked towards the study with the bag. "We need to keep these in a safe place. A place they will never find it."

Cindy followed Marty into the living room and Hadley could hear Marty explaining the program he was watching. Unable to know where to put the bag, Jace placed it on the couch and walked over to the table where the book was still open.

"The Witches Helpful Demonic Companions" Jace read out loud. "The famulus, latin for servant, feeds on their witches blood." Jace stopped reading and looked at Hadley and Kerry who had joined him at the table.

"Feeds on their witches blood, but the Orera took over a dying body. Therefore, she has no blood for it to feed upon." He said. "So the question is what is she feeding it? Familiars are not going to be able to go a year without a source of food. But she has no blood to give it and it still needs a source of food."

"Hadley?" Jace interrupted her train of thought. "You already said that."

"It needs a source of food." Kerry said through a laugh. "But you are right, I remember my mother telling me familiars need to be fed regularly for them to be able to be loyal to their master and follow their commands. Remember Cindy said she felt like an animal was on her when she went back to the Inn with Jace?"

Hadley bit her bottom lip, deep in thought as she listened to the others.

"Maybe it feeds her familiar just pure dark energy." Hadley proposed. Jace and Kerry stopped speaking between them and took a moment to think through Hadley's thought.

"That place sure is filled with dark energy. I honestly do not understand how people sit in there to drink all day."

All three turned their heads to see Cindy standing arms crossed at the door of the study.

"Cind's come in, we didn't want to interrupt mother son time." Hadley told her as she walked over and embraced her in a hug.

"We do love Care Bears. Well, I do." Cindy laughed as she hugged Hadley back. "He's fallen asleep so thought I would come see what you guys have discovered or undiscovered."

Hadley went over everything they had discussed as they walked over to the table, and she pointed to the book.

"Now that is something you don't want to find in your house." Cindy said as her face scrunched up.

"Find in your house?" Kerry repeated "The familiars coffin has to be hidden somewhere in the Inn." She added.

"One thing ladies, how are we going to find this coffin when the last time we went back to the Inn, I was thrown across the room and Cindy was attacked by the familiar?" Jace voiced.

Hadley fell onto the nearest chair with a groan. "He's right. How do we get in there without the Orera noticing us and not attacking us?" Hadley exhaustedly ran her fingers through her hair.

The rest of the afternoon and night was spent trying to convince Marty everything was under control. They all sat round the table for a family dinner before watching telly and playing board games before retiring to bed. Hadley snuggled up to Jace when they both finally got under the comfort of the duvet.

"I feel like we get somewhere and then hit a wall every time with this case." Hadley groaned to Jace as Chewy joined them on the bed.

"It is very frustrating." Jace agreed. "But we know its weakness now."

Hadley lifted her head from his chest and raised an eyebrow.

"Yes but how to use that weakness against it? Kerry said she would try and think of something, but I can tell she is exhausted as well."

"I am amazed you are both able to function, you both need rest with the amount of energy and magic you are having to use." Jace kissed her on the top of the head as she lay her head back onto his chest.

"Yeah I am tired, but there is so much to think about and process, my brain just cannot shut off." Hadley began stroking Chewy who was now lying in the small gap he had made between them.

"Sweetheart, I was thinking.." Jace began. Hadley mumbled a yeah as she continued to calm her emotions down by stroking the puppy's fur. "I think once the familiar is found we need to burn it." Hadley's body became stiff as she listened to her husbands words.

"Why?" She asked, wondering where he was going with his thoughts.

"If the Orera's strength and her weakness is its familiar, then we need to eradicate both."

"Why didn't we think of that?" Kerry said as she poured herself another mug of coffee the following morning.

"Jace has filled you in then?" Hadley asked as she entered the kitchen. Kerry turned round and nodded her head while pointing to her mug. "Yes please" Hadley answered. "Jace why did you let me sleep in?" She joined Jace and Cindy at the kitchen table, wiping away any sleep which remained in her eyes.

"Because you needed to rest and that is why you missed how we banish the demon." Jace took Hadley's hand in his and gave it a gentle squeeze. "I love you." He said with a sweet smile. Hadley nodded her head in agreement of his statement and mouthed 'I love you too' back to him.

"We are one step closer to ending this aren't we? Now we think we know how to defeat the Orera." Cindy said breaking the silence. Hadley took a sip of her coffee and looked at Cindy with a smile.

"I think so. We have a mixture of ideas, we just need to get them all into a plan." Hadley saw Kerrys face go solemn as she was skimming through the local newspaper. Jace and Cindy fixated onto Kerry, who sensed all eyes were on her and quickly turned the page.

"Just about the murders and a discussion whether the Halloween fair should continue."

"I am not surprised people are wondering whether they should allow their children to go to a fair; when a serial killer may be among them."

Hadley shook her head. "They would never cancel it. I know these people and this town. They will want everything to be as normal as possible." Hadley finished her coffee and got up for more. When she returned her face had become serious. "We have five days until the thirtieth. We have enough time to plan and prepare for what we need to do." Hadley saw all three nod their head in agreement.

"We need to decide where the familiars body may be buried." Kerry said. "It has to be in the actual Inn, I don't believe it will be in the grounds."

"Nor do I." Hadley agreed. "She would want to keep it close by and if she is unable to leave the Inn, then her familiar wouldn't be able to either." All four continued to throw out ideas.

"We can put the toilets out of the equation. They would have seen a coffin when they laid the pipes." Jace pointed out.

"Yeah, I found a renovation booklet when I had not long moved in." Cindy remembered. "The water mains were redone about a year or so ago. I think they would have noted that there was a coffin found."

Still unsure and without any leads or answers the group decided to take a break and freshen up for the day ahead.

"Marty?" Cindy called out to him as she walked up the stairs. "Come get dressed, you can continue to watch your cartoons once you have washed." Marty could be heard moaning and Hadley laughed as she left the kitchen and put her head round the living room door. Marty was sprawled out on the sofa in his racing car pyjamas, both animals lying either side.

"Come on you little terror. Your mother wants you to get washed up." She looked at the television and saw he was watching an episode of the Smurfs while completely ignoring her.

"Hey come on Mr." She asked again with no response. "Oh no, Marty must have become deaf because he can not seem to hear a word I am saying to him." She saw Martys eyes fall onto her, a small smirk forming in the corners of his mouth.

"Well" She said as she walked towards the telly. "If he cannot hear me, I guess he doesn't want to do something fun today." Marty stayed in his position on the couch, but Hadley knew his attention had now switched to her. "Oh well, looks like I will have to go on my own." She shrugged leaving the living room and headed to the staircase.

"What fun thing?" Marty said smiling as he rushed past her and stopped two steps ahead.

"Go and get washed up with your mommy and then I will tell you." Hadley laughed as she poked him playfully in the stomach. Marty nodded his head and raced up the stairs to join his mother.

Smiling, Hadley walked into her bedroom and waited for the shower to become free.

Jace came back into the master bedroom, a towel wrapped around his waist. Hadley noticed his bruised ribs had turned to a more sickening yellow than the black and purple it had been for over a week. Jace caught Hadley staring and smiled when her mouth began to fall at the corners.

"It's ok my darlin', I'm feeling better all of a sudden and it's not as swollen. Still sore but bearable. It just doesn't look nice." Hadley rose from the bed and gently put her arms around his waist. She leaned back so she could look at his face.

"I don't know what I would do without you." She placed a hand on his cheek and placed a soft kiss on his lips.

"I love you." He said as he looked into her eyes. Hadley managed to smile as a feeling of dread rushed through her body.

"I love you too." She said back as she fell back into his embrace. Hadley saw the door of the bedroom slowly open and a wet nose was soon felt on her leg.

"Remember you can always speak to me about how you are feeling." Jace reminded her. Hadley let one arm drop from Jace's waist to pet Chewy on the head.

"I know." She sighed "I know." Hadley felt Jace kiss her on the top of her head and she finally let her other arm fall from his waist.

"Suppose I should go shower." Jace nodded and sat on the bed as Hadley walked to the door to leave the room. Before she left she looked back and saw Jace take Chewy's face into his hands and kiss him on the nose.

"Hadley you aren't even ready." Marty frowned as he met her on the landing.

"Give me ten minutes and I will be." Hadley promised as she quickly walked into the bathroom and locked the door. The bathroom was still steamy and warm from the pervious user. The room smelt strongly of Finesse shampoo and conditioner. Once out the shower Hadley wrapped herself up in a bath towel and walked over to the mirror to begin detangling her freshly washed hair. She was unable to deny stress was not doing her any harm. Her reflection showed her teenage acne redeveloping around her chin. The dark circles under her eyes were proving to become much darker and more permanent. As she bit down on her lip again, her tongue could feel the cracks and dryness. Not wanting to stare at herself for much longer, Hadley quickly turned away from the mirror and dried her hair.

"You were longer than ten minutes." Marty announced as he sat on the floor arms crossed.

"I was ten minutes you little terror." Hadley was able to muster up a laugh and told him to go watch some more cartoons while she got dressed.

CHAPTER SEVENTEEN

Hadley made her way back down the stairs after dressing in a warm black long sleeved winter dress. Marty had taken her advice and was again watching cartoons on the television with everyone else.

"What is the fun thing we are doing Hadley?" Marty beamed upon seeing her enter the room. Hadley smiled and perched herself on the arm of the sofa next to Jace.

"Well, I don't know about the rest of you," she began "but Halloween is nearly here and I am certain Marty has not got a costume yet."

Hadley looked at Marty whose smile grew into a goofy grin.

"I didn't forget." He announced. Hadley could see three pairs of eyes staring at her in confusion, but she shook it off with a shake of her head.

"Well, what do you say we go get one today?"

Marty suddenly jumped off the sofa, scaring the animals with the sudden movement. Everyone watched Marty run out the living room to retrieve his shoes and coat, as a sense of unease filled the room.

"Are you sure this is a good idea?" Cindy asked. "We have two children already.." Cindy stopped speaking, so she could lower her voice to a whisper "killed."

Hadley felt herself wince as she heard the word killed, but composed herself quickly as Cindy finished the word.

"Look, you want to keep Marty away from all this. But how can we when we aren't being normal?" Hadley replied.

"Since Sarah was found outside we have done nothing but be surrounded by death, and we need something. I mean I know I need something to take my mind of it for a few hours." Hadley felt Jace wrap his arms around her as she buried her face into his chest and sighed. "Do you think it's a bad idea?" She asked Jace as she tilted her head back to look at his face.

"It will show the town we have nothing to hide." Jace said. "If we spend all our time locked up in the house, it looks as though we have something to hide. Plus I agree with Hadley, we all need some time out of the house." He placed a kiss on her forehead and gave her a tight squeeze. "Lets go and get things for halloween." He said enthusiastically.

Kerry stood and clasped her hands together. "You're right, we need a bit of normal. And I would like to check in and see about my shop, as well as pick up a few supplies." Hadley nodded as she pulled away from Jace "Thank you."

"Are we going then?" Marty squealed as he ran back into the living room.

"Mommy I want to be a vampire, no, a mummy. No, a werewolf!" He announced as he ran up to Cindy with a smile.

"You can be whatever you want to be baby boy." Cindy told him as she caught him mid-jump. "Now let us get our coats on, and we can walk down to the high street."

Jace locked the front door as everyone made their way onto the front porch.

"I'm so excited, can we get pumpkins as well? And stuff to make halloween cookies?"

Cindy smiled and nodded her head as she took Marty's hand and began walking the country lanes to the high street. Hadley felt her confidence dwindle as they got nearer to the centre of the village.

"Are you okay darlin?" Jace whispered suddenly sensing his wife begin to tense and slow her walking pace.

"Guess my nerves are beginning to get the better of me." Hadley sighed.

"Sweet, you're putting too much pressure on yourself. Just enjoy the moment and remember I am always here to help keep you grounded." Jace lifted their hands and placed a reassuring kiss on Hadley's.

"I love you." She told him.

"I love you too. Now lets catch up with the rest of them." Jace and Hadley began catching up with the others as they turned the corner onto the high street.

"Wow." Kerry expressed. "Everyone is acting so normal." Hadley looked around the high street and nodded in agreement.

"Maybe living in a town where people suddenly go missing or killed is nothing new." She shrugged as a shiver went down her spine.

Cindy looked at them both and sighed. "Be normal right." She said as she ruffled Marty's hair. "Come on let's go find you a costume." Hadley watched as Cindy took Marty further into the crowds towards the costume shop.

"Hadley, Jace, Kerry. What a lovely surprise to see you out today." A mans voice startled them as they began catching up with Cindy. Jace turned around and saw Officer Miller rearranging his police hat to a more professional manner.

"Officer Miller." Jace spat.

"Now now Mr Fernsby. No need to cause a scene." Officer Miller chuckled. Hadley saw Jace's hands ball up into fists and quickly placed her hand onto his forearm.

"Officer Miller, what a lovely coincidence it is that we should see you here." Hadley smiled as she stepped in front of Jace.

"Mrs Fernsby, it is surprising we are seeing you out here when there is no crime occurring." He waved his hand in the air to indicate the ever so normal scene around them.

"Yes well neither I nor anyone in our group are responsible for the murders that have recently occurred, which you very well know Officer Miller." Hadley said. Hadley felt Jace relax as he put his hand on the small of her back.

"Yes, well, just remember I will be keeping my eyes on all of you." The officer mumbled before grunting and walking away. Hadley saw Kerry huff as he turned to leave.

"Kill them with kindness Kez." She said as she wrapped her arm around Kerrys shoulders.

"Yes, well, I will leave that job to you. For now, I am going to go check on my shop. I have a new window to order." With that Kerry wandered off towards Spiritual

Awakenings. Hadley sighed and brushed her hand through her hair.

"Lets go find Cindy and Marty." Jace suggested as he put his arm around her waist.

A short walk down the high street they entered Weirdorama, the costume shop which was bustling with children trying to find their halloween outfits. Hadley felt a sense of nostalgia as she walked down the isles. The shop had been spilt into sections, scary costumes, funny costumes, child and adult costumes. The walls were painted a bright yellow which donned photos of children and adults. Each photo showed groups laughing and smiling in a different array of dress up. Hadley looked round for Cindy and Marty through the sea of excited children and exhausted looking parents. Hadley picked up a costume and showed it to Jace with a chuckle.

"I want to suck your blood." She said with her best Slavic accent. A group of children laughed as they walked past watching Jace do his best impression of being scared. Hadley placed the costume back on the rack and carried on walking to the back of the shop. Every horror film had a costume, The Exorcist, Halloween, Carrie and one that caught Hadley's attention. A spectacular collection of costumes from The Rocky Horror Picture Show.

"Hadley, Jace, over here" Marty shouted running up to them with a clown mask on.

"Wow don't you look scary." Hadley smiled when he finally reached them. Marty pulled the mask off, his face red and wet from sweat.

"Are you having fun?" She asked as she took the mask from him and placed it down on a shelf.

"What did you pick then Marty?" Jace asked as he smoothed down his sweaty hair.

"It's a secret, mommy is paying for it now." Marty pointed over to the cash register and Hadley saw Cindy smiling and chatting away to the shop attendant.

"Come on, we will wait for her near the front." Jace suggested as he picked Marty up and placed him on his shoulders. Hadley got Cindy's attention and pointed towards the door. With a nod Cindy turned back to the cashier and paid for Martys costume.

"Duck." Jace told Marty as they exited the shop and walked back onto the high street.

"All done" Cindy announced as she joined them. "Did you keep the secret Marty?" She asked as she held up a plastic bag. Hadley saw Marty nod as he put his second finger up to his mouth.

"We should probably go see how Kerry is getting on." Hadley suggested to the others. She led them to where the crime scene was, not so long ago. The glass which had scattered the floor and the crime tape which shut off the area had all gone, so the public could carry on with their day. Hadley noticed a few flowers and teddy of a green dinosaur had been placed by the lamppost just outside Kerrys window with a note which read *'forever in our hearts, our dearest son.'*

"Let's go in." She told them as she held open the door of the shop.

"Thank god you are here." Kerry expressed as they entered the shop.

"What's happened?" Jace asked as he lowered Marty from his shoulders but keeping him close as he scanned the shop.

"The man on the phone from the window company won't listen to me. I have been trying for…." Jace and Marty both jumped back as Kerry threw a phone book across the room.

"Kerry it's okay, let me sort it out." Jace said as he raised his hands in surrender. His expression softening as he approached the checkout desk. Hadley joined him and placed her hand on Kerrys.

"Kez, it's okay." She reassured her with a hand squeeze. "Let Jace sort this out, and we can sort out the other reason we needed to come here." Hadley saw Kerrys eyes begin to shine and become watery.

"It's okay." Hadley told her again. Kerry nodded her head and with a sigh as she wiped away the tears with her dress sleeve. Jace collected the phone book and brought it back to the counter.

"Right. Let's get this sorted for you."

Kerry swapped places with Jace and straightened her dress before walking to the sofa area and picking up her notebook.

"Is everything okay?" Cindy asked, concern coating her tone.

"Yeah it's all fine, and I am so sorry if I scared you then Marty." Kerry looked at Marty who was huddled next to his mother. Hadley joined them and saw Marty nod.

"He is okay, I think he is just tired." Cindy said as she wrapped her arm around her son.

Kerry began flipping through her notes as she explained her worries to the others. Hadley sat silent as she listened to Kerry and watched Cindy's reactions.

"Marty is still in danger isn't he?" Cindy said as her grip on her son became tighter. Hadley and Kerry made eye contact before both facing Cindy and nodding.

"We think so." Hadley said sombrely. "But we can attempt to do a spell which should protect him. We were going to do it before the fair, but we think we should do it now." Hadley said.

Hadley could see Cindy become uneasy with the thought of a spell being cast on her son.

"We don't need to do this. We have protected him this far without it." Hadley told her.

"I don't know if it is a good idea." Cindy confessed as she wiped a hand down her face, sweat forming on her forehead.

"Mommy, it's okay. I want Hadley and Kerry to do this." Marty said.

"Marty." Cindy shocked with her sons response.

"Mommy, I know what is happening. I have listened to your conversations and I have seen the pictures of the demons. I want to grow up and be like Hadley and Kerry and Jace. But I can't if something happens to me." Marty explained.

"You have seen the pictures?" Kerry asked shocked, though her expression showed she was impressed with the courage Marty was showing. Hadley opened her mouth to say something, but closed it when she realised she was speechless. Marty stood up and stomped his foot in annoyance to the silence his speech received.

"Marty?" Hadley said. "Are you sure you want us to do this spell on you?"

Marty looked at his mother before looking Hadley straight in the eye and nodded his head. Hadley looked over at Cindy.

"If he is okay with it, then I will allow it." Cindy said, pulling Marty into a hug. Hadley nodded and looked over to Kerry who had already stood up.

"We shall do it here in the back room." Kerry suggested. She led them past Jace and through the purple curtain into a corridor. Candles gave off dim light but it was just enough to see the way. Kerry gestured for everyone to enter through the next curtain, and they entered into a large room. Kerry gave Hadley a box of matches and instructed her where to light the first candle. She pointed to a tall white candle in the far right corner of the room. Hadley took a match out of the box as she walked over to the candle and struck the match with her right hand. Protecting the flame with her left, she felt the heat on her palm as the flame grew bigger. As Hadley found the wick, she took in a deep breath and blew the flame onto the candle wick. Hadley watched as each candle grew a blue flame before turning a bright yellow. Cindy gasped.

"Are you okay?" Kerry asked as she put her hand on Cindy's arm.

"That was cool." Marty said, his eyes wide in amazement as he saw a cauldron, big enough for a small animal to fit inside. Hadley smiled as she returned to the centre of the room.

"Hadley, please go and collect a black candle, some parchment paper and rosemary incense from the shop." Hadley nodded to Kerry and walked out the room. Cindy watched as Kerry walked over to a cupboard and took out a silver chalice encrusted with purple stones.

"What is that for?" Cindy asked as she watched Kerry pull out a black handled knife.

"It is called an athame." Kerry explained. "It is a ceremonial blade which we use in rituals such as this." She placed the athame down on a table and walked out of the room holding the chalice.

"I have everything." Hadley said as she reentered the room. "Where is Kerry?" She asked as she looked round the room.

"She took the cup out the room." Marty replied. Hadley nodded.

"She must have gone to fill it with water." She told him.

"Marty." Hadley crouched down, so she could be eye level with him and took hold of his hands. "I just want to be certain you are sure about this. Kerry and I will of course, be doing the spell, but it requires help from you."

Martys brows furrowed as he took in her words. "Help from me? How?"

"We will cast the circle and do the banishing spell for you. But if you want this to really work, when Kerry is saying the spell I want you to draw the banishing pentacle over this pentacle." She held out a wooden circle with a pentacle carved into it.

"Banishing pentacle?" Marty asked again as he scratched his head. Hadley showed him how the traditional pentacle is drawn; starting from the top point to the lower-left point and continued in one go. "Okay I can do that." Marty said and copied what Hadley had shown him. Hadley smiled before explaining how to draw the banishing pentacle.

"Okay so start at the lower-left point up to the top point and continue drawing it, in one go again." Marty watched as Hadley demonstrated how to do it correctly. With a nod, she handed the pentacle over to him and watched as he drew the banishing pentacle.

"Perfect Marty." She said as she gave him a hug of encouragement. "Kerry and me will be in the circle with you, so you have nothing to worry about. But when I tell you to draw the pentacle. I need you to dip your hand in the rosemary oil I brought in and draw it with that". When Hadley had finished, Kerry reentered the room with the chalice filled with water and smiled when she saw Hadley and Marty. Hadley saw Kerry whisper something to Cindy which made her leave the room with a hug and a smile.

"Shall we begin?" Kerry said.

Hadley took Martys hand and guided him into the centre of the room where Kerry was placing the black candle into the cauldron. Hadley walked over to the table to pour the oil into a small dish for Marty to use. Kerry joined her to help bring over the chalice, the oil, the athame, the incense and the pen and paper.

"You ready Marty?" Kerry asked as she and Hadley returned to the centre of the room. Marty nodded and placed the pentacle in front of him on the floor.

Marty watched Kerry walk clockwise round the circle, a sphere of energy formed around them all.

"I cast the sacred circle. I am between the worlds." She came to a stop next to Hadley who was facing north of the circle facing outwards ready to call the quarters. "I call the spirit of the North. Please join me and lend me the power of the earth."

Moving around the circle clockwise she continued, "I call the spirit of the East. Please join me and lend me the power of air. I call the spirit of the South. Please join me and lend me the power of water. I call the spirit of the West. Please join me and lend me the power of fire."

After the circle was cast and the quarters were called, Hadley and Kerry both sparked their matches in unison. Kerry walked over to the cauldron and placed the candle inside.

! Soon after, a strong scent of rosemary filled the room. "Goddess Hel, please join us as we seek to remove negativity from the young boys life and let him embark on a new path." Both women said. Kerry pointed the athame at the filled chalice as Hadley went and sat next to Marty. Hadley told Marty to watch the chalice as a white light flowed down and filled the cup. Marty gasped as Hadley took his hand and whispered everything is okay.

"I charge this water by your spirit to banish the negativity which is plaguing his soul. Let your light fill its place." Hadley patted Martys hand with her free hand and gently loosened her grip to pick up the black pen. Marty watched as Hadley pulled closer the parchment paper and began writing, 'Marty, curse, demon.'

Hadley looked up from her writing as the curtain blew inwards with a hiss. She noticed Kerry had turned in the direction, her arms held out in front of her.

"Hadley quickly" Kerry demanded as darkness began evolving around the outside of the circle.

"What's happening Hadley?" Marty cried as the sound of scratching floorboards echoed around the room.

"You are not welcome here." Kerry declared. "You may not enter the circle." Hadley ran over the cauldron and hovered the piece of paper over the flame. "No more will he be held back by this negativity." Hadley lowered the paper onto the flame and turned to nod at Marty.

"Now Marty!" She shouted over the growing screeches. As the paper burnt in the cauldron Marty dipped his finger in the oil and began drawing the banishing pentacle just as Hadley had shown him. Hadley saw his lips move but could not make out what he was saying. "Let light replace the darkness in his life." Kerry picked up the chalice and handed it to Marty to drink. Hadley walked over to Kerry.

"Thank you goddess Hel, for helping us rid his negativity. Thank you for letting us leave his negativity on the old road, and letting him pass onto the new road. Stay if you will, go if you must. Farewell and blessed be."

As quickly as the darkness entered the room, Hadley saw it leave with a final piercing scream. Hadley ran back over to Marty who had his hands over his ears and wrapped her arms around him.

"Kerry don't close the circle yet, we have to wait for the black candle to burn out." Hadley shouted as she tried to cover her ears. Kerry had crouched down and placed her head on her knees, fighting back the urge to scream. Hadley could feel Marty sink further into her chest as a tornado of shrieks and cold air skimmed on the edge of the circle.

"You can not harm him anymore." Hadley screamed "You are not welcome here, we banish you from this place. With the goddess and god on our side we demand you to leave." Hadley continued to scream until the room went silent and the cold air settled. Hadley felt Marty twitch between her arms and loosened her embrace, so he could look around the room.

"Kerry you okay?" Hadley croaked as her eyes adjusted to the calmness. She heard a thud as Kerry sank further onto the floor struggling to control her breathing.

"Kerry?" Hadley said softly as she checked Marty over. Hadley flinched as a hand touched her shoulder.

"It's me." Kerry reassured her. "I'm okay. Are you both okay?" After checking Marty over for a second time Hadley nodded her head.

"Let's close the circle and get out of here." Kerry suggested.

> "Thank you, spirit of the North for joining us and lending us the power of Earth
> Thank you, spirit of the East for joining us and lending us the power of Air
> Thank you, spirit of the West for joining us and lending us the power of water
> Thank you, spirit of the South for lending us the power of Fire"

CHAPTER EIGHTEEN

"How the hell did that thing get inside my shop?" Kerry spat as she chugged back a bottle of beer. Hadley wiped her eyes in frustration as they discussed what happened in the shop during the spell.

"My poor baby." Cindy whispered to herself as she sunk further into her chair.

"We are sorry Cinds. That was never meant to happen." Hadley said to Cindy as she took her hand and gave it a slight squeeze.

"It wasn't your fault. And no damage is done. He is safely in bed now." Cindy placed her free hand over Hadley's and squeezed it back. Kerry walked out the study and Hadley could hear the fridge open and bottles rattling against each other.

"Honestly neither of you heard, saw or felt the presence in the shop?" Hadley turned to Jace who was sitting on the couch. He leant forward and rubbed both his hands down his face.

"No we didn't know anything was going on." Jace told her and Cindy nodded in agreement.

"Here." Kerry said as she walked back into the study, carrying 4 opened cold beer bottles. "I think we could all use some more after today." She sighed as she sat back down and took a long sip of her drink.

"I had a protection spell on my shop." Kerry moaned as she placed her head in her hands "How could whatever that thing was get pass my spell?" She mumbled.

Hadley picked at the label, her teeth digging deeper into the inside of her lip.

"Maybe it's because the demon was able to enter the shop in the dream?" Jace suggested just at the very time he joined the women at the table.

"Yeah," Cindy added "Maybe because you entered the dream controlled by a demon, your powers no longer worked." Hadley and Kerry stared at Cindy in confusion, and she looked at Jace for support. Jace smiled and nodded his head in reassurance for her to carry on.

"What I mean is. When the demon smashed through your window, the salt protection, the protection spell was broken. If in the dream the window was smashed, and it was smashed in the present time. Then your protection in the present time is useless until you do it again." Cindy shrugged and took a sip of her beer.

Hadley had stopped stripping the label and sat with her eyebrows raised in surprise. She looked over to Kerry who had pushed out her bottom lip, looking deep in thought. Cindy smiled at their reaction and turned to Jace who gave her wink.

"What do you think?" Cindy asked.

"Makes sense." Kerry finally said.

"I agree." Hadley added before she looked at Kerry. "Tomorrow when the window is fitted, we will both go and redo the protection spell." Hadley watched as Kerry nodded and finished off her beer. "Right," Hadley said as she stood from the table. "I am going to let Chewy out before bed."

"And I am coming with you." Jace told her, concern filing his eyes. Hadley furrowed her brows but then nodded and took his hand when he reached her at the study door. Kerry sighed when the two left the study.

"Lets clean up before we go bed." Cindy finished her beer and began helping Kerry collect the empty beer bottles and plates from the table. With a clink, the beer bottles were placed onto the kitchen counter and Kerry quickly washed up the plates and put them on the rack.

"Thank you." Cindy said as she stood by the kitchen door. Kerry turned and saw Cindy smiling at her.

"What for?" she asked, confused of the soft tone.

"For helping Marty and me, I don't know what we have done to deserve friends like you, Hadley or Jace. I have always questioned what I believe in, but whoever brought you three to us, I am thankful to them and to you guys for staying and helping us." Cindy told her.

Kerry placed the tea towel down and put her arms around Cindy who instantly returned the gesture.

"You never have to thank us, we are here for you and for Marty, and we will never let anything harm either of you." Kerry reassured her. "Hadley and I are going to end this, and everyone who has been involved in the past are going to see justice."

"See justice and give the children the voice they deserve." Hadley interrupted as she and Jace walked through the kitchen back door. Hadley wiped Chewy down with a towel and kicked off her boots.

"Cindy are you okay? What's wrong?" she asked, worried when she saw Kerry and Cindy loosen their hug.

"I'm fine, I promise." Cindy told her and opened her arms to encourage Hadley to join in with the hug. Without hesitation Hadley walked over to the girls and placed her arms around both of them.

That night Hadley tossed and turned between the sheets, unable to fall into a light sleep. She felt her body not able to relax as she eventually laid on her back and stared at the ceiling. She focused on her breathing, she noticed her heart begin to beat hard against her chest. The soft sound of Jace sleeping next to her brought some comfort, but also a sting of jealousy stirred in the pit of her stomach. Hadley sighed and sat up to check the clock on her dresser. One toe touched the cold wooden floor as nine others followed before she pulled her other leg out of the warmth of the covers.

"Chewy" Hadley hissed after wiping her eyes and seeing her dog staring out the bedroom window. A cold wave rode over her body and she turned to look at Jace to see him twitch but quickly settle back into his sleep.

"Chewy come away from the window." She demanded in a hushed whisper, surprised he was ignoring her. Unsure whether he had just not heard her, she stood up and tiptoed across the bedroom to the window. As she got closer she noticed Chewy's fur was standing up, his body was rigid and his nose was pressed up to the window. Every breath he took caused a white puff of air to form onto the glass.

"Chewy." Hadley said as she saw Chewy take another breath on the window. She could hear a slight whine coming from him with every inhale he took. As she continued to watch him she could see clumps of hair falling off him and landing in piles on the floor. Unsure what to do Hadley looked back at Jace who was still in his deep sleep. Chewy's whining was becoming louder, his rigid body had moved into more of an attack stance.

"Chewy" Hadley said again as she took another step towards him.

Hadley heard a snarl form in Chewy's expression, his lips turned up revealing his sharp puppy teeth. Froth forming as saliva dripped from his mouth. His breathing became more heavy and deep. The snarls became more aggressive, until a growl left his mouth causing Hadley to jump back in fright. Hadley fell onto the floor, her heart racing as she scrambled to her feet and ran over to Chewy. Jace joined her at the window, confusion and horror radiating from his aura.

"What is going on?" Jace shouted as he tried to calm down the dog down, pulling him away from the window. Hadley caught her breath and shook her head, unable to get a sound to leave her body. Chewy's growls and snarls soon turned into hallow cries which filled the quietness of the house.

"Hadley" Jace called out as he began shushing and comforting their dog. Hadley had walked over to the window where Chewy had been just moments before and took in a deep gasp as her hand covered her mouth. The bedroom door swung open and a blurry eyed Kerry ran into the room carrying a metal bat in her hands. Cindy soon followed in moving quickly around Kerry so not to be attacked, and eyed the commotion in the room.

Kerry lowered her arm bringing the bat to her side and slowly walked over to Hadley. Jace was cradling Chewy's head trying to lower the dogs whimpers by shushing him.

"Had's" Cindy called out as she stood behind Kerry. She nudged Kerry to move closer, trembling while she studied Hadley's rigid, unmoving body.

"Hadley what is going on?" Kerry asked, finally getting the courage to walk around and stand in front of her friend. Hadley's eyes were wide and dilated, the hair on her arms had stood up and Kerry could see droplets of sweat falling from her forehead. Unease began to fill Kerry as she continued to examine her friend. A soft cry left Hadley's slightly opened mouth.

Kerry turned to face the window, the colour drained from her face as her eyes registered to the sight outside.

"Hadley, get away from the window." Kerry hissed as she took a step back, slightly pulling Hadley with her.

Hadley snapped back as she realised she was walking backwards. She felt the bed frame on her palms as she stopped herself from falling back and Jace's arms wrapped around her for support. Hadley moved along the bed frame until she felt the full embrace of Jace and sunk into his arms. He began stroking her hair as he looked to Kerry for answers. Kerry nodded her head to the window, her eyebrows furrowed with uncertain.

"Take a look for yourself Jace." She said as she walked over to Cindy who had crouched down to continue comforting Chewy. Knowing Kerry didn't know how to explain the situation Jace kissed Hadley's forehead, and walked across the room to the window.

The clear midnight blue sky gave way for the nearly full moon, illuminating the surrounding area. The odd faint light from the village could still be seen from behind the curtains. Yet, the street lamp lights seemed dimmer than usual and the odd breeze was still allowing the autumn leaves to fall to the ground, to decay and die. Nighttime clouds soon passed over the moon, the outside, fell into complete darkness. Jace felt cold fingers entwine with his, and he turned his face to Hadley with a slight smile. He could see the colour coming back into her cheeks, yet the dark circles underneath her eyes stood out. He watched as she turned her head to face his and saw her struggle to copy his reassuring smile. Jace gave her hand a squeeze as the clouds moved along and five figures emerged from the black. Jace felt Hadley's body tense up as she moved behind his arm.

"It's them." Hadley told them, her voice hoarse and raspy. Jace looked at his wife and then back to the window with squinted eyes, trying hard to focus on who was outside.

"Who's them?" Cindy asked being careful not to spook an already fragile Hadley as she walked behind her and Jace.

"Jace who is it?"

"It's Evelyn, Father, Benjamin, Annie and Jane." Hadley replied her voice now back to normal. Cindy gasped, her hand quickly covered her mouth to hold in her piercing scream.

Jace let go off Hadley's hand. "Oi!" he began banging on the glass "Oi! What are you doing out there?" His raised voice shook the room and made the three women and Chewy jump in shock.

"Jace" Hadley grabbed his fist before he could hit the glass again. "They won't answer you. They haven't moved since I first saw them." She grabbed his face between her hands and mouthed, 'It's okay, Chewy and me are okay now.' Hadley felt his head begin to nod as his eyes darted between her and their dog. When Hadley looked over to check on Cindy, Kerry had already gone over to her and put her arm around her shoulders.

"Why are they not moving?" Cindy asked, "Is this the Orera?"

Kerry guided Cindy to the bed and sat beside her with a sigh.

"I think so." Kerry replied looking at Hadley and Jace for backup. They both nodded their head when they saw Cindy look to them for an answer.

"They are standing there because they can't get past the protection spell." Hadley ran her hand through her hair, frustration and anger still lingering on the tone of her voice. Jace looked back outside and stopped Hadley walking away with his hand, unsure as to why he wouldn't let her move away she followed his gaze. Hadley tightened her jaw as she watched Evelyn take a few steps towards the house and eventually look up to the window. She continued to stare at Jace and Hadley then continued her steps until the invisible barrier stopped her from walking up the porch steps. Hadley let out a breath she did not realise she was holding, as Evelyn confirmed her protection spell was still strong. They watched as Evelyn's body attempted to take another step but only her upper body made any sort of movement. When they knew Evelyn realised she would not break through the barrier, they watched as her head snapped back up to look at them. Her eyes showed nothing but sinister darkness. Her mouth was nothing but a thin line which curled up when she made eye contact with both Jace and Hadley.

"Mommy what's going on?" Everyone in the room turned to the bedroom door and saw Marty rubbing his tired eyes, his teddy hooked under his left arm. Before Cindy could answer, a harrowing screech arose from outside; which made everyone cover their ears to block out the piercing sound. Hadley watched Cindy race to the bedroom door and cover Martys ears with her hands. She saw Kerry hold back a now frantic Chewy with one hand while still trying to cover at least one ear with the other. She looked to Jace who was standing closest to window collapse into himself, wincing in pain as the scream was threatening to burst his eardrums.

"Everyone go to the other side of the house now!" Hadley screamed. She pushed her husband to the direction of the door and began following before stopping. Hadley felt a need to go back and look out of the window. The others were still standing there, their arms down, their focus purely on a screaming, thrashing Evelyn. Her arms were banging against nothing that could not be seen, her legs kicking into the air. When Hadley could no longer take the pain, she ran to join to the others and slammed the door shut.

CHAPTER NINETEEN

Hadley woke up with her head resting on Jace's shoulder and Chewy's head slumped on her legs. A stiffness had taken hold of her body as she sat upright on the floor and stretched her neck from left to right. Checking the time on the bedside clock, she realised they all must have passed out at some point during the night. On the bed, on top of the sheets was Marty safely wrapped in Cindy's arms, both still in a deep sombre sleep. In the single armchair slept Kerry, her hands guarding her cat from what ever she feared was outside the night before.

Chewy had noticed Hadley moving and was already eager to get out the room and head downstairs. Not wanting to wake the others Hadley quietly pushed herself up from the floor and felt the need to stretch out her whole body. Putting her hands together she lifted her arms and pushed out her chest until she felt a crack and the endorphins race through her body. She noticed she had an audience as Kerrys cat was now watching her along with Chewy still at the door. With a stretch of their own, both animals followed her out the room.

Hadley reached the kitchen quickly, ready to curb her caffeine craving. The aroma of fresh coffee filled her senses as she walked to the backdoor to let Chewy out. The morning air was bitter and damp, a thick fog covered the village in the distance. Hadley called out to Chewy when she could no longer see him and ran onto the wet grass after him. Flashbacks raced through her mind of the events she saw the previous night. She remembered the look on Evelyn's face when she was trying to break through the protection spell. She remembered the fear she felt when she realised the strength and power the Orera must have over the people she thought she knew. She heard the screech that filled all their ears again as her vision became blurred and restricted. The fog began to dance as black dots swirled in front of her. Hadley felt her eyes fill with water when the thoughts of what had happened paralysed her to the spot. The screech still filled her head as she frantically searched for Chewy; her eyes darting in every direction. Through the noise she thought she could hear someone calling out to her, a voice she knew and was familiar with. Hadley felt her knees give way as she forced herself to move.

"I got you." She heard as warm arms wrapped around her, just before she reached the ground. "I got you." She heard again as her senses came back into focus. Hadley smelt him before her vision confirmed it. "Hadley" Jace took her head in his hands, his brows furrowed with concern. "Hadley, speak to me."

"You don't hear it?" She whispered wincing in pain. Jace shook his head as he surveyed the area before looking back into Hadley's eyes.

"There is nothing there." He reassured her. Hadley slowly came back into the present, her eyes never leaving Jace until every feature came into focus.

"Chewy, where's Chewy?" Hadley tried to stand up as she shouted for her dog to come back out of the fog. Jace followed her, never letting go of her arms for balance and support. He caught her again when Hadley tried to take a few steps forward.

"Hadley calm down," he told her. "Chewy is back in the house."

Hadley let Jace help her turn towards the house and saw Kerry, Cindy and Marty all looking concerned on the back porch. Her eyes moved to Martys arm and saw Chewy happily being stroked on the top of his head.

Hadley clung to Jace when she realised everyone was safe in the house.

"But I saw him run off, I saw him…."

Hadley broke down and fell back onto the wet ground. Her clothes from the day before absorbed the dampness and clung to her body.

"Hadley lets get you inside." Jace scooped her up in his arms and carried her up the back porch and inside the safety of their home. By the time he entered the living room, Hadley had fallen unconscious. Jace walked back into the kitchen after placing Hadley on the sofa and covering her with a blanket.

 Cindy was preparing breakfast for Marty who was sitting silently at the kitchen table with Kerry. The silence continued as they all drank their morning coffee, unable to make eye contact with each other. Jace looked up from his mug and saw Cindy and Kerry both deep in thought, their expressions mirroring one another, unaware of anything outside their own uncertain bubble. A clink of metal hitting the floor which made everyone jump and stand ready to attack.

"Sorry mommy" Marty whispered, fear and sincerity spread across his face. Cindy jumped to her son and knelt down to pick up his spoon which was now being cleaned by Chewy.

"It's okay baby." She told him, putting her hand on his cheek and kissing his forehead. "It's okay, I think we are all just a bit jumpy today." Marty looked around the table and focused on Jace.

"Is Hadley going to be alright?"

Jace sat forward and rested his forearms on the table. "She will be alright kiddo. Why don't you go play upstairs while we clean up down here?"

Marty scooted his chair back and called for Chewy to follow him up the stairs into his bedroom.

"Thank you." Cindy said as she collected the breakfast dishes. Jace nodded and pushed his empty mug to Kerry.

"Fine." Kerry sighed with a slight laugh, picking up the mug and refilling everyone's drink. "So," she said placing the mug down in front of Jace "How do you really think Hadley is doing?"

Jace wiped his hand down his face and rubbed his eyes with his thumb and second finger. "She is burnt out." He admitted. "I have never seen her like this. We have done hundreds of cases and never once have I seen her.." Jace stopped and his head dropped into his hands.

Cindy left the dishes in the sink and walked over to Jace. She raised her eyebrows at Kerry and tilted her head, pleading for her to say something to Jace.

"Jace" Kerry began. "Hadley will be okay." Jace lifted his head, his expression bleak. Kerry quickly made eye contact with Cindy, who was scowling at her.

"What I mean is, you are right. She is burnt out, and we have let her overwork herself. She needs to rest, at least for today."

Jace sighed as Cindy rubbed his upper arm.

"She won't agree with that, she will say there is too much to do." He reminded them.

"Well, she is asleep now, and it looks like she will be for a while." Cindy stated. "What do you think she would say we needed to do today?" Cindy asked.

"She would say we need to go visit Evelyn and the others and find out if they remember anything about last night." Kerry replied. "But I doubt they do and even if they did, they are not going to admit it to us."

"Well, if that is what she would do. Then that's the best plan we have." Cindy said. "I am happy to stay here with Marty and Hadley."

Kerry nodded and left the kitchen to get changed. Jace hung back.

"Hey," Cindy said. "Go get ready, I promise I'll keep watch of her. She would want you to go." Cindy hugged Jace until she felt him duplicate the gesture.

"Thank you." She heard him whisper before letting go and letting him walk up the stairs. Feeling overwhelmed

Cindy took some deep breaths and continued to clean up the kitchen.

When the last bowl and mug were put away, Cindy went upstairs and changed out of the clothes she had worn the day before. Marty had already changed into fresh clothes and had fallen asleep watching his favourite cartoons. Not to wake him, she quickly grabbed what she was going to change into and headed in the bathroom. Someone had already showered, the mirrors were still steamed up and the warmth from the shower water still filled the room. Once she had washed and changed, Cindy made her way back down the stairs and checked in on Hadley.

The living room felt cold and uninviting, so Cindy quickly got the fireplace working hoping it would make Hadley more comfortable. Hadley stirred as the cold air was replaced by the warmth and quickly fell back into her deep sleep. As she walked out the living room, she was startled when saw Kerry standing by the door, reading the newspaper.

"Sorry, I didn't mean to startle you." Kerry smiled aware of Cindy's reaction. "How is she?" She asked looking up from the paper.

"Still sleeping." Cindy told her, refusing to take the paper Kerry was handing to her.

"I don't like reading it anymore. Not with the murders, it seems to be full of horror lately."

Kerry pulled back her arm and gave Cindy an understanding nod.

"True, but soon we will see those responsible on the cover. Besides look." Kerry showed Cindy the page she was reading. Photos of bright orange pumpkins filled the page with families all gathered in a field. "This is where they will be today. No matter what, they have to keep up appearances around the village. "As Kerry and Cindy spoke in hushed voices Jace made his way down the stairs.

"So where are we going?" He asked, intrigued with their whispered conversation. Kerry showed him the newspaper. "We are going pumpkin picking."

The drive to the local farm shop was the perfect opportunity to talk tactics. Once the plan was set they spent the rest of the drive in silence, both full of their worries and concerns for the ones they loved. As Jace turned into the car park, a familiar face showed up at the car window.

"Mr Fernsby, Miss Knight, nice to see you out supporting your community."

Kerry saw Jace grip onto the steering wheel tighter and look at the man.

"Officer." Jace greeted him. Sensing he would not get anything else out of him, he inspected the car and raised his eyebrows when he realised there was no one else in the car.

"Just the two of you then?" The officer noted. "Four pounds to enter and park the car, follow the directions to an empty spot." Jace collected the spare change from inside the car and handed it over while keeping his eyes forward. The officer snorted as Jace dropped the money into his hand and he made a gesture for the car to move forward. Jace followed the signs until a teenage boy started waving them to move up into the overflow car park. As the weather had been wet and drizzly the last couple of days, it had made the mud in the overflow car park sinkable and a hazard to walk on. Jace offered Kerry his arm as she struggled to pick up her feet in the slosh that was the path.

"Thank you." Kerry said as she put her weight onto Jace and pulled her left foot free. Jace smiled as he watched others struggle to maintain their balance, yet still eager to reach the entrance to the farm.

"Don't mention it." He casually said as he steadied Kerry on the last few steps in the mud. When they both made it to the walkable path and to the entrance of the farm, Kerry felt Jace tense up and his pace become slower.

"Ready." She told him rather than asking him. A mother and father struggled to control their three children as they ran past a rather placid looking Jace. Kerry took his arm and walked him into the field.

"Jace, we are doing this to help Hadley, get a grip. She would want us to be helping." Kerry snapped.

Jace stopped, a look of shock and anger filled his face.

"Get a grip." Jace snarled. "My wife passed out from over working, we are facing the worst demon we have ever gone against, and you want me to get a grip?"

His face turned red and his fists balled up as he dug his finger nails into his palms. Kerry stood there taken aback from his outburst.

"Jace I'm sorry. I shouldn't have said that to you, you love Hadley. I love her too, just as much as I love you, Cindy and Marty. I know she is the only one who is going to be able to banish the Orera. If we are to protect the ones we love, if we are to protect and help Hadley, we need to do this." Kerry explained to him. "Let me buy you a coffee as a peace offering." The edges of Jace's lips began to turn up.

"A slice of cake, and we are even."

Jace saw a table by the window come free and made a dash before someone else took the only free table. The farm café smelt of strong ground coffee and a mix of pastries, fresh bread and soup. Out the window Jace saw families huddled together picking out the perfect pumpkin to take home.

"One coffee and a slice of I apologise again carrot cake." Kerry placed the tray on the table and handed over the peace offering to Jace with a smile.

"Thank you, and I am sorry for snapping at you Kerry. You have done so much to help us and I don't want you to feel unappreciated." Kerry gave an acceptive nod as she put a forkful of cake in her mouth.

When the last crumbs were eaten Kerry caught a glimpse of two people chatting outside in the field.

"Jace look." She said as she pointed in the direction of her eyesight. Jace turned in his chair and saw Evelyn and Father Anderson, happily exchanging pleasantries with Wotton-Under-Edge locals. Jace finished his coffee and suggested it was time to put the plan into action. As they left the warm café, the chilly autumn wind gently blew past them, making Kerrys nose run instantly with the change in temperature. Together they walked onto the pumpkin patch to Evelyn and Father Anderson.

"We need to talk to you." Jace calmly said as they stopped just feet away.

CHAPTER TWENTY

Evelyn turned round and gave a guarded smile to Jace and Kerry. Father Anderson turned round to them after saying goodbye to a young couple who had been in deep conversation with him.

"How lovely to see you both here" Father Anderson said, putting his hand out to greet them. Jace stared at the Fathers hand and left it there without extending his own.

"Very well." Father Anderson muttered as he put his down and composed himself with poise and pride.

"Jace, you said you needed to talk to us. Why don't we walk round the fields?" Evelyn suggested. Jace nodded and gestured for them all to start walking up the lines of pumpkins.

"Last night we had an incident at the house which we would like to discuss with both of you" Jace began, putting his hands into his pockets and his eyes remained staring into the distance.

"An incident you say? And what has this got to do with us?" Father Anderson questioned. Kerry huffed, unsure whether his question was full of ignorance or arrogance.

"You really don't know why we are here speaking to you?" Kerry challenged equally annoyed. As she was when Evelyn suggested walking round the fields.

"Miss Knight why would I be asking if I knew the answer?" Father Anderson implied while waving to a family who were on their way to pay for their pumpkins. Benjamin, Annie and Jane joined the group ignoring Jace and Kerry.

"Alright, enough" Jace stopped walking and stood his ground until all three stopped and turned to him. "Last night we were woken up and saw you two, Benjamin and tweedle dee and tweedle dum here outside our house."

Kerry walked to stand by Jace. She wanted to study all their expressions. Jace began retelling them the events which happened the previous night. Kerry continuously moved her eyes to assess each of their faces as they listened to Jace. She had zoned out of listening to Jace herself, her only focus was on if their facial expressions changed. If their body language became guarded or defensive.

"Okay there Doctor?" Kerry interrupted Jace. Jace turned to look at Kerry who was standing with her arms crossed. "Remembering anything from last night?" she asked.

"Maybe that you woke up with muddy feet?" Jace put his gaze back onto the group and raised his eyebrow to them all. "Well, did you?" He asked them.

Father Anderson kept his face stern, his stare never leaving Jace. Benjamin had managed to get his composure back before Jace could look at him.

"What about you two?" Jace turned to Annie and Jane. They both looked up from staring at the ground, neither could look him in the eyes.

"So how did you get mud on your feet ladies?" Neither answered, except to look at each other, nod and lower their heads again.

"I believe Jace asked you a question." Kerry snarled at the group. Her frustration intensifying as she watched Father Anderson continue to keep up the good appearance.

"Enough!" Kerry snapped. Pushing the Father's arm down with force, that he had raised up to wave at a passing family. Other families surrounding them stopped looking at the pumpkins and started to become interested in the commotion happening in front of them.

Father Anderson turned with rage, his lips turned up into a snarl towards Kerry. She could see the sweat running down his red swollen cheeks.

"How dare you touch me in public like that." He hissed. Kerry remained placid as she raised her eyebrows in response.

"It's okay everyone, please carry on and enjoy your time here." Father Anderson announced after taking some deep breaths, before turning back around with a smile on his face. Kerry looked at Jace and nodded.

"We came here for answers, and answers are what we are going to get." Kerry said in hushed tones.

"So you don't have to answer you can simply nod your head. Did you wake up with muddy feet last night?". All the women nodded their heads.

"Still don't want to answer Ben, what about you Father?" Kerry muttered. "Oh well, we know you were all there." She shrugged. "Do you remember being there?" She asked again. No one nodded their head "And Evelyn how did you get them bruises on your head?" Kerry walked over to

Evelyn and lifted her hat. Kerry turned to Jace as she still held up Evelyn's hat.

"What do you think Jace?" Kerry slowly turned to face Evelyn again before letting her hat fall back down. "How do you think it happened?" She began as she walked round the group and stopped by Jace. "When Evelyn here," she pointed her finger at Evelyn "was unable to get through the protection and continuously banged the side of her forehead." She finished by leaning her head to the side and raised her eyebrows.

Evelyn raised her hand to where the bruises were forming under her hat and shook her head. Kerry and Jace saw her mumble something under her breath and her eyes fill with water.

"Something you want to say Evelyn?" Jace asked.

"We don't remember being there last night, but yes, when we woke up, we all had evidence that we had left the house."

Jace put his hands in his coat pockets and sighed.

"Kerry can I have a word with you please?" Jace asked as he walked a few feet away from the others. Kerry smiled before joining him and asked what was wrong.

"Do you believe they don't remember?" He asked Kerry.

"I don't know." Kerry confessed. She turned to look at the group who were whispering to each other. Kerry felt a hand grip her arm.

"What are you going to say?" Jace whispered. Kerry pulled free and ignored him, a fire inside her was sending heat all through her body with every step towards them.

"You idiots." Kerry swore. "You honestly have no idea what you have been dealing with do you? And now because you didn't carry on the barbaric act you and your ancestors started, you have made yourself open to its forces."

"We have this under control." Benjamin barked.

"Under control. Good god!" Kerry screeched. She saw Father Anderson curl his lips for her blasphemy wording and Jace came to join her.

"You have learnt nothing. All you have done is feed this demon to make her stronger and more powerful. You have messed with something that you could never have understood or controlled." Jace argued. "One more child is going to die, look around you, any of these children could be the one you feed to her."

"But I suppose you already have children's blood on your hands, what's one more?" Kerry spat, anger and disgust radiating out of her.

"We have until the thirtieth, then one of you will strike again. So you are going to listen to Jace and I." Kerry told them, not waiting for either of them to respond.

"On the twenty-eighth all of you will come to the Fernsby home where we will take precautions to prevent you from harming anyone else.." Kerry was cut off.

"And what, you are going to keep us locked up like animals?" Benjamin questioned.

"What Kerry was saying before you interrupted her Doctor, is we will keep you secure in the house until the Demon is banished from this realm. It is obvious she has a strong connection to you all and that means we have to stop her from telepathically getting to you." Jace looked at Kerry and they both turned to look away.

"Wait." Evelyn stopped them after whispering with the others. "What's going to happen to the town, to us?"

Kerry shook her head in shock and Jace rubbed his hand down his face.

"I think you have lost all your rights in deciding what happens to the town and to yourselves." With that Jace and Kerry walked away without looking back.

"Mommy, is Hadley going to be okay?" Cindy was busy in the kitchen preparing ingredients for dinner, she closed the cupboard and put the can of Spam on the counter. "She will be fine baby. She just needs to rest." She reassured him.

"She has been resting all day." He quizzed her.

"Marty, you know there are bad things happening?" He nodded.

"Hadley, Jace and Kerry are doing everything to help stop that bad thing and protect you." Marty took a sip of his drink and carefully placed it back on the kitchen table.

"But mommy why protect me?" He asked not taking his eyes of the coke can.

"Because you deserve to be protected Marty."

Cindy and Marty both turned to the kitchen door to see Hadley standing there. She looked dishevelled and uneasy on her feet.

"Hadley!" Marty ran over to her and wrapped his arms around her waist.

"I was waiting for you to wake up, our show is going to be on soon."

He smiled up at her before resting his head back onto her stomach.

"How are you feeling?" Cindy asked walking over to Hadley and pulling her top half into a hug.

"Stiff, but I'm okay." Hadley told her.

"Well why don't you go shower, freshen up and I'll make dinner?" Cindy suggested

"And then we can watch our show." Marty smiled up at her. Hadley nodded her head and left to go upstairs. Cindy ruffled Martys hair.

"Want to help me cook while you wait for Hadley?"

As Marty stirred in the Spam to the diced potatoes, Hadley walked back into the kitchen.

"You look better." Cindy noted.

"I feel it." Hadley agreed "Wow and what are you cooking for us Marty?"

Marty looked up from what he was doing. "Potato hash with Spam, mommy always makes it good."

Cindy kissed Marty on the top of his head and told him to go and sit with Hadley in the living room.

Cindy rubbed her hands over face before finishing the prep for dinner and putting the final product into the oven.

Walking out the kitchen she popped her head round the living room door and saw Hadley and Marty asleep on the sofa. Knowing she should not bother them, she made her way into the study. The lights flickered on once she found the switch, and she made her way over to the bookshelf.

'No more being scared Cindy.' She said to herself and pulled out a variety of books. Each filled with notes and stories of different demons, paranormal beings, hauntings and spells. What to look at first she thought as her hands hovered over the covers.

Cindy began reading old cases Hadley and Jace had been involved in. Every so often she would gasp at the horror in which they were put into. She would feel tears forming as she read what families had been through and, she would find herself smiling at the victories they achieved. Once she felt she had a better understanding of the job Hadley and Jace had, a sudden sense of guilt filled her. She picked up another book and inspected the cover, she knew she recognised it from the other day when Hadley and the others were searching for the Orera name. Each page was filled with terrifying comments and pictures of beings from the darker realm. *"How could I have been so blind to the things around me?"* Cindy mumbled to herself.

"Because there is already enough evil in the world. And sometimes it is better to not know what other evil is out there." Hadley stood by the study doorway looking at Cindy with a weak smile.

"What you reading?" Hadley asked as she walked over to sit next to Cindy at the table.

Cindy shrugged and sighed, "I don't know why I am reading these. I just feel like I am not helping at all, and I have put all you in real danger and I can't do anything to help because I don't know any of this." Cindy let out a breath after realising she spoke all at once.

Hadley laughed and placed her hand on Cindy's shoulder.

"Cinds' you help more than you realise. But if you want to learn about any of this all you have to do is ask."

Hadley picked up the book Cindy had in her lap and put it onto the table.

"So what was you reading about?" She asked Cindy.

"I was looking at your past paranormal cases." Cindy told Hadley who smiled back at her.

"Then I was looking at the different types of Demons. I was looking into the one that possessed your mother and.." Cindy paused and gave Hadley an apologetic look.

"It's okay, I have made peace with my gods and goddesses. Sometimes even those in the highest of realms can not always save you." Hadley stopped and looked down at the picture of the demon which had possessed her mother all them years ago.

"But they should have protected your mother and you. How can you forgive them so easily and still believe?"

Hadley took some moments to herself, she thought back to what her mother use to tell her about the gods and goddesses they honoured.

"My mother always used to say our gods and goddesses come with both evil and good. You can not just blame one for good and put all your anger into another because something bad happens to you. Freya is the goddess of love, fertility and battle. When my mother first knew there was something wrong with her, she understood Freya could help her battle the demon but not destroy it. When the demon finally won, I did curse my gods but what happened to my mother was not their fault. They can not save us from things, they simply help us while our souls are in this realm."

"So that's why you use herbs and certain things for your spells?" Cindy asked.

"Yes we use what they would want and channel their energy. But at the end of the day, their energy, their magic would not work without us channeling and summoning outwards." Hadley explained.

Cindy nodded understanding her words. Cindy looked back over the books lost in her thoughts.

"Cinds'?" Hadley said.

"Yeah" Cindy mumbled back.

"If you want to learn more about our beliefs, want to be a part of it. We can help you." Hadley took Cindy's hands. "You don't have to fight demons or paranormal things, but you can still help us in other ways."

Cindy nodded and looked at Hadley.

"Maybe I can fight easy ghosts with you lot."

Hadley laughed and Cindy soon joined in.

"I think that is a good idea." Hadley agreed. "You have three people to teach you. Wow three, and with you that's four. Our coven sure has grown." Hadley smiled "The pagan path branches off into many directions, as you know Jace does not use magic. But I have a good feeling, I think you were born to be a witch. Just remember all Wiccans are pagans, but not all pagans are Wiccans. Remember you have already done the first thing." Hadley smiled.

Cindy, half smiled a look of confusion on her face "The first thing?"

"Yes, you discovered your calling. Many people are born into this path. Jace, Kerry and me were all from Pagan families. But others discover it. They suddenly get a calling, they realise they are in tune with nature and with the surrounding energies." Hadley stood up and walked to the bookcase.

She reached the least stacked shelf and picked up a plain unused black leather book. Hadley turned to walk back to the table smiling.

"Here" She held the book out to Cindy, who accepted the book with furrowed brows. Seeing Cindy's expression Hadley laughed and sat back down.

"It is for you Cinds'. This book will be yours and yours alone to write in. This will be your book of shadows, where you can write your thoughts, spells which work, rituals you feel work for you. But generally this is your journal."

Cindy opened the book to the first plain page. "How do I start writing in it, do you and Kerry have one?"

Hadley nodded her head. "We do, but I think we should eventually create one together, I shall speak to Kerry about it. I think its time to bring back my mothers coven."

"Why is there no coven anymore?"

"After she became possessed, she sent all the coven members on their way to protect them. The tree stump outside is our sacred altar."

"Why the tree stump? I noticed it is the only one. Does the coven have a name?"

Hadley smiled. "When we connect to the gods and goddesses outside a white light emerges from the stump, it is beautiful and powerful. My mother was the high priestess and named us The White Tree Coven… Anyway, on how you start your book of shadows."

Hadley retrieved a pen and handed it over to Cindy.

"On the first page simply write; This book of shadows is hereby blessed, for it is sacred above all rest. No curse nor hex shall see below, or they shall face quite a foe. Except mine, no eyes shall see. So merry part and blessed be."

Hadley watched as Cindy finished writing and gently placed the pen down and closed the book.

Cindy took a few moments to herself before turning to Hadley and beamed at her.

"Thank you so much, I know this is the right path for me." Cindy stopped talking and began looking concerned.

"What about Marty?"

Hadley looked back towards the kitchen and frowned thinking about what Marty had already been through. Before turning back to Cindy she put on a smile and shook the bad thoughts out of her head.

"Marty is a smart boy Cinds'. He has been exposed to the darker side of life from an early age. Yet, he is still questioning everything, he wants to learn about these things." Cindy laughed at Hadley's comment.

"I know he has, he wants to grow up to be like Jace and you. The fearsome demon hunters he calls you." Hadley could not help but smile.

"Well, that's fine for the future. However, at the moment he wants to learn about paganism, and since me and Jace are here , I can always help out there. We are family now, we help and learn from each other." Hadley reassured her. "One thing for sure is that your son is not going after demons, vampires, werewolves or anything like that for a long time".

Cindy shook her head. "I still can't get my head around that. I remember when I was younger, I snuck into the living room to watch The Beast Must Die behind the sofa." Cindy laughed at the memory. "But seriously thank you for letting us stay here." Hadley put her hands in the air.

"Nope, no more thanking us, you are family now, and I love having a full house." Hadley told her. "So shall we go set up for dinner? The others should be back soon."

CHAPTER TWENTY-ONE

"We're back." Kerry shouted from the hallway. "And we bring pumpkins."

Marty ran out the kitchen and straight to Kerry, his mouth open in excitement and awe at the number and size of the pumpkins Jace and Kerry had brought back with them. Hadley walked down the stairs and took a heavy looking pumpkin off Kerry and placed it further into the hallway.

"Wow, did we go a little overboard this year?" Hadley laughed as she continued to help bring in the pumpkins.

"Kerry made a fair point, although the people who run the town are sadistic murderers. It's not the farmers fault, so we should help them out."

Jace groaned as he stretched his back. "And that's the last of them. Let me just lock up the car and I'll be right in."

"Mom, mommy, look at all the pumpkins Kerry and Jace got." Marty squealed. Cindy finished the dinner set up and walked into the hallway.

"Wow." Cindy expressed trying to meet Martys enthusiasm. She caught Marty mid-jump in to her arms and kissed him on the cheek.

"We are going to have a lot of fun carving these." Cindy said.

"I was thinking of using one for food." Jace said as he walked through the front door and locked it behind him. Marty pulled a face which made Jace laugh

"Don't worry just one." He told Marty as he ruffled his hair on his way to the kitchen. After a while of chit chat, Cindy announced dinner was ready and everyone made their way into the kitchen for another family meal. As the night went on, they all found themselves sharing halloween stories, old pumpkin carving stories and watching whatever Marty picked on television.

"Right Marty time for bed, say goodnight to everyone." Marty sighed as he moved off the sofa and went round the room kissing everyone goodnight.

"Mommy can we let Chewy out and he come sleep with me while you all stay down here?" Cindy looked at Hadley who nodded and told Chewy to go outside with Marty and Cindy.

When the backdoor opened and closed, Hadley looked over to Jace and Kerry with squinted eyes.

"So, did it go well?"

Jace and Kerry gave each other a knowing look and nodded to each other.

"Define well." Jace sighed. "We believe them when they said they do not remember coming here last night. But they did acknowledge they woke up with muddy feet and Evelyn woke up with bruises on her forehead."

Hadley pushed her lips out in thought. "Well, I suppose at least they admitted to waking up in a weird state."

"Yeah, but they were still the stubborn you know what, which we have grown to hate." Kerry added.

"So did you make a plan? What are we going to do?" Hadley asked biting her bottom lip.

"Maybe we should wait for Cindy." Jace suggested.

"No need to wait, I'm here, shall we go into the study?" Cindy said from the living room door.

As they made their way to the study and began sitting around the table. Kerry stood up and walked out towards to the kitchen. Everyone looked at each confused until they heard the fridge door open and bottles clink against each other.

"Sorry, I just thought this would be appropriate with what we need to tell you." Kerry said as she walked back into the study and handed everyone a bottle of beer.

"Jace I think you should tell them our plan." Kerry said before taking a swig of the drink. Jace put his bottle on the table and sighed.

"So after speaking to them, we believe they do not know how they can be controlled by the Orera. We already established she can not get past our protection shield. So I suggested all those involved in feeding the Orera for all these years; will come here on twenty-eighth and stay here until the Orera is banished." Jace explained to Hadley and Cindy.

Hadley and Cindy remained quiet as they processed Jace's plan. Hadley rubbed her hands over her face as she pictured the plan in her head.

"Did they agree?" Hadley asked.

"We think so." Kerry replied "Jace was pretty stern and scary, so I think they will come."

Hadley found a plain piece of paper and began jotting down notes .

"Okay, so we need to decide what we are going to do whilst they are here. Also, how we plan to find the familiar and destroy it." Hadley thought out loud.

"Well, I was thinking you have a basement don't you? We could keep them in there, that way they can't escape."

"Ruthless Cindy, I love it. Write it down Hadley." Kerry laughed.

"Okay, if they are going to be in there, we need to clean it out and add some extra protection down there. We also need to protect ourselves from them." Hadley said looking up from her note making.

"I don't know if you two have ever used them, but I read about poppets in one of the books." Cindy said.

Hadley looked at Cindy. "Go on, what do we do with a poppet?" She quizzed.

Cindy took a deep breath as she tried to remember what she had read.

"Well, from what I can remember reading, it says poppets can be used for anything, love, healing. So I assume we can use them to bind someone right? What if we made one for each of them?" Cindy stopped talking and looked around the table. Kerry stared at her, her eyes wide. When she realised Cindy was staring at her, Kerry coughed and composed herself.

"I think that's a brilliant idea." Kerry confessed "But wait, how did you read about them? I don't think I have ever made one before."

Cindy looked at Hadley for reassurance.

"Cindy has had a calling and wants to join us, but even I didn't realise you took in information so quickly." Hadley announced.

Kerry gasped and put her hands together. "I knew it!" She squealed while pushing out her chair and flung her arms around Cindy's shoulders. "We are going to be a force not to be messed with, with miss brain over here." Kerry said tapping the top of Cindy's head.

Hadley and Jace laughed as Cindy blushed with all the the attention.

"So Cinds', how do we make them and what do we need?" Hadley asked when they had all settled down.

"We can make them with clay, fabric, wax, even sticks. I think we should use fabric, quicker, easier, and we can add herbs and something belonging to them inside it." Cindy explained. Hadley made more notes.

"I can get the stuff from my shop and bring it back here." Kerry offered.

"Perfect." Hadley said.

"Jace?" Hadley called, looking up at him. "You know the Inn more than me, so I want you to sit down with Cindy and draw up some kind of floor plan. If the familiar is where we believe it is, we need to know how long it will take us to get there and where the others need to be to distract the Orera and so on." Hadley listed off.

"Fine by me." Jace said smiling.

"One more thing, any of them that do not turn up, you have to bring them here." Hadley told him. Jace leant back on his chair and put his hands behind his head.

"That darlin, will be very fun." He said with a wink.

"What does all this mean? Do we have a little coven now?" Kerry said. Hadley looked at Kerry and Cindy.

"It looks like the White Tree Coven is back. Which means Cindy and all of us need an initiation."

CHAPTER TWENTY TWO

The following night Hadley helped Cindy prepare for her initiation.

"Are you excited?"

"I think I am." Cindy laughed.

"Hadley before we can begin, we need a high priestess of the coven. And I think it should be you." Kerry said.

"Why me? Do you not want the honour?"

"No you have to be it. You brought us together and this is your mothers coven. It belongs to you."

After it was decided, Hadley and Kerry prepared everything outside. In their large secluded garden stood the tree stump Hadley, her mother and their coven used to use when they would give their offerings to gods and goddesses.

Kerry placed candles around the area to produce a circle. After carefully placing each candle she then placed four candles within the circle to indicate north, west, east and south.

On the tree alter, a white candle stood between a bowl of water. A bowl of salt was placed next to the chalice which was filled to the brim with wine. On one side of the stump the rune Ansuz was placed for Woden and on the other was placed the rune Fehu. The first rune, of the first Aett, for the goddess Freya.

"Here it is." Jace handed Hadley the athame, and she placed it on the stump above the new book of shadows, which they would all sign.

Hadley quickly ran into the house to get changed with Kerry and Cindy.

"You both look amazing."

Kerry and Cindy turned to look at Hadley.

"Good thing Kerry always looks prepared." Cindy said as she stared at her reflection. They had both changed into black lingerie, Cindy wore a delicate babydoll set while Kerry wore a satin chemise.

"Hadley you look like a true priestess." Kerry beamed when Hadley changed into a pure white cami set.

"Thank you, but I am taking a cardigan with me until we start." Hadley laughed as she covered herself up.

Jace and Marty had placed more candles outside the circle, making the garden glow in a soft orange light.

"It looks amazing out here." Hadley said as she walked over to Jace.

"You look amazing, your mother would be so proud of you. Are you ready to become a high priestess for your coven?" Hadley looked up at Jace and smiled.

"If I have you by my side.." Jace cut her off by lowering his head and meeting her lips.

"Sorry to interrupt this lovely moment. But we are ready to begin." Jace and Hadley looked at Kerry with matching grins.

"Let's start then."

Hadley entered the circle on her own as the others watched from the outside.

"I cast the sacred circle. I am between the worlds." She came to a stop next to Hadley who was facing north of the circle facing outwards ready to call the quarters.

"I call the spirit of the North. Please join me and lend me the power of the earth." Moving around the circle clockwise she continued. "I call the spirit of the East. Please join me and lend me the power of air. I call the spirit of the South. Please join me and lend me the power of water. I call the spirit of the West. Please join me and lend me the power of fire."

Picking up the salt water mixture, Hadley anointed herself and kneeled before the altar.

"Jace what is she doing?" Marty whispered as he sat nearer the house with Jace.

"She is meditating, she is showing the god and goddess that she is willing to dedicate herself to them."

Hadley stood up and raised her arms above the altar.

"Woden and Freya, hear me now. I am here, a simple pagan holding thee in honour. For have I journeyed and long have I searched seeking that which I desire above all things. I am of the trees and of the fields. I am of the woods and of the springs; the streams and the hills. I am of thee; and thee of me. Grant me that which I desire. Permit me to worship the gods and all that the gods represent. Make me a lover of life in all things. Well, do I know the creed. That if I do not have that spark of love within me, then I will never find it without me. Love is the law and love is the bond. All this do I honour above aught else."

Hadley lowered her arms and picked up the athame before kissing the blade. She held the blade up to the dark sky.

"Woden and Freya, here do I stand before. Skin bared to dedicate myself to the thine honour. Ever will I protect you and that which is yours. Let none speak ill of you, forever will I defend you. You are my life, and I am yours from the day forth. So mote it be."

Hadley lowered the athame and kissed the blade once more. Delicately she pressed the blade to her palm and made a clean cut to drip the blood into the chalice. With a bloody hand, she picked up the chalice.

"As this wine drains from this chalice, so let the blood drain from my body should I ever do aught to harm the gods, or those in kinship with their love. Woden and Freya, so be it."

Hadley signed her name in the new book of shadows. She turned to see Kerry wipe a tear away as she smiled at her .

"Kerry, are you ready to sign yourself to this coven and again to Woden and Freya?"

Kerry nodded her head and took Hadley's hand.

"And Cindy are you ready to sign your name to this coven and to the gods and goddesses?"

Without hesitating Cindy nodded her hand took Hadley's other hand.

"Then you may enter."

Hadley brought them both to the altar and told them to kneel after pouring more wine into the chalice.

"I am she who speaks for Woden, what is thy name?"

In unison Kerry and Cindy said their name. Hadley dipped her finger in the salt water and asked Kerry to stand to be anointed. Hadley locked eyes with Kerry and they both smiled as Hadley ran her finger down from Kerrys forehead to her sternum. Moving to stand in front of Cindy she performed the same anointment.

"In the names of Woden and of Freya may this sacred water cleanse you. Let it drive out all impurities. All sadness and all hate."

Hadley placed the water back onto the altar and turned to place a gentle kiss on Kerrys and Cindy's lips.

"In the names of Woden and Freya may you be filled with the love that should be borne by and for all things."

Hadley held out her hands for both of them to take. "Both answer me, what are the names of the gods?"

"We know them as Woden and Freya."

"Are these the gods you wish to worship above all else?"

"Yes, they are."

"Do you promise faithfully to attend the rites held in their honour, so far as you are able?"

"I do."

"Do you promise to defend them from those who would speak them ill?"

"I do."

"Do you promise to love and honour thy brothers and sisters of the craft. To aid them when in distress, to care for them when sick, to protect and defend them from their enemies, so far as you are able?"

"I do."

"Know then, that in all these things are we equal. In all things do we seek for the good of us all. Love is the law, and love is the bond."

"Love is the law and love is the bond."

Hadley kissed Kerry and Cindy again.

"Kerry, you okay to go first?" Hadley said as she passed the athame to her. Kerry nodded and did a small slice on her palm. Letting the blood trickle into the chalice Hadley was holding, Kerry passed the athame to Cindy, so she could perform the same act.

"As this wine drains from the chalice, so may the blood drain from your body should ever you do aught to harm the gods. Or those in kinship with their love. Woden and Freya so mote it be."

"So mote it be."

CHAPTER TWENTY-THREE

"Can I ask something?" Cindy said while sitting in the study the following evening. "Who is going to go in the Inn and do this?"

Jace, Hadley and Kerry all looked at each other.

"Well," Jace said. "It will be us three. You have Marty to think about, and we are not going to put you in that sort of danger." Cindy nodded, disappointment on her face.

"Well, I guess I have to do as much as I can before then, then don't I." Cindy told them.

She watched as they all nodded their heads. Hadley began biting her nails again as a thought raced through her mind.

"We are going to have to make light bombs, anything that will distract the Orera when we get in there. So we can start preparing them tomorrow." Hadley said.

"Light bombs?" Cindy asked.

"It is a spell which releases a bright light when smashed." Hadley finished with a yawn. "One thing I know, we are going to defeat this, and everyone involved will be punished."

The next morning everyone apart from Marty was up and dressed for the day.

"Okay, so I will go get what we need for the poppets. Do you already have the herbs?" Kerry asked as she started getting ready to leave the house.

"Yes, we agreed we would use cayanne pepper." Hadley replied. "Be safe." Hadley told Kerry as she hugged her by the front door.

"I'll be fine, Im just going to get stuff for the spells. Also, some food, it's going to be long day." She told Hadley and walked into the rain.

Hadley watched her go until she could no longer see her and closed the front door.

"Hadley I have a great idea." Cindy said as she struggled to put on her boots. "I am going to run over to Mikes and get a horseshoe. We can put it over the basements' door, what do you think?"

Hadley began to open her mouth but was cut off.

"Or is that a bad idea, will we be able to enter? I know it is to keep witches out."

Hadley sat next to Cindy on the stairs and put her hand on her arm to bring her back into the now.

"I think that's a good idea, and do not worry." Hadley laughed. "It is used to keep out witches but not our kind." Hadley reassured her. "But who is Mike?"

Cindy stood up and grabbed her coat of one of the hangers. "You remember the one who started calling you satanists in the pub when you first came in. Well, he is a farmer and although he is a drunk. I trust him." Cindy explained while zipping up her coat.

Before Hadley could say anything, Cindy was shouting bye and closing the front door behind her.

Hadley sighed shaking her head and made her way back into the kitchen where Jace was feeding the animals. "Where did they go"? He asked. Hadley explained Kerry had gone to her shop to pick up supplies for the poppets and anything extra they may need. And Cindy had gone to see Mike to ask for a horseshoe to hang it on the basement door. Hadley stopped talking when she realised Jace was not listening to her. He had slumped down onto the kitchen floor and was cuddling Chewy. Hadley walked over to him and sat down beside him taking one of his hands in hers.

"My love." Hadley whispered to him.

Jace sighed and lifted their hands to plant a kiss on top of hers.

"I know this is what we do, we choose to go down the path of demons. But thinking of you in danger" Jace caught a sob in throat, "I can't lose you."

Hadley squeezed his hand and rested her head on his shoulder.

"Do you remember when we were in university, and we were on our second or third investigation. We were in an Inn at night in the Grassmarket. And we kept hearing doors bang and the professors were even getting spooked. But you know what I remember from that place?" She looked up at Jace who was already looking at her. "I remember you and I went exploring to the back and one of the floorboards kept creaking even when we stopped walking.

So you took hold of my hand and pulled me closer because I was freaking out."

Jace smiled remembering the story "I remember." He told her.

"Do you remember what happened next. When we started walking again. We heard a crack and then felt something running towards us. You pushed me out the way and fell through the floorboards." Hadley stopped and smiled when the image appeared in her mind. "We heard a low laugh, but I crawled over to you through the dust and debris. You gripped onto the floorboards not wanting to fall into the basement. I was so scared when I saw you. But it wasn't because of the sounds or the sinister energies I felt. I was scared because I thought I would lose you. I couldn't lose you because I already knew then, that I loved you with every fibre in my body."

Hadley turned her whole body towards Jace and placed her hands on his cheeks.

"We have always put ourselves in danger whether we mean to or not. But really the only thing that scares me is the thought I might lose you."

Jace rested her forehead onto Hadley's.

"I love you." He whispered and pressed his lips onto her.

They stayed that way until they both came apart for air and Hadley rested her head back onto his shoulder.

"Thank god the professors and the others in the team came over, no way would you have been able to pull me up." Jace smirked.

Hadley playfully smacked his shoulder before agreeing to his statement. When the laughter died down, they both fell into silence.

"We will be all right my darlin this isn't our first demon and it won't be our last."

CHAPTER TWENTY-FOUR

Kerry was grateful for the calm winds as she made her way to the town's high street under her umbrella. The town's shops were preparing to open and she noticed a few of the workers wave to her through their shop windows. Unsure of what to do, Kerry waved back and smiled before continuing on.

As she reached further up the high street, she crossed the road and lowered her stare as she walked past the church.

"No fighting talk today" She heard someone cheerfully call to her.

Kerry stopped and turned to see Father Anderson standing outside the town's most popular café.

"I have nothing to say to you Father, you know what you have to do. I shall see you on the twenty-eighth." Kerry told him, her voice platonic.

"Maybe if you came to church one Sunday you would understand why this needs to be done. Look at the town, it is as old as any and yet still flourishing. That's because…" Kerry bit her tongue and turned away.

"I shall see you on twenty-eighth, at the Fernsby's Father." Kerry said again and didn't look back.

Rounding the corner to where her store stood, two young girls ran up to her smiling.

"Morning Kerry." They said in unison.

Taken aback by the sudden friendly human communication, Kerry jumped back, dropping her umbrella in a puddle.

"Dammit" She hissed to herself.

"Sorry Kerry, let me get that for you." One of the girls said.

"Oh no it's okay." Kerry told her, but the girl had already picked up the umbrella and was shaking off the excess water.

"Thank you and I'm sorry I freaked out like that." She told the girls.

"It's okay, we just wanted to come to the shop and see you. We also want to do a ritual for Samhain, but we don't have anything yet."

Kerry saw the crumbled piece of paper in one of the girls hands and asked if she could take a look. After reading it over Kerry smiled and told the girls to follow her.

"Oh no" One of the girls gasped.

Kerry looked at what the girls were looking at and took a deep breath in and pinched the bridge of her nose.

"Kerry why would someone do that to your shop? What even are these symbols?" Kerry sighed as she took in the amount of graffiti on the front of her store.

"They are Satanic symbols. Someone is obviously trying to play a practical joke on me?"

"Well, I don't think it is a very funny prank do you Sally?"

"No, it is not Becky. We are sorry Kerry."

"It is okay girls, come on inside, we don't want an audience of people seeing you walk inside." Kerry told them.

Kerry saw both girls frown by her sentence.

"We don't care if people see us, we know you are not a Satanist and neither are we." Becky said as she skipped happily into the store as Kerry held the door open for them.

Kerry looked back over the list the girls had made and began collecting the supplies as she walked round the shop.

"This is your first time isn't girls?" Kerry pointed out.

Both girls nodded "Yes, if our list is wrong, or you think anything else needs to be added, we are happy to add it; aren't we Becky?" Sally said.

"Yes, please let us know how to do it correctly." Becky said straight after.

Kerry finished filling the basket and made her way over to the counter.

"Okay so that comes to twenty pounds. I have also added in some extra black candles for you, make sure you light them when the sunsets and place it next to a window." Kerry saw the girls faces turn into confusion and smiled. "On Samhain the veil between this realm and the others are at there thinest. Therefore, those who are lost can find the light and hopefully pass through."

Both girls nodded, showing great interest in Kerrys words.

"Two more things, maybe you should head to the farmers market and collect some apples, acorns, even pumpkins to decorate your altar while you do your ritual. The final thing I want to ask is if you have your passage for your ancestors on paper?" Becky and Sally shook their heads.

"We wanted to know if what we had matched yours." Sally sheepishly admitted.

"Could you help us with it?" Becky asked.

Kerry pulled over a note pad and pen and wrote;

'This is the night when the gateway between our world and the spirit world is thinnest. Tonight I honour my ancestors spirits of my father and mother. I call to you, and welcome you to join me for this night. You watch over me always, protecting and guiding me and tonight I thank you. Your blood runs in my veins, your spirit is in my heart, your memories are in my soul.'

Both girls thanked Kerry while paying and started heading out the door.

"Oh and girls?"

Sally and Becky both stopped at the door and faced Kerry.

"Let me know how it goes, be safe and blessed be." Kerry called to them.

"Blessed be to you Kerry." They said in unison and left the shop happily looking into in to their filled bag.

The girls left the shop and Kerry began collecting everything she needed to make the poppets.

Cindy made her way to Mikes farmhouse on the outskirts of the village. The cold crisp air highlighted her sense of dread and unease, which she had been feeling ever since she came to Wotton-Under-Edge. As she came to the lane which led to Mikes driveway, she stopped by the gate and looked down. Her brows furrowed as she pulled her leg back as to not step on what looked like a dead bird.

Bending down, the bird showed no signs of injury, there was no blood and no feathers had been pulled from the corpse. Cindy found herself drawn to the eyes of the bird. She realised there was no life there, however, the birds eyes had not clouded over. Sadness filled her as she pushed herself up and widened her eyes. Slowly but carefully she made her way up the driveway. Stepping around clumps and straddlers of dead bird corpses. When she reached the top of the driveway she could hear a deep muttering coming from the open garage.

"Mike?" Cindy called.

Mike walked near the entrance of the garage holding a shovel in his left hand.

"Cindy what you doing here?" Mike snorted, annoyed and intrigued by Cindy's appearance.

"Hey, Mike, erm there are loads of dead birds all up your driveway."

"I have seen." Mike interrupted her "Happens every year. Like they get to this area and just drop dead. But this year, I have never seen it like this, Ravens. All of them are I checked." Mike told her.

"You don't know why they do this?" Cindy asked.

"Tried to speak to the police to get them to speak to the environmental people. But I got laughed out of the station." Mike shrugged and walked over to a steel trash container and began shovelling up the dead birds and placing them into the trash can.

"Just burn them and wait to see if it happens again." Mike stopped shovelling and looked at Cindy, whose eyes followed the shovel to the trash can and back to the birds. "What are you doing here Cindy? Your Inn still isn't open, shame that is. But I know you haven't come all this way to ask where I am currently drinking." Mike leaned on the handle of the shovel and raised his eyebrows. "So?" He asked again.

Cindy moved her eyes from the birds and the trashcan and finally looked up at Mike.

"You are right. I didn't come here for that. I came to ask for something." Cindy replied with a sheepish smile. "I was wondering if I could have one of your horseshoes that you no longer need?" Cindy asked.

"A horseshoe?" Mike let out friendly laugh and lent the shovel against the trashcan. He flicked his head in a direction and began walking without saying anything to Cindy. Cindy followed him around to the stables and stopped at one of the stables when Mike told her he would go find one.

"Hey, aren't you a pretty thing" Cindy softly spoke. A beautiful grey horse raised its head and arched its neck at the sound of Cindy's voice. "Aren't you beautiful." She spoke again. The horse began walking to the gate of its stable with its muzzle down. "You can come here, I just want to say hi." Cindy watched as the horse flipped its head and circled the surrounding air with its nose. "You are so gorgeous, how are you today?" The horse flipped its head again and dropped its muzzle down to be closer to Cindy's hand.

"Seems like Georgie likes you." Mike said as he walked back towards Cindy. Cindy smiled, still stroking Georgie's muzzle.

"Well, I like you too Georgie." The horse flipped its muzzle in the air as a response.

"He's an old boy now, but still owns the fields round here." Mike said as he admired the horse. "Anyway, here" He held out a silver horseshoe to Cindy.

"Thank you so much Mike." Cindy told him as she accepted and took it out of his hands.

"It's alright, come now. I will walk you back to the road." Cindy said her goodbyes to Georgie and followed Mike out of the stables. "You and Marty staying at the Fernsby's place aren't you?" Mike broke the silence.

Cindy nodded her head.

"When do you think the Inn will be back open?"

Cindy didn't answer straight away, making sure she avoided stepping on any dead birds.

"I'm not sure." She confessed when they reached the end of the driveway. "I will let you know when I do." Cindy told him with a smile. Mike gave her one nod.

"Good, that place needs something doing to it, always had a bad vibe. But can't moan when the alcohol is there."

Mike sighed and looked at Cindy. "Look, I don't know what has been going on with that place, but I do know it's had more owners than I can count on my fingers. I am glad you have stuck around."

Cindy placed her hand on Mikes shoulder, she knew they had become good friends since she first moved to the town. She had a soft place in her heart for him, ever since he defended her when a group of men tried to cause a racial argument in the Inn. She thought back on that memory, he was already drunk, slumped over his fourth pint trying to read an out of date newspaper. But when the customers she were serving started making racial slurs, he was the first one to defend her and get them out of her Inn.

"Thank you, Mike. You are a good friend." Cindy said and gave his shoulder a squeeze. They said their goodbyes and Cindy took off back towards to the Fernsby's home.

Cindy was the last to arrive back late in the afternoon. The house was full of activity and the strong aroma of sandalwood filled the entire downstairs.

"Cindy is that you? We are in the study." Hadley called out.

Cindy hung her coat back up and stopped at the door which led to the basement. Hearing voices down there, she gripped the banister and descended the stairs. The smell of damp overtook the calmness of the sandalwood.

"Mommy!" Marty ran over to hug Cindy smiling "I've been helping Jace." He told her proudly.

Cindy smiled while she looked round the basement. All but one wall had been covered with wood panelling, leaving a stark contrast to the rock wall. The wooden flooring looked worn but intact and a humidifier could be heard humming in one of the corners. Light bulbs hung from the ceiling which gave the basement a warm but uninviting atmosphere.

"Luckily, Hadley's mom sorted out the drainage and added the paneling before she passed." Jace said. "Can't get rid of that damp smell though." He shrugged.

"They will live." Cindy said coldly as she walked around the basement. "So are we nearly done down here."

Jace gave one nod. "Aye, just need to bring down the cots and the food supplies. Kerry, Hadley and you will come down before they arrive and cast the protection room spell." He told her. "Come on kid, let's go get a drink, we have deserved a break." Jace said as he scooped up

Marty over his shoulder and both went laughing up the stairs.

Cindy followed the two out of the basement and shut the door behind her.

"Hey you okay?" Kerry asked her while walking out the kitchen with three drinks in her hands. Cindy blinked herself back into the present and nodded.

"Yeah sorry" She replied as she took one of the drinks from her friend.

"Hey, if you are worried, that's okay. But we can do this." Kerry told her. "Come on, we are about to start the poppets."

Cindy took a sip of the cold refreshing drink Kerry handed her and followed her into the study.

"You're back" Hadley said smiling as she saw Cindy walk in behind Kerry.

"Did you get what you went out for?"

Cindy walked over and placed her drink and bag onto the table.

"Hmmm" Cindy replied as she began rummaging through her bag. "Here" Cindy said as she handed over the horseshoe to the others.

"Did Mike wonder why you wanted it?" Kerry asked as she passed the horseshoe over to Hadley to look at.

"Not really no, but there was something strange over on his farm."

Hadley and Kerry both looked up and listened as Cindy told them about the dead birds and how there were more than there has ever been.

"Do you think it is something to do with the Orera?" Cindy asked after finishing off the details of her day. Hadley and Kerry both nodded their head.

"You said they were black?" Hadley asked. Cindy nodded her head

"Yeah, Mike was certain all of them were ravens."

"I fear for Hugin that he come not back. Nevertheless, more anxious am I for Munin." Hadley whispered.

"What does this mean?" Cindy asked.

"It is part of an old poem, ravens are the birds who tell Woden everything they see as they travel across the world at dawn." Kerry explained.

Jace had joined them in the study with a concerned and angry look on his face.

"It's a sign, she is showing us she is trying to block out the gods and making sure none of our souls leave this plane." Jace snarled.

Jace ran his hand through his hair sighing "Let's keep preparing." He suggested to the others. The women all nodded and Kerry began pulling black fabric out of her shopping bag.

"Right, so we need to make five of these. The easiest way is to make them into gingerbread men shape. Hadley you have a cutter right?"

Hadley nodded and went to fetch the cutter from one of the kitchens drawers. Once she came back into the study, Kerry got a white marker and began tracing ten gingerbread shapes. She gave each a piece of fabric with the two stencils neatly drawn on, and they all began cutting out the shapes. Cindy watched Kerry as she demonstrated how to do the close stitches, as to avoid bleeding of the poppet. Once Kerry was happy with everyone's stitching, she handed them each a black tourmaline and a teaspoon of birch bark. Watching everyone place the crystal and botanicals into the poppet, Kerry nodded, pleased with everything.

"Okay we will sew them up when they arrive, but last thing we need to do is draw on the sigil for banishing." Kerry demonstrated to Cindy as they watched her draw on the legs of the poppet.

"Perfect." She told them, when everything looked finished.

"Great, let me put these away somewhere Chewy can not eat them." Hadley said as she collected the figures and placed them in a locked cupboard below her altar. "Right." Hadley turned around as she clasped her hands together.

"Cindy we are going to show you how we make the light bombs." Jace saw Cindy look at the time and placed his hand on her shoulder

"Don't worry, i'll look after him tonight. We can drive and pick up some food and I'll even sort the animals out." Jace said.

"My hero" Hadley gushed bringing her hand to her heart. Cindy laughed and thanked Jace before going to tell Marty the plan for the evening.

Once they heard the front door shut the women congregated in the kitchen as they began prepping for their next assignment. Hadley brought the cauldron over and Kerry helped her lift it onto the countertop.

"Right, this will not harm her. But confuse and hopefully stun her. Which should give us enough time to get to the fireplace, find the coffin, stab the familiar and burn it" Hadley listed off.

"Is that all?" Kerry nudged Cindy with her elbow smiling. As quickly as the smile came across Kerrys face, it quickly disappeared.

Breaking the tension Hadley went over to the parlour and collected a large tub of water. She saw Cindy watching as she emptied the whole contents into the cauldron.

"It is moon water." Hadley explained "The moon was full and luckily, it was raining so Jace and I took the cauldron outside to collect it. We used it the night I dream hopped."

"But why the full moon?" Cindy asked as she wrote down notes.

"You can do this with any phase of the moon, but the full moon is best. It is when we release all that stands in our way, it will help protect us."

When the cauldron was full, Hadley asked Kerry to grind up some frankincense.

"Frankincense will give us protection. Spirituality and most importantly it is linked to the fire element." Hadley explained to Cindy as she watched Kerry grind the herb up with the pestle and mortar.

"So it will set alight?" Cindy asked looking up from her notes.

"No, no." Hadley explained, as Kerry handed her the mortar. "Because it is linked to the fire element, it will be the key to helping us set the familiar on fire. Once it is complete, we will pour our potion over the blade of the athame, and once stuck in the familiars body, we can then set it alight."

Cindy wrote more notes as she watched Hadley tip the frankincense into the cauldron. A cloud of white smoke rose into the kitchen and quickly disappeared.

"And that is another reason we are using frankincense." Kerry laughed. "When we throw them, that smoke will stop that Orera in her tracks."

Cindy nodded and drew an illustration of smoke coming from the cauldron.

"Lastly, we need two labradorite crystals." Hadley told Kerry. Kerry nodded and pulled out two crystals which had a dark base with metallic blues, greens and yellows inside.

"Wow they are beautiful." Cindy said, putting her hand out to hold one. Kerry handed her one of the crystals and placed the other on the counter top.

"What is the story behind these?" Cindy asked, still memorised by the beauty of the crystal.

"Well, legend says the Aurora Borealis became trapped inside when a warrior tried to break the rocks to free the light. But it caused the light to crystallise inside them forever." Kerry told her.

"Yes, and that light inside is what we need for these." Hadley found two tea towels and two hammers and placed them in front of Kerry and Cindy.

"Place the crystal on the tea towel and fold it in half." Hadley instructed "Now bang it into as many pieces as you can. But do not open the tea towel."

Kerry and Cindy began smashing the hammer against the crystal until they could feel tiny shrapnels through the cloth.

"Excellent" Hadley said as she picked up one of the tea towels carefully, without exposing the crystal pieces to the air she poured the pieces into the potion. Cindy watched as small shimmering lights began swimming around the inside of the cauldron.

"Wow" Cindy gasped as she watched Hadley tipped in Kerrys crystal pieces.

Hadley began stirring the potion.

"Cindy can you go and grab a few white potion balls and a few white potion bottles please?"

When Cindy returned after a few trips Hadley called her over to the cauldron and placed one hand in Kerrys and the other in Cindy's.

"Okay repeat after me," Hadley instructed them.

"Goddess Freya, mother of love and battle. Bless this potion for what is to come. Endow it with power and positive energy. Guide us through this battle with Woden by your side. Now bless this potion, So mote it be".

The three women watched as the potion bubbled and the light from the crystal fragments shined brighter.

"Right, lets fill up the balls and the bottles." Hadley instructed. When the potion was emptied, the women placed all the filled bottles and glass balls safely in Hadley's walk in altar room.

CHAPTER TWENTY-FIVE

"Make sure the horseshoe ends are pointing downwards." Cindy told Marty as she helped him pin it to the basement door.

"What do you think Jace?" Marty asked as he jumped down from the chair to admire his handiwork. Jace ruffled Martys curly hair, which had come to be a regular gesture since Marty moved in.

"No one could have done it better than you." He responded. "Now help me carry the supplies down to the basement. Hadley and Kerry should be done with blessing the room by now."

Marty picked up two pillows and followed Jace down into the basement.

"Are we ok to come down?" Jace called as he stopped halfway down.

"Yeah you can come down." Hadley called back.

Hadley and Kerry had spent hours preparing the basement and going back through their old books of what really worked to warn off witches centuries ago. With help from Cindy, they were able to collect hazelnuts which they placed under each cot. Cindy was able to find a large collection of used brass bells in an overcrowded antique shop. Which they decided to place one on each step going down to the basement. On the walls they painted protective symbols and opposite the cots they placed a wooden table and a few chairs.

"Cindy can you draw a pentacle on the floor by the table and chairs please?" Hadley asked as she handed over a small tin of white paint and paint brush.

Cindy nodded and drew the pentacle without taking the paintbrush off the floor.

"I shall be right back." Hadley told the others and quickly walked up the basement stairs. The house had a calm atmosphere which was only interrupted by the sounds of Chewy's paws scrapping across the wooden hallway floor as he slept.

Hadley took a deep breath and walked into the study, a purpose took over her stance, she knew what she came in for, yet a small voice in her head was trying to flood her with doubt. As she lifted the clip on an old wooden box, an old pagan tune her mother used to hum to her when she couldn't sleep played. The dark velvet lining still shimmered when light touched it. The only thing which lay on top of the lining was an old silver skeleton key; which she hadn't seen since her mother died.

The key looked old, used far too many times, passed down for centuries by hers and her mothers ancestors. Hadley took the key out the box and walked over to the far side of room. Tracing her finger along the wooden panelling of the walls, Hadley stopped and crouched as her finger found a thin piece of covering. Feeling the burn in her knees as she crouched there longer than she wanted to, Hadley eventually ripped off the covering revealing a pure silver lock. With shaking hands, Hadley entered the key into the lock and turned until she heard a soft click. The door opened to a tiny black space, Hadley could see old dust covering the no longer liveable spiderwebs and an untouched layer of dust which covered the floor. Leaning in so her fingers could sweep the walls to find the light switch, Hadley coughed as a cobweb fell from the roof and landed in front of her face.

Eventually, the light flickered on and Hadley saw what she had opened the secret room for. A dozen witch bottles which had been passed down. The oldest bottle was filled with urine and menstrual blood, along with bones and teeth. Hadley smiled at the memory of her mother explaining why these bottles were made and hidden in secrecy. Hadley took a breath in through her nose and sighed. She knew they were used for protection and although her and Kerry had done everything possible to protect themselves within their home. She couldn't resist the call from her ancestors about using her witch bottle.

"Kerry, Cindy, can you come up here?" She shouted.

Within seconds Kerry and Cindy both rushed into the study, their breaths heavy after running up the stairs.

"What's wrong?" Kerry said breathless. Hadley folded her lips in to stop a laugh escaping as she watched Cindy panting against the study doorframe.

"I am so sorry, I didn't mean for it to come out as an emergency. I just wanted you guys up here." Hadley apologetically told them as she held out her hands to them. Cindy and Kerry walked over concerned but each took one of Hadley's hands.

"Look." Hadley said pulling them closer, so they would also be having to sit on the floor with her. Cindy pushed her head forward wanting to get a better view of inside the dimly lit space.

"What are these?" She asked, while pulling out one of the bottles. The bottle was old, filled with a brown coloured liquid. The top was sealed shut with wax proving it had never been opened.

"Witches bottles." Kerry said as she took another one out. Kerry examined the contents of the bottle, the liquid looked clear.

"That one was my mothers." Hadley smiled. "It has seawater, a skeleton key, some pine needles, a few drops of her blood and chips of black obsidian."

"So who does this one belong to and why does it look all..?" Cindy pulled a disgusted face as she continued to examine the bottle.

"This one," Hadley told her "belonged to one of my ancestors. My mother told me inside that one is urine, menstrual blood, teeth, a key, some needles and I have never seen it, but apparently there are some bones of a dead animal in there." Hadley smiled as she saw Cindy look up, wide eyed and her mouth parting as she processed the information Hadley had just told her. Kerry laughed and took it off Cindy to examine it herself.

"Why is there urine and blood in there?" Cindy asked, wiping her hands on her clothes.

"Many believe that the maker of the jar should add his or her urine, and if the woman is bleeding, well then that made the jar even more powerful." Kerry explained. "And you're right, I don't see any bones in there, but teeth and what looks like a broken mirror." Kerry put the bottle back in the space.

"So I think we should make our own." Hadley smiled. "What do you think? I have the perfect bottles for us to use."

Kerry smiled and nodded her head, when Hadley turned to look at Cindy a light joyful laugh filled the room.

"Don't worry, we new present day witches don't use urine or menstrual blood." Hadley reassured her. "However, if you are on…"

Kerry laughed at Cindy's face as she helped Hadley put all the witches bottles back in their secret confined place. Hadley locked the door and placed the skeleton key in her pocket.

"Come, lets make our own." Hadley said as she led them into the kitchen. Jace and Marty were sitting at the table drinking something hot which smelt like vanilla. Marty smiled as he saw his mother walk in.

"Mommy, Jace made me some hot milk but put some vanilla in." He told her with glee. Cindy walked over and kissed him on the top of his head.

"It smells define, can I taste?" Cindy asked. Marty happily handed over the mug and watched as his mother took a sip of his drink.

"It is lovely, but you enjoy it." Cindy told him as she placed the mug back onto the table. Hadley had gathered three round small glass bottles and placed them on the kitchen counter.

"Okay girls, or should I say witches." Hadley announced.

Cindy laughed as Kerry rolled her eyes with a faint smile. Hadley showed them how they must first add the needles and pins to the halfway point. She watched them do the same and continued with showing them to add the salt to purify the rusty nails and needles. After, she then added in the rosemary and finished by pouring in the red wine.

"Okay now we need to mark the jars as our territory." Cindy burrowed her eyebrows.

"This isn't where we pee in the bottle is it?" Cindy said.

Hadley shook her head and pricked her finger with a sharp needle, letting a few drops fall into the bottle.

"Come on Cind's" Kerry encouraged her by passing her the needle. "You need to consecrate the wine and let a few drops of blood fall." Kerry told her. Cindy nodded and let her blood fall into the bottle.

"Perfect, now we need to seal the lid." Hadley said as she lit a black candle and dripped the hot wax around, making sure the wax firmly held the lid in place. Hadley handed the candle to the others, and they all followed Hadley's instructions.

"Now we place them with the others." Hadley said while walking out the kitchen back into the study.

When all three witch bottles were safely locked away, they all joined Jace and Marty back in the kitchen.

"Hadley?" Marty said. Hadley smiled as she sat next to Jace

"Yes, Marty?" She asked, knowing his curiosity could not be tamed.

"Why did you put all that in a jar?" Hadley put her forearms on the table and lent forward.

"Well, it is said the needles and pins once purified by the salt, will capture the evil by impaling them. And because they are impaled they will drown in the wine and then be removed by the rosemary." Hadley leaned back and rested her head on Jace's shoulder.

"So did you finish the basement?" Kerry asked.

"Aye, it is all done. All we have to do now is wait for them to come."

The mood suddenly dropped as everyone thought of what was to come in the next few days.

"Hey I know." Cindy said trying to cut the tension. "Why don't we carve them pumpkins Kerry and Jace brought back? It is Halloween in a couple of days after all."

Marty shot up excited with the prospect of pumpkin carving.

"I think that's a braw idea, ready to see who carves the best pumpkins you wee rascal?" Jace teased as he started bringing the pumpkins to the kitchen table.

Kerry had placed old newspaper down as a table covering, while Cindy collected knives and spoons for the activity.

"I'll sort the animals out." Hadley announced as she moved away from the table and collected the animals' food bowls. When the metal scoop went inside the dog food bag, Chewy came running in closely followed by Kerrys cat. Hadley loved how normal the small simple things felt, however, she knew if the animals waited any longer all hell would break loose. Giving Chewy the command to sit, she placed the bowl on his mat and quickly filled the cat bowl with kibble and placed it next to Chewy. Once certain the animals were taken care off, Hadley joined the others round the kitchen table. The smell of pumpkin filled the room, as everyone began scooping and placing the once insides in a pile soaking through the newspaper. Chewy made his way under the table, scoffing down anything Marty dropped on the floor. Once the Pumpkins were nothing more than shells, Jace handed out pens and everyone began predesigning their pumpkins, before using the knives.

"They look great." Cindy smiled, after Jace had lit the last candle and placed the top back onto one of the pumpkins. They all stood in front of the house as their pumpkins filled up the stairs and front porch.

"What do you think Marty?" Cindy asked as she huddled up to her son. Marty looked round at the group who were all smiling at him and began crying.

"Hey, hey, hey, what's wrong? Do you not like them?" Cindy asked bending down to be eye level with him. Through sobs Marty shook his head and began wiping his nose with his coat sleeve.

"No, I like them." He replied, clearly embarrassed as he hid his face in his mothers shoulder.

"Then why are you crying?" Cindy said putting her arms around him and rubbing his back.

"They look really cool, but we are doing it early because of the demon aren't we?" Marty said, lifting his head to look round at the group. "What if we don't get to do this again, or someone gets hurt?" Martys words took everyone by surprise, and a feeling of guilt rippled through them all.

"Marty" Hadley said. "We will be able to do this again, I promise." Hadley knelt down to take the Marty into a hug. "Shall we go in and get some hot chocolate, now we have seen our pumpkins come to life?" Marty nodded and let Hadley lead him inside the house. Jace walked into the house next until Cindy and Kerry were the only ones left outside.

"Okay hun?" Kerry asked.

Cindy rubbed her hands over her face and nodded her head. Knowing Cindy was lying, Kerry wrapped her arm over Cindy's shoulders and walked her inside the house.

As soon as they walked in the house, the atmosphere instantly changed to calm. Marty could be heard laughing in the kitchen with Jace and Hadley. The animals were lounging in the living room, and Kerry had sat on the stairs to remove her boots.

"You can talk to us, you know?" Kerry said, pulling Cindy out of her mind. "You are not alone anymore, we are a coven now, a family. Hadley, you and I are sisters. And sisters do not let their sisters go through things alone. Personal, spiritual and everything in-between" Cindy wrapped her arms around herself, as she let the words Kerry had told her sink in.

"I just hate my baby feeling all these emotions. Emotions a child should never have to feel." Cindy leant up against the hallway wall and closed her eyes.

"True." Kerry agreed. "Hadley saw a demon kill her mother from the inside, our ancestors watched their villages be burnt to the ground, some were murdered, some were raped, others were taken as slaves. But if all of them let that destroy their souls. They wouldn't have survived, we wouldn't have the stories. Marty is a strong child, with a strong group of protectors around him." Kerry stood up and looked towards the kitchen. "Listen to that, he is already laughing, and he will sleep safely tonight. I think he would make great demonologist." Kerry nudged Cindy with her elbow and smiled. Cindy sighed and began walking towards the kitchen.

"Do not let him hear you say that." She pointed her finger to Kerry. Kerry demonstrated zipping her lips shut as she joined the others in the kitchen.

Hadley woke up early the morning the invited guests were to come round. As she left the main bathroom she ran into Kerry who was already washed and dressed.

"Couldn't sleep either?" Hadley smiled as she took note of Kerrys outfit.

"Like it?" Kerry did a twirl to show her black and purple long sleeved dress.

"Its beautiful" Hadley noted. "I'm gonna go get changed, can you put the coffee machine on please?"

Kerry nodded, called the animals and walked down the stairs. Hadley knew she wanted to make the impression of authority when Evelyn and the others came. Quietly, as to not wake up Jace, she crossed the bedroom to open up her wardrobe. She pulled out her favourite black ritual dress and quickly slipped it on and left Jace to sleep a little longer.

"Wow, you look amazing." Kerry said as she poured two mugs of coffee. Hadley smiled and thanked her. She took the mug off the counter and walked out of the kitchen into the study with Kerry close behind her.

"Are we sure everything is ready?" Hadley asked, frantically going over the notes they had produced over the last couple of days.

"Yes, we checked and checked, and then we checked again. Hadley we got this." Kerry reassured her. "We have even topped up the protection around the house, we have extended the protection line so Chewy can still go outside. Everything is prepared."

Hadley nodded and sat on one of the chairs.

"This is the easy part right?" Hadley spoke to the room.

"Think so." Kerry shrugged.

Hadley pulled the book which contained the Orera over to her and began flicking through the pages.

"I would give anything for this to be over."

Kerry walked over to look at the page Hadley had stopped on and closed the book.

"The gods and goddesses will be with us, wishing for something else will not make it happen." Chewy walked in to the study and placed his head on Hadley's thigh.

"I know" She said. "We should get the others up, they will be here soon."

CHAPTER TWENTY-SIX

After a few hours of debating whether anyone would show up, a knock on the front door made everyone except for Marty walk into the hallway. Hadley got to the front door first and looked behind her before she opened. With encouraging nods, Hadley turned back to the door and casually opened it. Hadley began counting how many were stood on her front porch.

"Five, thank you for all coming." Hadley said.

Evelyn began to walk inside until Hadley put a hand up to stop her.

"Before you come in, there are rules in which you will all need to follow."

Father Anderson scoffed and crossed his arms over his chest.

"As I was saying, you will come into the house one at a time. Once in, you will be led to the bathroom, where you will shower and salt cleanse yourselves."

"This is ridiculous!" Benjamin snarled.

"You will do as you are asked. You have given up your right when it comes to dealing with the Orera".

Hadley turned to Cindy, ignoring the eruption on the porch. "Can you please take Evelyn and show her what she needs to do." Cindy nodded and led Evelyn into the main bathroom on the ground floor. "Kerry, Jace and I will keep watch out here, until the next one is called in. Please sit." Hadley gestured to the front porch furniture.

"Why must we have a shower with salt? I have never heard anything so ridiculous in my life." Annie protested.

"The salt shower will cleanse you, before you are taken into the protected locked room. You will also be putting on some old clothes we found which will have no connection to the Orera." Kerry told them.

Cindy opened the door and called for Jane to come into the house. When she wouldn't stand Hadley stood up and glared at her until she eventually followed Cindy inside.

"I am not going along with this." Father Anderson muttered to Benjamin.

"Oh but you are." Hadley said. "If we have to force you into that house, we will. We do not want to cause harm to any of you. But if you do not do what we ask, we will use what ever means we have." Father Anderson sat up straight his eyes never leaving Hadley's.

"Okay next one." Cindy called.

Eventually, everyone was in the basement except the Father and Jace.

"You expect us to sleep down here?" Benjamin said as he made his way down the basement stairs.

"Sit down on what ever cot you want and be quiet." Kerry ordered.

Hadley kept her eyes on the women, they were all wearing clothes Hadley had picked up from a local charity shop a few days prior. The twins usual elegant persona was now washed away as they looked round the room. The symbols drawn on the walls and floors stood out and Hadley saw Evelyn eyeing the poppets on the table.

"What are they?" Evelyn asked. But Hadley ignored her as Jace brought the Father down. Father Andersons eyes opened wide.

"Satanists! You aren't here to stop the Orera, you are probably working with her."

Hadley saw Kerry roll her eyes and laughed. "Father, you know we are not satanists. Wiccan, Pagan, yes. But Satanists, no. And we aren't going to sacrifice you, human sacrifice has long been drawn out in our beliefs. Besides, we wouldn't sacrifice a monster like you to our gods. Now sit." She ordered.

Hadley passed a pair of scissors to Kerry.

"So, I am supposed to ask some questions before either of us cast a spell. Kerry and Cindy will help me answer them, Jace will be watching in case either of you do not let Kerry cut a piece of your hair."

"What?"

Hadley put her hand in the air. "First question, what are the possible outcomes of this spell? Cindy what do you think?"

Cindy tilted her head to the side as she watched Kerry cut a lock of Evelyn's hair. "The possible outcome is we stop another murder."

"I think that's a good answer don't you?" Hadley spoke to everyone in the room. "Next question, are we manipulating someone else's free will? Kerry, you can answer this one." Kerry snipped a lock of Janes hair.

"We might be, but I am sure the gods and goddesses will forgive us if we save someone else's life."

Hadley nodded "Would I be willing to cause the outcome without a spell? Let's ask Jace." Hadley noticed Jace had not taken his eyes off of Benjamin or the Father since they came down to the basement.

"Jace"? Hadley said.

"Sorry sweetheart" He smiled at her. "Would we be willing to cause the outcome without the spell? Absolutely not."

"Thank you." Hadley smiled. "And lastly, is there an easier way to do this?" Hadley watched Kerry cut the mens finger nails and walk back to her.

"No, there isn't. This is the only way we think we can stop this." Hadley took a deep breath and stood up.

"Thank you, Kerry."

Kerry put the hair and finger nails in front of each poppet. Hadley picked up the first one and the lock of hair placed in front of it.

"These are called poppets." Hadley held up the little figure in her hand. "Kerry snipped your hair or cut your nails because we need a piece of you to link to the poppet." Hadley held up the lock of hair in her other hand. "Who does this belong to Kerry?"

Kerry looked at it and pointed to Evelyn. Hadley nodded her head and smiled.

"What we do now is we add the hair into the poppet like so." Hadley reached back to the table and picked up the needle and thread and quickly closed the opening.

"Now this is connected to you Evelyn. Cindy, can you please pass me the black cord."

Everyone stared at Hadley as Cindy passed her a black cord, she could see terror and anger in each of their eyes.

"Evelyn, you are bound to cause no harm, not to me, not to yourself and not to others. Evelyn, you are bound to cause no harm, not to me, not to yourself and not to others. Evelyn, you are bound to cause no harm, not to me, not to yourself and not to others."

Hadley repeated the binding spell until the whole poppet was covered with the black cord. Once she had finished the first poppet, Hadley placed it in a woven basket and did the same spell on the three other poppets.

"You should be paraded through the streets, and sent to the gallows." Father Anderson spat as he watched Hadley place his finger nails into the final poppet.

"Father, the last woman to be hung in the United Kingdom for witchcraft was in 1727. Your ancestors may be proud of you for saying that. But how could they if they too were feeding children to a demon witch?" Hadley sewed up the poppet and began binding the poppet.

"Father, you are bound to cause no harm, not to me, not to yourself and not to others. Father, you are bound to cause no harm, not to me, not to yourself and not to others. Father, you are bound to cause no harm, not to me, not to yourself and not to others"

When she finished she gave the basket to Kerry and Cindy.

"Go bury these outside, each one in a separate grave and a rock placed on top." They both nodded and left the basement. "Now that is done, you will not be able to harm another child in this town. And in two days time, we are going to send the Orera back into the dark realm and let those children's souls finally be free."

"So we just have to stay down here like prisoners?" Benjamin snarled.

Jace moved closer to Hadley and placed his hand on the small of the back.

"I think this will be the last nice place you will sleep in, for a very long time." Hadley told them and let Jace guide her up the basement stairs.

"You can't leave us down here. Please Hadley." Evelyn said standing at the bottom of the stairs. Hadley turned back to the basement as anger boiled up inside her. Jace tried to stop her but she turned her head to stop him.

In his defence Jace held up his hands and stayed on the stairs as Hadley marched back down.

"Please Hadley. Please Hadley. You do not get to plead." She hissed at Evelyn.

Evelyn looked taken aback and moved back towards the cots and the others.

"What would your god and goddess think of you?" Evelyn asked.

Jace had walked down after hearing Evelyn's remark and stood next to Hadley.

"What do you know of our gods? Do you think yours will forgive all of you for what you have done?" Hadley said.

"We won't know until that time comes, but we have protected more lives by eliminating others." Father Anderson added.

"How can you justify any of this? You can't play god. And you will stay in this basement until we sort out the mess you have continued."

"Just like her mother."

"What did you just say"? Hadley walked closer to the Benjamin.

"Don't you dare speak of my mother."

Jace grabbed Hadley by the waist and moved her towards the stairs.

"She believed her powers could save this town and look what happened to her." Benjamin called out.

Jace gripped Hadley tightly and carried her up the stairs as she tried to wriggle herself out of his grasp.

"What is going on?" Kerry said as she and Cindy stood in the hallway.

"Shut and lock the door." Jace ordered as he moved a screaming Hadley further away from the basement. Kerry ran to the basement door and once shut she locked it. Cindy walked over to Kerry unsure what do to as Jace tried to calm down Hadley.

"Mommy, what's happening?" Marty said from the stairs looking through the railing. Cindy and Kerry both looked up surprised by the new voice.

"It's okay, Hadley is just a little upset." Cindy tried to assure him, through the continuous screams which were leaving the study. Kerry bit her bottom lip, before deciding to take charge of the situation. She told Cindy to take Marty and go pick up something for them all to eat, and she would sort the animals out. As she made her way into the kitchen she whistled and waited a couple of seconds. As the seconds passed, Kerry could hear Hadley screaming along with things smashing in the study.

"Hey buddy," She said to Chewy as he came running into the kitchen followed by Nugget. "Shall we get you guys some food?" The animals both looked up and sat obediently waiting for Kerry to put their food bowls down on the floor. Once that task was done, Kerry took some breaths and opened the door to the study.

"How dare they mention my mother." Hadley said putting her head in her hands.

"Hadley you are giving them what they want. They want you to get angry, so you make a mistake and they can carry on doing what they have always done."

Hadley looked up and saw Kerry cleaning up the destruction she had created.

"Kez, you don't need to do that." Hadley stood up and took the books off Kerry.

"You're right I don't. Which is why you are going to sort this mess out, and I am going to make you some camomile tea." With a smile, Kerry left the study and headed to the kitchen.

"What just happened?" Hadley said, her face solemn. Jace lifted her chin and placed a soft kiss on her lips.

"Talk to me."

Hadley sighed at his question and shook her head.

"I don't know. I know my mom tried to help and look what happened, she opened another portal and let another demon in. She was a strong witch Jace."

She rested her head on Jace's chest, and he brought his arms up to wrap around her.

"I know, but she didn't know what she was up against. And you have your sisters to help you." Jace reassured her.

"You should believe him Had's. We are going to do this, and we are going to make your mother proud." Kerry told her as she walked in with the tea tray. "Here, this will calm you." Kerry told her as she poured three cups of camomile tea. Hadley finished cleaning up the study then joined Jace and Kerry at the table.

"Where is Cindy and Marty?" Jace asked.

"I sent them on a food run, they should be back soon."

"Wonder if them lot down there will enjoy the rations we left for them."

"Hadley" Kerry laughed.

Hadley shrugged and looked towards the basement door.

"When do you think the Orera will notice she can't get to them?" Kerry asked. Hadley turned back round and placed her elbows on the table to rest her head on her hands.

"I think she may realise something is not right tonight. She will attempt to connect with them tomorrow and come the thirtieth; she will be in complete panic mode when she cannot connect to any of them." Hadley bit her bottom lip as she thought about her words. "That's when we go in and end this." Kerry and Jace nodded their heads in unison.

"Woden will guide us in this battle." Kerry said.

"Aye, the all father, god of battle and wisdom will be with us." Jace told them. "I trow that I hung on a windy tree, swung there all nights of nine. Gashed with a blade bloodied by Woden, myself. An offering to myself knotted to that tree. No man knows whither the root of it runs. None gave me bread, none gave me drink. Down to the depths I peered to snatch up runes, with a roaring screech and fall in a dizzied faint. Wellbeing I won and wisdom too and grew and joyed in my growth. From a word to a word, I was led to a word. From a deed to another deed."

CHAPTER TWENTY-SEVEN

Rubbing her eyes as she made her way downstairs the following morning. Hadley abruptly stopped when she saw Jace by the basement door.

"Morning my love, do I dare ask what you are doing?" Jace kept his ear placed on the door and put his index finger up to his lips. Pulling up one of her eyebrows, Hadley joined Jace, pulled her hair away from her ear and placed it up against the door. Hadley closed her eyes hoping her hearing would help pick up whatever Jace was hearing

"Jace" She whispered, "I don't hear anything."

She saw Jace hold up his hand instead of answering her. Annoyed by his lack of communication she huffed and placed her ear back onto the door. After a few more minutes Hadley's eyes widened as she began hearing a rumble from the other side of the door. Wanting to hear more, she pressed her whole body up to the door and covered her free ear with one of her hands.

Hadley could feel her heartbeat pick up, she felt her breathing become shallow and her body involuntary begin to shake. She could see Jace was beginning to sweat, the muscles in his back had tensed as he listened to whatever was behind the basement door.

Faintly she could hear nails being scratched onto something solid until they began tapping in threes. A slow steady rhythm. Hadley could feel her throat begin to close up, saliva struggled to pass down her throat.

The tapping continued, the sound was getting closer to the door. Hadley wanted to move away from the door, but some part of her wanted to know what was happening. She could sense Jace also wanted to leave the door, but his body was stopping him as he remained pressed to the door.

Tap, tap, tap.

Hadley tried picturing what or who could be doing making the noise.

Tap, tap, tap.

The sound of the noise traveled up the basement stairs.

Tap, tap, tap.

Hadley felt hot, her hands had become clammy and her feet stuck to the wooden hallway floor. Tap, tap, tap. The top basement stair creaked. Hadley lost the ability to breathe. She was consumed with what was happening behind this locked door.

Tap Tap……

"What are you guys doing?"

Jace jumped back knocking Hadley off balance, and she fell to the floor. Cindy looked at them both confused and concerned.

"Are you two okay?" She held her hand to Hadley who finally let out a breath and accepted the help.

"There was" Hadley looked at Jace for what to say.

"Noise, there was a strange noise coming from the basement." He said wiping the sweat from his forehead.

Hadley pinched the bridge of her nose, "We need to all have a meeting." Hadley looked down at her damp sweat stained shirt and without saying another word went back upstairs and shut the bathroom door behind her.

"Jace why don't you go shower and change? I'll sort everyone out. We can speak about it when we are all ready." Cindy put a reassuring hand on Jace's arm as she looked at the basement door and back to Jace. "Go, everything will be fine."

Cindy left Jace in the hallway and started making breakfast for everyone, she fed the animals and took Chewy out into the garden. When she came back inside, no one had yet reemerged back downstairs. The look on both Hadley and Jace's face flashed in Cindy's mind as she stared through the kitchen door to the locked basement door. The house seemed quiet and Cindy could no longer stand there and wait for something to happen. Quickly she kicked off her outdoor shoes and ran into the study and pulled out a herbalism book.

She remembered reading about one particular herb which creates a barrier against negative energies, one they would sometimes use in exorcisms. Once she found the name, Cindy rushed to where Hadley kept all her herbs and frantically searched the cupboard. Cindy picked up the mortar and pestle and began crushing the herb into small fragments. Cindy was unsure as to whether this would work, but seeing her friends faces and knowing her son was living in this house. A surge of needing to protect the ones she loved overcame her. The sweet smell of the herb filled the room as she infused it with hot water.

'Protection against evil and negative spirits and energies. Attracts purely positive energies' she reminded herself as she took an empty jar outside to fill it with soil. Once back inside she checked the water had cooled down, when she was happy with the temperature Cindy mixed the herb water into the soil and mixed them together.

"Hail to Jord, mother of Thor who gave to her son her strength and her solidity. Goddess of dirt and sturdy stone, of moss and roots and buried bones. Of seed and stem, of cave and plain, of every patch on which we step, on which we live our lives. Upon your flesh we stand. We laugh and weep, couple and contend. Suffer the bitter and savour the sweet. Birth our babies, teach our children, bury our dead. All our joys and sorrows, all that we love and fear, all that we ever know, all comes from you. Mighty Jord, encompassing goddess, we honour you and I ask you to bless this soil. So mote it be."

Happy with the result, Cindy walked over to the basement door. Her left hand began to shake uncontrollably while she tried to unlock the door. A sickness inside of Cindy rose from her stomach and into her throat. She could feel her fingertips losing their grip on the glass jar as she fiddled with the lock on the basement door. Eventually, the lock pulled to the side, and the door clicked open. Taking a deep breath Cindy slightly opened the door, she could see the lights were on, but could hear no movement. Another deep breath, and she opened the door fully so she could see the top stair. Deciding now was the time, Cindy kneeled down and scooped out some mixture to spread across the floor. Scooping up a few more handfuls she threw the mixture down the stairs.

"What are you doing?"

Cindy jumped and looked to where the voice came from.

"Is there anything I can do to help?" Evelyn asked standing at the bottom of the stairs looking up to try and see what Cindy was doing. Cindy ignored her and inspected her work not wanting to look down at Evelyn.

"I'm sorry we tried to trick you and Marty."

Cindy stopped and thumped her fist down on the stair.

"You do not get to apologise to me or my son."

"Why bother talking to her Evelyn, she is one of them now. She should be hung like her sisters." Benjamin said to Evelyn as he walked behind her and looked up at Cindy.

Cindy stood up and scooped one more handful of the mixture in her hand and threw it to the bottom of the stairs. Not wanting to know if it hit them or not, Cindy made quick work of leaving the basement and locking the door behind her. Taking a different type of breath, one filled with satisfaction and a new sense of belonging, Cindy emptied the rest of her herb spell by putting the mixture on the frame of the door and finishing with the lock.

"Thank you for your blessing and your help during this time, so mote it be."

"So mote it be."

Cindy swirled round and saw Hadley and Kerry staring at her smiling.

"Angelica herb, also known as the holy ghost. I'm impressed" Kerry said.

"What gave you the idea to use such a powerful herb?" Hadley asked.

Cindy walked into the kitchen to clean up the mess she had made while putting together her spell.

"Well, seeing yours and Jace's face earlier made me realise I need to step up and do something. When I was doing the spell, I felt Goddess Jord. I felt her presence it felt amazing; I felt strong. When I was in the basement Benjamin said something about me joining her sisters now and.." Cindy shrugged unable to find a word to describe how she felt in that moment.

Hadley and Kerry smiled at each other and both wrapped their arms around her.

"So proud of you Cinds" Hadley told her.

Hadley and Kerry helped Cindy clean up the now cold breakfast and quickly cooked up something for Marty to eat before he started complaining.

"Cindy I heard you asked Goddess Jord for her blessing on a spell today" Jace said as they all sat around the kitchen table. Cindy smiled and nodded her head unable to speak due to still chewing the food in her mouth.

"How do you feel about being in a coven Kerry?" Everyone looked at Kerry

"Why do you ask that Jace?"

Jace smiled and shrugged, "Well I could ask Hadley as well, you are both used to being solidity witches, and now you are in a coven."

Hadley narrowed her eyes at Jace, confused at his questions.

"I guess I have been used to being a solitary witch for many years, but that is because I never found my true coven. Never trusted anyone, never clicked with anyone to call my sisters." Kerry stopped speaking and smiled at Hadley and Cindy.

"But I'm proud to be in our little coven and after tomorrow, we will be stronger than ever." Hadley raised her can of coke.

"To the White Tree Coven"

"To the White Tree Coven" everyone else cheered.

"I have put Marty to bed with Chewy, they're watching television with snacks." Cindy told the others when she walked into the study "Thank you for making today nice and easy for him, he knows what is going to happen tomorrow. So I wanted one more day of normal."

Hadley took Cindy's hand as she sat down and give a slight squeeze.

"You don't need to thank us, we all love Marty, and we promised we would keep him safe." Cindy put her other hand over Hadley's and thanked her.

"You ready Jace?" Kerry said looking behind her where Jace was setting up something.

"What is going on?" Cindy asked as she strained her neck to get a better view.

"Well, because you are one of us now, and us Pagans and Wiccans believe in art and how it can increase our power to protect us. We thought it was time you got your first taste of our culture." Hadley explained, "Jace was taught by his father, who was taught by his father and so on."

"So it's not a gun?" Cindy looked worried as she took in the information Hadley was telling her

"No, it's called stick and poke. Of course, you don't have to do this if you don't want to?"

Cindy looked at her new family and shook her head.

"No, I want to do this. I am proud of being one of you." Jace called her over and patted the seat he had set up for her.

"So what am I getting done, the same as you and Kerry?" Hadley and Kerry pulled chairs over and sat next to Cindy.

"Yeah, you'll get the same as us." Kerry told her, "The main one we want you to get is the anti possession one."

Kerry and Hadley both showed her the design they had on their chest. The symbol was a simple pentacle with two delicate wings on either side and the Algiz protection symbol connected to the bottom of the pentacle.

"Its beautiful" Cindy said as she studied the design. Cindy pulled off her jumper and sat back down in her vest top "Okay lets start."

As Jace got to work on marking Cindy, she winced and put her hand out for Hadley to grab hold of.

"Just squeeze if it gets to painful, it will be over soon."

Cindy nodded her head and closed her eyes, taking in deep breaths to try and disassociate from the constant prodding of the needle.

"Can we talk about something to try and distract me?" Cindy pleaded.

Kerry got up from her chair and told them she would be right back. Hadley rolled her eyes as she heard the fridge door open and close and the clink of the bottle tops hitting the kitchen counter.

"We cannot have a story without a drink, plus it looks like Cindy could do with trying to numb out some pain." Kerry laughed as she handed out a bottle of beer to everyone.

"I suppose I will tell the story." Kerry took a swig of her drink and got comfortable in her seat.

"It all started with an altercation between Alizon Device a woman who would spend most of her days in Trawden Forest. On one particular day a pedlar named John Law was going about his own business, when Alizon stopped him and asked him for some pins. No-one really knows what Alizon wanted the pins for. However, it was no secret they were commonly used for magical purposes. Particularly for healing, divination and love magic.

John refused to give Alizon the pins, people were told witches were evil and besides pins were of great value back then. So days passed with everything being fine. Alizon continued spending time near the Trawden Forest until news broke, that a man named John Law had suffered a horrendous stroke. Leaving him bed ridden and unable to care for himself, John spoke out and said he had met a strange woman while in the forest who asked him for some pins. According to John he believed because he refused her request the woman must have been a witch, and he had been cursed.

Alizon was put to trial in front of Judge Justice Nowell. She told him she had met Lucifer and made a deal with the devil. And that he could have her soul, so long as he brought harm to John. But Alizon didn't stop there, she went on to accuse her grandmother Elizabeth Southerns, who people called Old Demdike, her mother Elizabeth and brother James of witchcraft.

Alizon continued accusing others of the black arts, those people belonged to a rival family known as the Chattox. After the trial a horrific and barbaric time followed over the county of Lancaster on the commands of king James I.

On the twenty-seventh July 1612, Jannet Present was hung for witchcraft. On the eighteenth August Anne Whittle, Elizabeth and James Device were all hung for witchcraft. The following day Anne Redferne, June and

John Bulcock, Katherine Hewitt and Alizon Device were all found guilty of witchcraft and hung. Old Demdike never made it to trial, some say it may have been somewhat of a blessing."

"Why didn't she make it to the trial?"

"Because the prison which held all the accused proved to be too much for the fragile old woman."

"Them poor men and women"

"Yeah, they were accused of anything from hexing someone to cannibalism. However, there is no proof of this. But during the sixteenth century a book wrote by no other than the gracious king James made everyone feel uneasy. He made everyone look at witches with disgust. Because, everyone knows witches make a less sophisticated society."

"We are done."

"Wow they look amazing." Kerry said in an attempt to calm herself down. Hadley took her eyes away from Jace to examine his craft.

"They really do look good. Still haven't lost your touch my love."

Jace bowed as he began cleaning up and Cindy went to look in the bathroom mirror at her new appearance. Those left in the study heard Cindy shout she loves how they look before she returned to help clear up.

"I think everyone should try and get some sleep. We will go over everything tomorrow before the Halloween fair starts, and then we put the plan into action." Hadley told them. Kerry looked towards the study door.

"I think your extra spell worked wonders Cinds', haven't heard anything from down there all day."

"It was nothing" Cindy smiled.

Once the study was once again clean, Cindy wished everyone a goodnight and left the study to head towards her bedroom.

"Guess I'll head up as well" Kerry said with a yawn. Hadley gave her a hug and watched as she left the room.

"You okay sweetheart?" Jace asked while coming back into the study from the kitchen. Hadley nodded as she knew she was not going to be able to construct a full sentence. Hadley knew Jace would understand an instantly he showed her by taking her into his arms and letting her sink into his embrace. "We are going to be alright you know. I am not going to let anything happen to you." His voice was soft filled with passion and love. Hadley nodded again tightening her arms around his waist. "I love you."

"I love you too" Hadley whispered back.

CHAPTER TWENTY-EIGHT

"Hadley come on, everyone is waiting for us at the Ferris wheel." Hadley looked around at the bright lights in a daze. The smell of freshly cooked doughnuts and candy floss filled her senses. The sounds of families laughing and children screaming made her head feel weak and she stumbled forward.

"Hadley, come on."

She looked down and felt a child's hand grip hers, pulling her forward.

"We are all waiting for you. You took ages to get here. I think the others were starting to get restless."

Hadley tried to take in her surroundings as the child kept pulling her forward. Game stands with vendors calling out deals and lines of children and adults waiting to get on different rides which whizzed past her.

"What is going on?"

"Hadley why are you being silly? Mommy, Kerry and Jace are waiting for us."

Hadley continued to look around.

"Jace is here?"

"Of course he is, we are all here."

She tried to stop herself being pulled but the child's grip tightened on her hand.

"Marty, stop" A realisation came over Hadley.

"We can't stop Hadley, we have to go to the others" he said refusing to look at her.

She was pulled further into the fair, banners announced different types of shows: The Magical World of Dancing Hellhounds. See The Worlds Most Forbidding Manticore. Can You Face Bigfoot Himself?

"Marty, stop."

More stands went by with the sounds of balloons being popped, darts and water pistols being shoot. More vendors called out, encouraging all ages to step up and come inside their striped coloured tents.

"Marty please, you're hurting me."

"We are nearly there, can you not see it? We can ask to be left at the top."

Hadley put her arm out and grabbed onto one of the food carts in attempt to stop herself being pulled any further. Her fingers dug deep into one of the side grates. But Marty kept pulling and her grip started to loosen. She felt the pads of her fingers start to slice open.

"Marty what are you doing? Stop this now."

But her cries were met with more pulling. Through the window of the cart, Hadley's mouth began to water with the fresh smells of fried food.

"Marty, please stop pulling me, I can't carry on anymore."

Marty stopped, but he still refused to look at her. Hadley let go of the grate and examined her fingers, each finger perfused blood which streaked down onto her palm. Marty still held onto her other hand but as he stopped running Hadley was able to get a better hold of herself. Breathing heavily she continued to scan the fair, the crowds grew louder and the lights shined brighter.

"Do you want something?"

Hadley turned her head to look at who spoke to her. The food cart was empty.

"Do you want something? Do you want something? Do you want something? Do you want something?"

Hadley froze to the sound of the voice.

"Here."

Hadley looked down at the counter where a fresh doughnut in a styrofoam container had been placed.

The doughnut smelt fresh, she could see the hot air flowing from the plain sugared rounded treat. She put one bloody finger onto the sugar crust and felt the deep fried warmth.

"Hadley we need to go now."

Hadley looked at Marty who had dropped into a running stance.

"Not yet Marty"

A scream left Hadley's lungs before she could stop it. The fresh smelling doughnut still smelt right but the soft brown colour had now turned a sickening black and green. The sugar coating had dropped off and transformed into maggots swimming at the bottom of the styrofoam.Her finger which she had placed on top of the doughnut had sunken which brought up a black tar that bubbled as she pulled her finger out.

"Hadley we need to go on."

Before Hadley could respond her body was pulled away running and once again she found herself stumbling through the crowds. Her fingers were still bleeding and her index finger was still covered in tar. Her lungs were burning as Marty picked up speed.

Children in the shadows stepped out, their clothing modern to victorian. They all bared the same wounds, all showed the same horror in their expressions.

"Come on lass, toss a ring on a bottle, you won't win."

Hadley looked at the vendor who called out, but he had already turned away from her.

"Knock down a coconut, you won't win" another voice called out.

"Marty!" Hadley stumbled again losing her footing and scraping her knee.

"Hadley we're here" Marty squealed.

"Marty I'm hurt, please I need to leave."

Marty gripped her hand tighter and dragged her across the floor.

"Marty please stop."

"Hadley, finally you are here." Hadley held onto her bleeding knee with her free hand.

"We have been waiting for you sweet. Look we are at the front of the line."

Hadley's vision blurred and the pounding in her head brought bile up from her empty stomach. Marty let go of her hand and joined who she assumed was Cindy and Kerry.

Trying not to put pressure onto her injured knee, Hadley looked around for an escape. The hand Marty had held, felt raw. When she brought her hand up more tears fell when she saw the top layer of skin had been stripped. She watched as blisters formed on her palm and burst. Realising no one was paying attention, Hadley pushed through the pain and began to run.

"Oh no Hadley, it's time for us to go on the Ferris wheel."

Hadley heard a sickening crack as her shoulder dislodged from its socket. Unable to focus from the agonising pain. Hadley let out a whimper.

"Come now Hadley."

She felt hands grab her around the waist. Her senses became disoriented as she was flung over a shoulder.

"Jace is that you?" Hadley asked through deep breaths.

"We have been waiting for you Hadley."

Falling in and out of consciousness from the pain and the blood loss, she could no longer manage to construct a sentence.

"Put her next to me Jace. Mommy and Kerry are sitting in the one behind us."

"Okay, we have to make sure she stays awake."

Hadley was thrown into a cold metal seat that only needed a tiny movement to make it swing.

"See Hadley I told you I would bring you here."

Hadley felt Jace sit next to her and a single metal bar secure them into the ride.

"Hold on tight."

"Jace she isn't holding on."

Unable to move her arms, she felt her arms be lifted and placed onto the metal pole. A scream she thought she couldn't produce exploded from her as her swollen injured hands interacted with the cold metal.

"That's it Hadley, don't let go now."

Hadley felt her head fall forward but something inside her said she needed to look at Marty. She lifted her head from her chest and groaned with pain as she tried to move her head closer to Marty.

"Marty?"

Hadley's voice was all but a whisper that passed her dry chapped lips.

"Marty what's happening?"

"Look Hadley we're going to the top. We are going to be staying up here so you can see everything."

Hadley mumbled something inaudible as the Ferris wheel came to a stop at the top.

"Wow just look Jace."

Hadley felt the seat swing and the bitter cold air made her head lift.

"Jace she isn't opening her eyes."

She felt a small hand hit her cheek and an aching pain flushed her cheeks making her eyes pop open.

"There. Now look Hadley."

Hadley could not control her body swaying. Two large hands went on either side of her head pulling her up so she could see the fair from above. Hadley quietly sobbed as the pain in her shoulder intensified when Jace lent on her shoulder to keep her head up.

"Why are you doing this to me?" Hadley managed to say through sobs.

"We are not doing anything to you."

"Yeah, me and Jace aren't doing anything to you, we are just at the fair."

Marty flung his arms out and giggled.

"Look over there Hadley." Jace moved Hadley's head to where Marty was pointing. Hadley strained her eyes to see what Marty wanted her to look at.

"I can't see it Marty."

Jace let go of Hadley's head and watched in annoyance as it fell to her chest.

"Tut tut Hadley. We brought you up here for you to see all this and look how you are being."

She felt him poke her displaced shoulder

"Jace please" Hadley could feel herself losing. "You need to help me. Please I don't feel right."

Instead of a reassuring response Hadley heard nothing but laughter. Hadley felt tears run down her cheeks onto her chest as the laughter only got louder.

"Stop it, stop it, stop it, stop!" She screamed with the last of her energy. Hadley forced her head up and turned to face her husband.

"Jace."

Jace turned to face her and she jumped back in her seat, afraid and unsure she turned to Marty.

"What's the matter Hadley? Have you figured it out yet?"

Hadley felt her heart slow down as she looked into Martys eyes. They were the same as her husbands. The same as every demon she has ever faced.

"This is where you, along with everyone else will end up. This is how it all ends."

Hadley screamed as she fought against Jace and Marty.

"Hadley, it's okay".

Hadley could feel herself being shaken by her shoulders.

"It's okay sweetheart. You can wake up your safe here."

Hadley stared at Jace as she scanned his eyes and let out a breath she did not know she was holding in.

"Darlin, it's okay, you are okay."

Jace pulled Hadley up to a sitting position and cradled her in his arms. Hadley didn't realise she was shivering until she felt the warmth of Jace.

"Let's get you out of these pyjamas." He held Hadley at arms length. "You had a bad dream that's all it was."

Jace stood up and helped Hadley out of bed.

"I'll run you a hot bath, and we can talk about it."

Hadley nodded and followed Jace into the bathroom.

"Sit down while I get it ready." Jace put down the toilet seat and guided Hadley to sit down.

The warmth of the hot tap filled the room quickly, the steam made Hadley shiver, but made her feel more conscious of her surroundings. Hadley watched as Jace poured in the bubble bath and let the scent of lavender fill her senses.

"Here" Jace held out his hand for Hadley and helped her stand up and walk towards the bathtub. Gently he pulled her damp night shirt over her head and helped her get into the tub. Hadley let the hot water thaw her insides as she slid further down into the tub. Hadley closed her eyes as Jace got a jug and began pouring water over her hair.

"So you want to tell me what happened?"

Hadley instantly reached for her shoulder.

"Sweetheart?"

Hadley sighed so Jace put his arm around Hadley from behind.

"You haven't been like this since you kept dreaming of your mother. Please tell me what happened." He whispered in her ear. Hadley put her hand on Jace's arm and nodded.

For the next few minutes, Hadley went over the details of her dream to Jace. Jace had moved to sit at the side of the tub and took Hadley's hand as he listened without interrupting. When she struggled to describe a certain part, Jace gave her hand a squeeze to remind her it was okay. When she finished, Jace got up and brought over a fresh towel from the cabinet. Hadley stood up and got out the bath so Jace could wrap her up.

"I love you." He told her as he put his arms around her.

"I love you too." Hadley lifted her head just enough, so she could reach his lips.

"Thank you for listening and looking after me."

Jace kissed her softly on the lips. "I will always love you Hadley and I will never let anything happen to you."

CHAPTER TWENTY-NINE

"Today is the day."
Evelyn looked at Benjamin and scoffed.
"Did you not hear me, we need to get out of here."
Evelyn turned to face him. "We are not getting out of here."
"In case you have forgotten we have a job to do. What do you think our ancestors.."
"Our ancestors, our ancestors? I am sick and tired of hearing you go on about our ancestors. We have failed them, we have been caught for our actions and theirs."
As the ones in the basement argued, Hadley and Cindy quietly entered and stood at the bottom of the stairs.
"I am disappointed Evelyn. I thought you would feel some sadness for what you have done and not just because you got caught."
Hadley walked over the table and sat down on the spare chair.
"Not wanting to talk me. What about Cindy, will you speak to her?"
Cindy smiled and joined Hadley by the table.
"Oh you are probably wondering why I have a tray with me?" Cindy asked them. "We and the others were speaking this morning and we were trying to decide whether you were telling us the truth."
Hadley kept her eyes on all those locked in the basement.

"Neither of us could come to a decision, I mean if I was asked do you know if you are going to murder a child tonight. I would probably lie as well." Cindy shrugged. "But because we don't know, and you say you don't know. We have to take even more precautions."

Hadley saw the men flinch at Cindy's words

"Problem Father, Benjamin?"

"You already have us locked up like circus animals, and you want to do something else." Father Anderson snarled at Hadley.

Hadley raised her eyebrow and gestured for Cindy to carry on.

"As I was saying, we need to take extra measures because if the Orera can get to you. We need to make sure you can not leave."

Cindy poured tea into five cups and Hadley began handing them out.

"Drink now." Hadley ordered when she handed over the last cup.

"More witchcraft" Evelyn whispered to the others but drank when Hadley and Cindy looked at her.

"What is this going to do to us?" Jane asked.

"What you have just drank is Valerian mixed with passion flower. Soon you will start to feel drowsy and then go into a gentle sleep, so I suggest you all lie on your cots. Of course, we don't want it to weaken before the night comes. So we added just a touch of what you called witchcraft to it." Cindy felt powerful as she watched her tea take effect within seconds.

"I think you should listen to Cindy" Hadley said. "Looks like you are all need to lie down."

Cindy and Hadley helped all five get to their cots.

"One more thing" Hadley whispered into Father Andersons ear. "You will be tied to your cot."

Hadley saw his eyes go wide before slowly closing again.

"All done?" Hadley asked Cindy as she finished the final knot.

Cindy nodded and picked up the tray before leaving the basement.

"It's done." Hadley shouted after locking the basement door and walking into the study. Kerry and Jace were sitting at the study table, books and articles sprawled out in front of them. Hadley walked behind Jace and put her arms around him and peered at what he was reading.

"Jace we know the layout of the Inn now. We have gone over it a hundred times."

Jace ignored her and carried on studying the blueprint of the building.

"I know darling, but we only have a few hours until we go, and I do not want anything to go wrong."

Kerry looked up from her book and unintentionally scowled. "Jace we are going into a demon den which we and everyone we know has never faced before. No matter how much we plan. I don't think the plan will stick."

Hadley gave Kerry a look, and she quickly put her hands up.

"Sorry."

Jace nodded his head. "I know, it's okay. I'm just worried, Cindy is staying here to look after Marty and guard the basement door. And then us three are going into something as you said, we have no idea what. I just don't want anything bad to happen to either of ye."

Hadley kissed his cheek. "We will get through this my love. All of us."

Cindy walked in with a fresh pot of coffee, with Marty and Chewy closely behind her.

"I thought we might need some extra caffeine" she said as she placed the tray on the table. "I have also put something in the oven for everyone to eat before, well before it begins."

A tense cold feeling fell over the group. Marty put his arms round Cindy's waist and Chewy placed his head on Hadley's lap after she sat down.

"Cindy are you okay staying? And making sure they" Hadley nodded her head towards the basement door "don't do anything".

Cindy nodded and picked up the book she had been reading.

"Ha, I don't know about that, but I was looking at this." Cindy put the book in the middle of the table and pointed to the section she was reading.

"To help those who are lost." Kerry raised a sceptical eyebrow.

"I know what you're thinking, but Marty and me were talking last night, and he told me many of the children's souls the Orera has kept there are afraid or do not think they can leave." Cindy pointed to Marty "He got really upset last night, he said they're his friends, and he wants to help them."

Kerry, Jace and Hadley all looked at Marty who was sipping on hot chocolate, oblivious to the surrounding conversation.

"Okay, so how do we help them?" Hadley asked.

Cindy took back the book and skimmed over the page once more.

"First we need to make sure we can communicate with them. Therefore, we need silver and moonstone. The silver will influence the moonstones' ability for psychic ability and clairvoyance. After, we will need cedar to burn it in the Inn, the smoke will purify and revive the spirit."

"So it will give them the energy to no longer be locked on in this realm." Jace interrupted.

Cindy nodded in agreement and looked at the others "What do you think?"

Kerry stood from the table. "I have moonstone necklaces at the shop, we will need to activate them when I come back, but I think it sounds like a good plan."

Hadley agreed and went into the herb stock cupboard and pulled out two cedar smudge sticks.

"Okay" Hadley said as she walked back over to the table. "Kerry if you go and get the necklaces, Cindy and I will set up for the blessing." Hadley watched as Kerry began getting ready to leave the house. As she heard Kerry open the front door, Hadley ran into the hallway.

"Be careful, please."

Kerrys eyes twinkled, but her smile never reached her eyes. "I won't be long."

"Let's get the altar ready." Hadley said as she walked back into the study.

"I'll get the alcohol." Jace said as he made his way to the kitchen. Cindy looked at Hadley "Alcohol?"

"It's an offering to Woden" Hadley told her while scribbling names of herbs on a plain piece of paper. "Here" she said handing the note to Cindy.

"The nine sacred herbs" Cindy read. "Camomile, nettle, fennel, crab apple, mugwort, plantain, watercress, chervil and cockspur grass. Aren't these for healing?"

"Yes, but we are going to scatter them upon the altar, an added touch for the All Father when we say the blessing."

Cindy nodded her head and went to collect the herbs. Hadley opened up a cupboard near to her altar and searched for the pipe and tobacco.

"I love that smell." Jace said as he came up behind her with a bottle of mead in his hand.

"I know, you say it every time we get it out." Hadley laughed as she turned to face Jace.

"Well, I am not one to disappoint." Jace shrugged with a smile before planting a delicate kiss on Hadley's lips. She pulled him back for another, before walking to the altar door and stepping inside. Jace cleared the table while Hadley pulled out a red tablecloth and covered the whole table. She placed candles around the edges of the table, placed the pipe next to a bowl where she added the tobacco and told Jace to put the mead near the pipe. She pulled out the runes Dagaz, Ansuz and Othala and decided they would burn sandalwood.

For the finishing touches, Jace placed a delicately carved wooden wolf and Hadley placed a carved wooden Raven opposite. Lastly Hadley put a beautiful raw carnelian crystal next to the wooden Pentacle.

"It looks great." Cindy said as she walked into the altar room with the herbs in separate bags.

"Did we have them all?" Jace asked.

"All nine" Cindy replied holding them up to show him. "So we just put them round the table?"

Hadley nodded and took a bag from Cindy and began scattering the herbs over the altar.

As the last bag was being emptied upon the altar, the front door opened and closed.

"Wow, Woden will surely be thankful for his offering." Kerry said as she walked into the room. "But since we are asking for something bigger than we have ever asked before, I thought we should go above and beyond."

Jace, Cindy and Hadley turned to look at Kerry who was holding up a bag from the local food market.

"The best beef they had and some leeks and asparagus."

"Perfect" Hadley clasped her hands together smiling.

"I'll get a plate to put the feast on." Jace told them.

As he left the room, Hadley looked over Kerry.

"Hads, I am fine, nothing happened. I got to my shop and found the necklaces." Kerry held up four silver pendants each with a moonstone crystal presented in a drawstring pouch.

"Here is the plate." Jace said as he walked back in. The women watched as Jace made the food look presentable and pushed it into the centre of the table near the mead and tobacco.

"We shouldn't wait much longer." Kerry said as she looked at the time.

"Okay, let me just go check on Marty and tell him to stay in his room." Cindy quickly left the altar room while Hadley, Jace and Kerry prepared themselves for ritual.

"Is he okay?" Hadley asked as Cindy walked back into the room and closed the door behind her.

"Yeah he is fine, promised he would stay upstairs until told otherwise."

"Gid lad that boy is." Jace smiled as he took his place on a chair in front of the altar. The women joined him and began centring themselves before turning their attention to Woden. Hadley lit the candles and the incense and sat back down in silence. The room soon filled with the scent of sandalwood and a calming energy filled the room.

"Hail to Woden,
World Shaper, wisdom seeker,
Wyrd walker, wandering God.
Hail to he who brings
Both weal and woe
Who hung on the tree
Who gnawed upon his spear,

To tear a hole between the worlds.
Hail to he, who won the runes,
Who, burned by their fire,
Shrieked his spells,
And burned them all right back.
Hail to the All father,
Ruthless, fearless, mighty God,
Weapons wise and wondrous lord.
Bestow your blessings upon me here tonight,
And may my prayer be pleasing to you.
Hail Woden."

After they all recited the blessing, they sat in silence as they connected to Woden. Hadley felt connected to Woden by the core of her being. As she inhaled, she drank in his breath as she felt Woden breath into her. As she exhaled she breathed into him, continuously making the connection between her and Woden stronger. When she was no longer connected to her body, Hadley spoke in whispered tones.

"Woden, great All father. Please give us strength for the battle we are about to take. Guide us in the right direction and pass on your bravery and wisdom. The moonstone I shall wear around my neck, please bless it for protection and guidance for those who are lost."

Hadley drank in his breath and exhaled one last time before she reoriented herself back into her physical body and grounded herself once again. Hadley saw Jace, Cindy and Kerry nod their head, giving her the indication they were all back and grounded in their seat. Hadley watched Cindy, Kerry and Jace take turns in pouring out the mead and offering it to Woden. She waited for Jace to sit down before she got up and gracefully walked to the altar and poured the mead into an empty glass. As she placed the glass onto the table Hadley recited;

"Divine breath giver, I give this liquor to you in offering." She took some loose tobacco and placed it in the pipe. "I also give you this tobacco, for your pleasure. May these small gifts be pleasing to you, Hail, Woden."

Cindy picked up the horn and after honouring Woden passed it along to Kerry. Hadley was last to honour Woden and held onto it while they all recited the closing prayer.

> "Thank you, Woden.
> For your wisdom.
> I hail you now, All Father,
> And always
> Hail Woden."

Once the last word was spoken, Hadley walked over the altar and snuffed out the candles. When the last one had been put out, she turned to the others.

"Time we got going." Cindy gave her friends one last hug.

"Be safe, Blessed be my sisters and Jace."

"Blessed be." Kerry and Hadley told her as they all hugged in a group.

CHAPTER THIRTY

The sound of the Halloween fair could be heard as the three made their way through the village.

"Did you ever used to go there?" Kerry asked, thinking a distraction could do them all some good. Hadley went straight to her dream, the decaying food, the odd fair ground shows and the ones she loved with demon eyes. Instantly she put her hand to her shoulder and stopped to look in a shop window.

"Hadley, are you okay?" Jace walked back to her after realising she was no longer with them.

"Yeah sorry" She turned to Jace and took his hand to catch back up with Kerry. "Sorry, what did you ask?"

"I asked if you ever went to the fair when you were younger."

"Yeah, my mom used to take me every year. The toffee apples were always one of my favourite things." Hadley smiled at the memory as she spoke to the others, pushing the previous thought to the back of her mind.

As they continued walking, they went over their plan one more time, before they reached the road the Inn was on.

"Okay, we need to not be seen before we get in." Jace told them. He went into a crouching position as they reached the wall of the Inn and the others followed his lead. The Inn had an aura surrounding it, a dark strong aura which made it hard to not just turn around and leave. Hadley felt the Orera as soon as they reached the entrance to the court yard. The umbrellas which were still in their stands were ripped and broken, graffiti had been sprayed on the tables, the walls and the pavement. One which stuck out to Hadley was in bright red 'Evil inside, stay away.'

Hadley crept up to one of the windows and peered inside. The windows were covered in grime and dirt, the last of the autumn daylight struggled to penetrate the darkness which engulfed the entire Inn. Hadley could see no tables were standing upright, chairs were broken, their legs scattered over the floor. A bang caught Hadley's attention at one of the other windows, she instantly bent down and turned to face the others.

"She is panicking" Hadley whispered. Kerry craned her neck. "Kerry stay down. She is panicking because she can't connect to any of their minds." Hadley pushed Kerry back down. "She may know we are already here, but we don't want her to see us yet. She cannot leave the Inn listen."

Hadley motioned for Jace and Kerry to move back against the wall as the piercing sound of scratching at the windows moved to the one above them. Hadley held her breath as she felt Jace lace his fingers through hers 'we can do this' he mouthed to her. As the scratching at the window subsided and moved away, Kerry flicked her head to the entry and crawled in front of the others.

"If we don't move quickly who is to say she won't connect to someone else?"

Jace nodded "Let me go first." He passed Kerry and stopped at the door. Hadley could feel the coated knife pressing against her hip from her waistband.

"Remember, the familiar is just as dangerous as the Orera." Jace whispered, as he put his hand on the door handle. Hadley and Kerry both nodded.

"When I open the door, Kerry you throw in the first light bomb then we break away from each other and try and keep out of sight. Hadley do you remember the way to the fire place?" Hadley nodded as she gulped down a breath and her fingertips graced the handle of the knife.

"Open it." She told Jace when Kerry had got into position. The Inn door creaked as Jace pulled it open and the commotion inside stopped at the sound.

"Now."

On Hadley's command Kerry launched the light bomb into the Inn. Blinding white light filled the room as all three split up and crept to different parts of the Inn.

The smell of musk and decay filled their senses as the light dimmed to a calming glow. Hadley caught a glimpse of Jace as he made his way behind the bar. Kerry moved into the shadows and threw another light bomb into the middle of the Inn. As soon as the glass smashed, the blinding white light filled the room once again and Hadley crawled in the direction Cindy said the fireplace was.

The floor had become coated with a black tar substance, causing Hadley to go slower than she had planned. The tables and chairs thrown across the room became obstacles she quietly moved around before the light once again became a calming glow. When the light went out again Hadley hid behind a turned over table as the smell of sage began to fill the room.

A piercing scream filled the entire room as the Orera began scrambling over the mess she had created the night Cindy ran to the Fernsby home.

"Enough of this" a voice called out. "Do you think a new high priestess and a weak white witch can stop me?"

Hadley held her breath refusing to give up her location.

"I know you have done something to stop my people fulfilling my ritual. And now someone or someone's will have to pay. I will not leave this realm, Margaret invited me in 700 hundred years ago and neither of us are going to leave now."

Hadley shuddered as the Orera walked around throwing chairs in every direction.

"Hadley, Kerry, Jace. You should join us, it's better this side." The voice was different this time, more feminine, more delicate than the Orera's previous sinister tone. Hadley moved quietly to peer round the table and saw the Orera for the first time. Shock overtook her as she stared at a beautiful young woman dressed in a kirtle, her feet bare. Her long hair was tied into separate braids.

'Margaret'

Not able to look away Hadley watched as the beautiful woman disappeared leaving a grotesque crone like form. A blue tinge and glow overcame her, but her eyes always remained black.

Hadley waited for the next light bomb to go off but nothing happened. She could hear the Orera walking around the Inn. She knew she needed to get to the fireplace with or without the light bombs being a distraction. So when the Orera's back was turned, she crawled behind another table and caught a glimpse of the fireplace. She began moving again until she heard a purr which turned into a murderous hiss.

Quickly she moved back behind the table and waited, her body began shaking as it fell into flight or fight mode but the blade digging even more so, made her stay. Hadley heard the crash of another light bomb go off and moved quicker this time, letting her adrenaline take over until she was in the right position.

Jace could see Hadley had made it to where she needed to be

'Now it's distracting her until Hadley locates the familiar' Jace thought.

"How do you think you are going to beat me little Kerry?"

Jace froze as he saw the Orera move to where Kerry was hiding.

"And Jace what are you planning on doing? You have no powers. What do they call you and your wife demonologists?" The voice changed again and Jace saw the blue tinge fade out revealing a white tinge glow.

"I used to think like you. My sister, Alice, June and her mother thought we were on the right side. But they killed my sister. They burnt her body and branded her in front of everyone." Margaret moved closer to the bar and slammed her hand down. "We had to suffer for one man who thought he was a god. If only the townspeople listened to us, none of this would have happened. But of course, no one listened to women back then. We were meant to be seen and not heard, used for mens pleasures and then forced to cook and clean for the rest of our lives. But I couldn't stand that or them any longer. I did what I had to do and finally corrected my conjuring." The hand on the bar became blue again. "And when Margaret called me, I could not refuse. We sent Thomas Tuswell and his merry men right into the dark realm where they would be tortured forever by my kind." The Orera let out a devilish laugh. "I can still hear them screaming now."

The Orera stopped speaking when she heard a hiss coming from the corner of the room.

"Well, well, well, what has my precious found over here?"

Jace held his breath as he saw Kerry attempt to throw another light bomb before the Orera took hold of her wrist. The sound of hissing came again and Kerry screamed as blood began to trickle down her cheek. The moonlight gave little light but Jace caught Kerrys eyes as they widened.

'Help me' she mouthed as she held out her hand. Jace crawled to the end of the bar and held out his hand so only their fingertips touched. Moving further out of his hiding place he moved until he could take hold of her hand. Sweat dripped from his palms, the black tar substance on the floor made his knees slip. Jace screamed as a foot slammed down on his arm sending his whole body onto the floor. He could no longer see Kerry, but her scream

filled the entire room as her nails scratched on the dirty wooden floor.

"Jace!" Kerry screamed before her body hit the wall.

"Tut, tut Jace. I told you, you can not beat me. What are you expecting to do?" Jace looked up from the floor. The Orera's malicious smirk beamed down on him.

"Ah ah ah" She hissed as he tried to free his arm from under her foot. "You want to try and destroy me, and you think I should just let you go?" The Orera laughed as she lifted her foot and brought Jace to a standing position with her finger. "I will get my final sacrifice." She snarled.

Jace felt his windpipe close as he was lifted higher into the air. On instinct his hands went to his neck, there nothing could be felt but it was tightening with every breath he inhaled.

Kerry opened her eyes when a weight landed onto her stomach. She let out a soundless gasp as the weight shifted and blood began to leak from her chest. Using her inner strength Kerry put her hands up.

"With the power within me, I demand you to get off me." Kerry shouted in latin.

She felt the weight on her stomach leave with a hiss. With deep breaths, she rolled onto her side and saw Jace scrapping at his neck through the dimmed light of the light bomb. Using her arms to pull the top half of her body up she searched the floor for the remaining weapons they had brought.

By one of the broken chairs she found one of their backpacks and quickly unzipped it to find one of the spare potion bottles filled to the brim. The ache in her head produced a ringing in her ears and her blurry eyes made it hard for her to read the labels. She looked back to Jace, his eyes bulging yet pleading for her to focus and help.

'Come on Kerry, you can do this. Jace needs you.' After refocusing and pushing through the pain she pulled out a vial filled with white and silver specs. Pushing herself up on unsteady legs she rebalanced herself and took a few steps forward, "Goddess Freya, All Father Woden."

The Orera turned before she finished. "Maybe your powers are stronger than I first thought pathetic Kerry. But your gods and goddesses can not help you."

"With your strengths combined cause pain and discomfort to the evil one."

Kerry threw the vial before the demon could react and watched as the vial smashed into the Orera's chest. The vial exploded and the potion sizzled on the demons skin. She dropped Jace to the floor who eagerly gasped for air. The Orera let out a piercing scream as she called out to her familiar. Kerry heard tiny footsteps behind her and pulled out another vial, recited the same spell and threw it towards the footsteps. Without hesitating she ran towards Jace and checked he was breathing.

"You are getting stronger." Jace said through gasps.

"Yeah well lets hope Hadley's feeling this new strength, and she is nearly done." She whispered as she pulled Jace to a safer place.

Hadley could hear the commotion coming from areas of the Inn she was not able to see. After moving around more tables and broken chairs she swore when a sharp splinter pierced her hand.

"Keep going forward." She heard someone whisper in her ear. The voice was cold against her skin making the hairs on her arms stand up.

"Come on you are so close." The voice whispered again.

"Don't bother she can't hear us. No one but Marty has ever been able to hear us." Another voice whispered. Hadley stopped and turned her head. "You can help me?" She asked.

She lifted her head and standing next to her stood two of the children she remembered seeing in the courtyard. Both children looked at each other and smiled nodding their heads.

"Can you show me where the fire place is?" Hadley watched them as they crawled through the tables. When Hadley caught up with them, they had stopped and looked at her.

"It's here." One of them told her as they moved away, so Hadley could move closer. The children didn't leave as she unzipped her backpack and pulled out a small shovel.

"Do you know where I need to dig?" She asked.

One of them shook their head as the other nodded and pointed to the back of the fireplace. The floor there was soft but untouched and Hadley crawled further into the fireplace, careful not to make noise. Immediately Hadley began digging. Rapidly picking up speed until she hit something solid.

"I think I found it." She told the children who stood in the corner of the fireplace. Putting down the shovel Hadley began digging further down with her hands, she could feel her nails fill with soot. The children's eyes never left Hadley's hands as she unearthed bones and an old wooden box.

Hadley looked over to where Jace and Kerry were supposed to be hiding but could only hear cries of pain and snickering from the demon. The desperation to know what was happening overtook her. She needed to know if her husband and sister was okay. Without second guessing herself, Hadley crawled out the fireplace with the box and pulled a light bomb from her bag. Immediately she threw it into the middle of the room. The bright white light filled the room giving Hadley a chance to see the horror the others were going through.

As the light started to dim the Orera flipped her fingers sending Jace and Kerry to crash into the adjoining wall. Hadley screamed as tears began falling from her eyes. As Jace and Kerry hit the floor the Orera turned to Hadley, her eyes instantly going to the wooden box Hadley held in her hands.

"How dare you touch my belongings." The Orera screeched before she heard footsteps running to Jace and Kerry.

"You tedious pathetic children" she screeched as they helped Jace and Kerry to their feet.

With the distraction Hadley opened the wooden box and was confronted by a mummified cat wrapped in layers of yellow stained bandages lying in a bed of dead straw.

Hadley heard a snarl coming towards her as she quickly began pulling the knife from her waistband. The snarl turned into a growl and she felt her body fall back. Her vision blurred as her head made contact with the floor. Hadley screamed as something jumped onto her stomach, sharp nails began piercing her skin so sharp they teared through her clothes. With her hands she tried to free herself but to no prevail. She felt her clothes become warm as she started bathing in her crimson nightmare. Hadley tried to reach for the knife she dropped, but the pain from her stomach made her reach back to protect herself.

"Jace" Hadley screamed.

Jace joined the children to help Kerry up and checked her over.

"Jace" He turned to the sound of Hadley's voice and ran towards her.

"Hadley."

He felt a light bomb fly past him and saw Hadley when it exploded onto the floor. His heart sank as he saw her withering on the floor covered in blood.

"Hadley" He called out again as he dodged round the tables.

Hadley saw Jace running to her and felt a sudden wave of power rise within her

"With the power within me, I demand you to get off me" she screamed in Latin. She flicked her hand and she felt the weight on her stomach go. Instantly she sat up and reached for the knife.

"Jace look out" she screamed as she saw the Orera appear behind him. She watched as Jace stopped moving towards her and was lifted into the air with an arm wrapped around him. Hadley found the knife and held it above the mummified familiar.

"Don't be silly high priestess." The Orera warned, her black eyes showing no emotion.

"Don't listen to her Hadley this has to end." Jace shouted before the Orera's grip became tighter around him. She looked over at Kerry who was tiptoeing towards her with a potion blessed by the goddess of fire.

Hadley knew Jace could see her freeze, she could hear the familiar coming towards her once again. She could see the Orera smirking as she squeezed Jace tighter.

The room felt as if time had stopped, flecks of dust and dirt flickered over where the light bombs were wearing out. The knife in her hand began to slip as sweat began to build up under the pressure to save her husband while destroying the Orera's reign. Hadley felt her mouth dry up as she moved her eyes back to Jace.

'It's okay darlin, I love you' Jace mouthed as he nodded his head encouragingly.

Hadley placed the tip of the knife on the mummified familiar as she heard the children run in the direction of the familiar, stopping it from pouncing on her again. Without hesitation Hadley inserted the knife through the corpse.

"Goddess Freya, Goddess of war, battle and death. I ask you for your power and strength. Destroy this familiar, send it back along with its master to where it belongs. Kill it now with the strike of my knife. So mote it be."

She saw the Orera drop Jace and fall to the floor screaming in pain.

"Jace" she shouted.

"Hadley we have to finish this." Kerry ran to her with the potion and smashed it on top of the box. "By my power I send you back never to return."

The entirety of the familiar burst into hot flickering flames. Kerry and Hadley watched as the Orera held her head in her hands and hollered in pain. Slowly the blue light which surrounded the demon faded as she fell back into the dark realm. The black eyes which Hadley had seen many times turned a clear white and the white light which surrounded Margarets body dimmed, as her body decayed as the final flame burnt out.

CHAPTER THIRTY-ONE

Hadley ran over to the lifeless body which lay on the floor, surrounded by the children the Orera had kept hostage.

"Jace" Hadley cried as she fell to her knees. "Jace my love, wake up."

Hadley moved to his side and shook his body.

"Jace, baby please you can't leave me."

Kerry walked over to Hadley and placed her hand on Hadley's shoulder

"Hadley" Kerry saw a deep cut along Jace's neck. Hadley looked up at Kerry and the children, none of them would meet her eyes.

"Help me get him to a hospital." She screamed at them.

"Hadley" Kerry got down to Hadley's level and took her hands in hers. "I'm sorry, I am so sorry Had's. But he's with the gods now. He is in summer.."

"Don't. Don't you dare say he is in Summer-land. He can't be gone, he can't leave me. I can't do this without him." Hadley kissed Jace's lips. "Please my love wake up."

"Hadley."

"Get away." Hadley screamed in latin as she threw her hand out causing Kerry to fall backwards.

Hadley lay next to Jace refusing to move as she cradled his dead body.

"Come with me children, I can help you alone." Kerry said.

She bent down and gave Hadley a kiss on the cheek and walked somewhere more private within the wreckage that was the Inn. The children followed her, except for one who knelt down and whispered something into Hadley's ear before joining the others.

"Thank you all for helping us today. We know how scary it must have been to stand up to the demon who has kept some of you here for hundreds of years." Kerry stopped speaking and looked thoughtful for a moment

"May I ask you something?"

The children nodded in unison.

"Why are only some of you here when she has been here for 700 years?" The children looked at each other until one put their hand up.

"Miss, we are the last ones she killed every one hundred years. She said we are the trophies, if you hadn't come another would have joined us this night."

Kerry wiped a fresh tear from her cheek and placed the last candle on the floor. She had created a circle as they spoke and gestured for them to stand inside.

"I am so sorry this happened to all of you."

"We are sorry you lost your friend, and we couldn't help." Kerry felt a cold hand touch her cheek.

"Do not think the loss of Jace is your fault. He would be grateful you helped Hadley and me defeat the demon." The cold touch left her cheek and she looked up at whom it belonged to.

"You fought well, all of you did."

Kerry took out a box of matches and lit the match in one easy swipe. Protecting the flame with her left hand she felt her palm heat up and gently blew the flame onto the candle. The children watched amazed as all the candles began to glow with a bright yellow flame.

"Not all witches are bad." Kerry smiled as she watched their faces. "I am going to call the corners and cast the circle; I cast the sacred circle. I am between the worlds." She came to a stop next to Hadley who was facing north of the circle facing outwards ready to call the quarters.

"I call the spirit of the North. Please join me and lend me the power of the earth." Moving around the circle clockwise she continued. "I call the spirit of the East. Please join me and lend me the power of air. I call the spirit of the South. Please join me and lend me the power of water. I call the spirit of the West. Please join me and lend me the power of fire."

"Now are you ready to leave this place?"
She noticed some children seemed hesitant. "It is okay to be worried, but there has been a place waiting for all of you since your physical body was taken from you. I will help you get there." Kerry stood up and backed away from the circle.

"Will it hurt?" One of them whispered. Kerrys head tilted to the side and tried to blink away the tears.

"No, the Goddess Hel will guide you to where you need to go. She should not be feared, for you have done nothing unworthy."

She closed her eyes and put her arms out making sure her palms were facing upwards.

"I call upon you Goddess Hel, ruler of Niflheim. Judger of souls, granter of existence within your realm. Enter thy circle of peace and innocence and collect what belongs to you."

Kerry felt her palms warm up as the surrounding room radiated a satisfying heat. After a few moments the warmth died down and the coldness set in again. Kerry opened her eyes to see the candles of the circle still alight, but the children had gone.

"Thank you Goddess Hel,
Thank you, spirit of the North for joining us and lending us the power of Earth
Thank you, spirit of the East for joining us and lending us the power of Air
Thank you, spirit of the west for joining us and lending us the power of water
Thank you, spirit of the South for lending us the power of Fire."

"Hadley" Kerry sat down next to Hadley who was still lying next to Jace. "Hadley we need to contact the authorities. We can't leave Jace here like this." She placed a hand on Hadley's arm.

"This is all my fault." Hadley turned her head from Jace's shoulder to look at Kerry. Her face was raw and puffy.

"Had's this is not your fault. Jace would not want to be here."

"I can't leave him yet."

Kerry took a deep breath looking around the dimly lit Inn.

"There is a phone just outside the courtyard."

Hadley nodded and turned to rest her head back onto Jace. She ached to see his chest go up and down, to open his eyes and smirk at her for watching him sleep.

"You're getting cold Jace, your hands are so cold." She waited for him to answer.

"Not talking are we, well, why don't I tell you one of my favourite memories of us. It was the first Christmas we spent together at your parents, do you remember that. Your mom was worried I was a vegetarian because someone hinted I may have been."

She laughed and looked up at Jace's motionless face. "Yeah you were always doing things like that. What about the time we were on an investigation and we needed to get a train to Cornwall and when we had to switch trains you kept looking behind and asking why I was following you. You kept saying you didn't know me and that carriage was so crowded. All those people thought I was some strange stalker until you turned around and kissed me."

She lifted her head and noticed she had been resting on his blood.

"I don't know how I am going to go on without you. What am I going to tell your mom, your dad and your brother? I brought you here and now you are gone. Jace I am sorry, I love you." Hadley's eyes rolled back as the tiredness of crying and the loss of blood she had encountered overtook her.

Hadley woke up to a brightly lit room, the smell of disinfectant and the beep of machines made her question where she was. She tried to sit up but winced and her hands went to her stomach. Looking down she noticed she had been put in a green and white gown. The vein on her right hand had been inserted with a cannula, round her neck was a delicate Topaz pendant. She lifted her gown and saw her stomach covered in bandages which were tender to touch.

"Hadley how are you feeling?"

Hadley let go of her gown and looked up to see a nurse standing at the end of her bed.

"Can I get you anything?"

Hadley realised her mouth was dry and asked for water. The nurse soon returned with a jug of water and poured some out in a glass and handed it over to her. The water drenched her mouth and throat, Hadley didn't stop drinking until the glass became empty.

"Thank you."

The nurse smiled at her and refilled the glass. "Your friends are waiting outside. I will let them know they can see you now."

Hadley tried to sit into a more comfortable position as the nurse left the room. Hadley's heart sank as she realised one person would not be outside waiting to come in. All her emotions came back to her as her eyes filled with new tears.

"Hadley" Cindy cried as she wrapped her arms around her shoulders. Hadley fell into her embrace as she continued to cry. Kerry put her arm around Marty whose tears were mixing into his running nose.

When the tears dried out Cindy loosened her embrace and held Hadley at arms length.

"We are so happy you are okay."

Hadley noticed all their faces were red, their eyes tired and their skin showed signs of stress. She closed her eyes and half smiled.

"Thank you." She looked at Kerry.

"Did you dig up the poppets and release the.."

Kerry nodded "Yeah as soon as I knew you were safe here I went back to the house and let Cindy know everything. Then we both dug up the poppets and took the papers Jace got, confirming all the murders and who was responsible."

Hadley flinched at the sound of Jace's name.

"So are they?"

"They won't be able to cause anymore harm to anyone again." Kerry reassured her.

"And Jace?" It was just a whisper but Kerry knew what Hadley wanted to know.

"Well, when we dug up the poppets we needed them to be in the place of the crime. So we guided them to the Inn and shortly after, the police found them all standing near Jace's body with the papers in a bag next to him."

Hadley nodded her head, when tears began to fall again she wiped her face with her hand and put her arms out to Marty

"Come here and give aunty Hadley a cuddle."

Marty carefully jumped on the bed next to Hadley and snuggled by her side.

"I looked after Chewy for you and Jace like I promised." Hadley kissed the top of his head.

"I never doubted you would do anything less. He would be proud of you."

She made eye contact with Kerry and Cindy.

"I am going to send every malicious, ugly, disgusting demon back to the dark realm. They have already taken two loved ones from me and I will avenge them and not let anyone else suffer this pain. This pain I am.."

"Visiting time is over now, but the doctors said we can discharge Hadley tomorrow." The nurse said as she walked back into the room.

"We will be back tomorrow morning." Kerry kissed Hadley on the cheek, followed by another embrace from Cindy. Marty kissed Hadley on the forehead and jumped off the bed. Hadley settled in for the night as the nurse checked her wounds and re-bandaged her back up.

"Can I get some pain killers before I go to sleep?" The nurse nodded and went off to get Hadley's request. She returned a short while after with the pills.

"Nurse, can I ask something?"

"Hmm of course, ask away." The nurse replied as she reached the door.

"What happened to Jace?"

The nurse turned to look at her with pure sadness in her eyes. "He was brought here as a DOA and he's currently in the morgue that's all I know."

Hadley stared out of the window as the nurse quietly left the room, leaving her alone with her thoughts of Jace. With tears falling silently down her cheeks and her reflection showing someone she did not recognise, she recited.

> 'Mother Goddess, Father God, I release myself from those who have left this plane. And let them walk the blessed gardens of Summer-land.'

Printed in Great Britain
by Amazon